DANIELLE STEEL

44 CHARLES STREET

A Novel

CORGI BOOKS

TRANSWORLD PUBLISHERS
61–63 Uxbridge Road, London W5 5SA
A Random House Group Company
www.transworldbooks.co.uk

44 CHARLES STREET
A CORGI BOOK: 9780552158992

First published in the United States
in 2011 by Delacorte Press,
an imprint of The Random House Publishing Group,
a division of Random House, Inc., New York

First published in Great Britain
in 2011 by Bantam Press
an imprint of Transworld Publishers
Corgi edition published 2012

Addresses for Random House Group Ltd companies outside the UK
can be found at: www.randomhouse.co.uk
The Random House Group Ltd Reg. No. 954009

Penguin Random House is committed to a sustainable future for
our business, our readers and our planet. This book is made from
Forest Stewardship Council® certified paper.

MIX
Paper from
responsible sources
FSC® C018179

Typeset in Garamond by Falcon Oast Graphic Art Ltd.
Printed and bound in Great Britain by Clays Ltd, St Ives plc

44 Charles Street

www.daniellesteel.com

For more information on Danielle Steel and her books,
see her website at www.daniellesteel.com

Danielle Steel is one of the world's most popular and highly acclaimed authors, with eighty international best-selling novels in print and 600 million copies sold. She is also the author of *His Bright Light*, the story of her son Nick Traina's life and death. She lives in California and Paris.

44 Charles Street

Chapter 1

Francesca Thayer sat at her desk until the figures started to blur before her eyes. She had been over them a thousand times in the past two months – and had just spent the entire weekend trying to crunch numbers. They always came out the same. It was three o'clock in the morning and her long wavy blond hair was a tangled mess as she unconsciously ran her hands through it again. She was trying to save her business and her house, and so far she hadn't been able to come up with a solution. Her stomach turned over as she thought of losing both.

She and Todd had started the business together four years ago. They'd opened an art gallery in New York's West Village where they specialized in showing the work of emerging artists at extremely reasonable prices. She

Danielle Steel

had a deep commitment to the artists she represented. Her experience in the art world had been extensive, although Todd had none at all. Before that, she had run two other galleries, one uptown after she graduated, and the other in Tribeca. But this gallery that they had started together was her dream. She had a degree in fine arts, her father was a well-known artist who had become very successful in recent years, and the gallery she shared with Todd had gotten excellent reviews. Todd was an avid collector of contemporary work, and he thought that helping her start the gallery would be fun. At the time, Todd was tired of his own career on Wall Street as an attorney. He had a considerable amount of money saved and figured he could coast for a few years. The business plan he had developed for them showed them making money within three years. He hadn't counted on Francesca's passion for less expensive work by entirely unknown artists, helping them whenever possible, nor had he realized that her main goal was showcasing the work, but not necessarily making a lot of money at it. Her hunger for financial success was far more limited than his. She was as much a patron of the arts as a gallerist. Todd was in it to make money. He thought it would be exciting and a welcome change of career for him after years of doing tax and estate work for an

10

important law firm. But now he said he was tired of listening to their bleeding-heart artists, watching his nest egg dwindle to next to nothing, and being poor. As far as Todd was concerned, this was no longer fun. He was forty years old, and wanted to make real money again. When he talked to her about it he had already lined up a job at a Wall Street firm. They were promising him a partnership within a year. As far as selling art was concerned, he was done.

Francesca wanted to stick with it and make the gallery a success, whatever it took. And unlike Todd, she didn't mind being broke. But in the past year, their relationship had begun to unravel, which made their business even less appealing to him. They argued about everything, what they did, who they saw, what to do about the gallery. She found the artists, worked with them, and curated the shows. Todd handled the money end of things and paid the bills.

The worst of it was that their relationship was over now too. They had been together for five years. Francesca had just turned thirty when she met him, and Todd was thirty-five.

It was hard for her to believe that a relationship that had seemed so solid could fall apart so totally in a year. They had never wanted to get married and now they disagreed about that too. When Todd hit forty, he suddenly decided he wanted a conventional life. Marriage was sounding good to him and he didn't want to wait much longer to have kids. At thirty-five, she still wanted what she had when they met five years before. They had talked about maybe having kids one day, but she wanted to turn their gallery into a success first. Francesca had been very honest with him about marriage when they met, that she had an aversion to it. She had had a front-row seat all her life to her mother's obsession with getting married – and she watched her screw it up five times. Francesca had spent her entire life trying not to make the same mistakes. Her mother had always been an embarrassment to her. And she had no desire whatsoever to start emulating her now.

Francesca's parents had gotten divorced when she was six. She had also watched her extremely handsome, charming, irresponsible father drift in and out of relationships, usually with very young girls who never lasted in his life for more than six months. That, combined with her mother's fetish for marriage, had made Francesca commitment-phobic until she met Todd. His parents' own bitter divorce when he was fourteen had made him skittish about marriage too. They had had that in common, but now he had begun to think that marriage made sense. He told her he was tired of their bohemian lifestyle where people lived together and thought it was fine to have kids without getting married. As soon as Todd blew out the candles on his fortieth birthday cake, it was as if a switch were turned on, and without any warning, he turned traditional on her. Francesca preferred things exactly as they were and had always been.

Now suddenly, in recent months, all of Todd's friends seemed to live uptown. He complained about the West Village where they lived, and which she loved. He thought the neighborhood and people in it looked scuzzy. To complicate matters further, not long after they opened the gallery, they had fallen in love with a house that was in serious disrepair. They had discovered it on a snowy December afternoon and were instantly excited, and had gotten it at a great price because of the condition it was in. They restored it together, doing most of the work themselves. If they weren't working in the gallery, they were busy with the house, and within a year everything in it gleamed. They bought furniture at garage sales, and little by little they had turned it into a home they loved. Now Todd claimed that he had spent all of the last four years lying under a leaky sink, or making repairs. He wanted an easy modern condominium where someone else did all the work. Francesca was desperately fighting for the life of their business and the house. Despite the failure of the relationship, she wanted to keep both, and didn't see how she could. It was bad enough losing Todd without losing the gallery and her home too.

They had both tried everything they could to save the relationship, to no avail. They had gone to couples counseling and individual therapy. They had taken a two-month break. They had talked and communicated until they were blue in the face. They had compromised on everything they could. But he wanted to close or sell the gallery, which would have broken her heart. And he wanted to get married and have kids and she didn't, or at least not yet – and maybe never. The idea of marriage still made her cringe, even to a man she loved. She thought his new friends were dreary beyond belief. He thought their old ones were limited and trite. He said he was tired of vegans, starving artists, and what he considered left-wing ideals. She had no idea how they had grown so far apart in a few short years, but they had.

They had spent last summer apart, doing different things. Instead of sailing in Maine as they usually did, she spent three weeks in an artists' colony, while he went to Europe and traveled with friends and went to the Hamptons on weekends. By September, a year after the fighting had begun, they both knew it was hopeless and agreed to give up. What they couldn't agree on was what to do about the gallery and the house. She had put everything she had and could scrape up into her half of the house, and now if she wanted to keep it, he expected her to buy him out, or agree to sell it. They had less invested in the business, and what he wanted from her was fair. The problem was that she just didn't have it. He was giving her time to figure it out. Now it was November, and she was no closer to a solution than she had been two months before. He was waiting for her to get sensible and finally give up.

Todd wanted to sell the house by the end of the year, or recoup his share. And he wanted to be out of the business by then too. He was still helping her on weekends when he had time, but his heart was no longer in it, and it was becoming increasingly stressful for both of them to live under one roof in a relationship that was dead. They hadn't slept with each other in months, and whenever possible he spent the weekend with friends. It was sad for both of them. Francesca was upset about ending the relationship, but she was equally stressed about the gallery and the house. She had the bitter taste of defeat in her mouth, and she hated everything about it. It was bad enough that their relationship had failed –

five years seemed like a long time to wind up at ground zero in her life again. Closing the gallery, or selling it, and losing the house was just more than she could bear. But as she sat staring at the numbers, in an old sweatshirt and jeans, she could find no magic there. No matter how she added, subtracted, or multiplied, she just didn't have the money to buy him out. Tears rolled down her cheeks as she looked at the amounts again.

She knew exactly what her mother was going to say. She had been vehemently opposed to Francesca going into business and buying a house with a man she loved but didn't intend to marry. She thought it was the worst possible combination of investment and romance. 'And what happens when you break up?' her mother had asked, assuming it was inevitable, since all of her own relationships had ended in divorce. 'How will you work that out, with no alimony and no settlement?' Her mother thought that all relationships had to start with a prenup and end with spousal support.

'We'd work it out just like your divorces, Mom,' Francesca had answered, annoyed by the suggestion, as she was by most of what her mother said. 'With good lawyers, and as much love for each other as we can muster at that point, if that happens, and good manners and respect.'

All of her mother's divorces had been on decent terms, and she was friendly with all her former husbands, and they still adored her. Thalia Hamish Anders Thayer Johnson di San Giovane was beautiful, chic, spoiled, self-centered, larger than life, glamorous, and a little crazy by most people's standards. Francesca referred to her as 'colorful' when she was trying to be nice about her. But in fact, her mother had been an agonizing humiliation for her all her life. She had married three Americans and two Europeans. Both of her European husbands, one British and one Italian, had titles. She had been divorced four times, and widowed the last time. Her husbands had been a very successful writer, Francesca's father, the artist, the scion of a famous British banking family, a Texas land developer who left her comfortable with a big settlement and two shopping malls, which in turn had allowed her to marry a penniless but extremely charming Italian count, who died eight months later in a terrible car accident in Rome in his Ferrari.

As far as Francesca was concerned, her mother came from another planet. The two women had nothing in common. And now of course she would say 'I told you so' when Francesca told her that the relationship was over, which Francesca hadn't had the guts to do yet. She didn't want to hear what she would have to say about it.

Her mother hadn't offered to help her when Francesca bought the house and opened the gallery, and she knew she wouldn't help her now. She thought the house a fool-hardy investment and didn't like the neighborhood, and like Todd, she would advise Francesca to sell it. If they did, they would both make a profit. But Francesca didn't want the money, she wanted to stay in the house, and she was convinced there was a way to do it. She just hadn't found it yet. And her mother would be no help with that. She never was. Francesca's mother wasn't a practical woman. She had relied on men all her life, and used the alimony and settlements they gave her to support her jet-set lifestyle. She had never made a penny on her own, only by getting married or divorced, which seemed like prostitution to Francesca.

Francesca was totally independent and wanted to stay that way. Watching her mother's life had made her determined never to rely on anyone – and particularly not a man. She was an only child. Her father, Henry Thayer, was no more sensible than her mother. He had been a starving artist for years, a charming flake and a womanizer, until, eleven years ago, he had the incredible good fortune to meet Avery Willis, when he was fifty-four. He had hired her as an attorney to help him with a lawsuit, which she won for him, against an art dealer who had cheated him out of money. She then helped him invest it instead of letting him spend it on women. And with the only genius he had ever shown, in Francesca's opinion, he had married Avery a year later, she for the first time at fifty, and in ten years she had helped him build a solid fortune, with an investment portfolio and some excellent real estate. She talked him into buying a building in SoHo, where he and Avery still lived and he still painted. They also had a weekend house in Connecticut now. Avery had become his agent and his prices had skyrocketed along with his financial affairs. And for the first time in his life he had been smart enough to be faithful. Henry thought his wife walked on water – he adored her. Other than Francesca's mother, she was the only woman he'd committed to by marrying her. Avery was as different from Thalia as two women could ever get.

Avery had a respectable career as a lawyer, and never had to be dependent on a man. Her husband was her only client now. She wasn't glamorous, although she was good-looking, and she was a solid, practical person with an excellent mind. She and Francesca had been crazy about each other from the first time they met. She was old enough to be Francesca's mother, but didn't want to be one. She had no children of her own, and until she got

19

married she had the same distrust of marriage that Francesca did. She also had what she referred to as crazy parents. Francesca and her stepmother had been close friends for the last ten years. At sixty, Avery still looked natural and youthful. She was only two years younger than Francesca's mother, but Thalia was an entirely different breed.

All Thalia wanted now at sixty-two was to find another husband. She was convinced that her sixth would be her final and best one. Francesca wasn't as sure, and hoped she'd have the brains not to do it again. She was sure that her mother's determined search for number six had frightened all possible candidates away. It was hard to believe she had been widowed and unmarried for sixteen years now, despite a flurry of affairs. And she was still a pretty woman. Her mother had had five husbands by the time she was forty-five. She always said wistfully that she wished she were fifty again, which she felt would have given her a better chance to find another husband than at the age she was now.

Avery was totally happy just as she was, married to a man she adored, and whose quirks she tolerated with good humor. She had no illusions about how badly behaved her husband had been before her. He had slept with hundreds of women on both coasts and throughout

Europe. He liked to say he'd been a 'bad boy' before he met Avery, and Francesca knew how right he was. He had been bad, in terms of how irresponsible he had been, and a lousy husband and father, and he would be a 'boy' till the day he died, even if he lived to be ninety. Her father was a child, despite his enormous artistic talent, and her mother wasn't much better, only she didn't have the talent.

Avery was the only sensible person in Francesca's life, with both feet on the ground. And she had been a huge blessing to Francesca's father, and to her as well. She wanted Avery's advice now, but hadn't had the guts to call her yet either. It was so hard admitting she had failed on every front. In her relationship, and in her struggling business, particularly if she had to close it or sell it. She couldn't even keep the house she loved on Charles Street unless she could find the money to pay Todd. And how the hell was she going to do that? Bottom line, she just didn't have the money. And even Avery couldn't work magic with that.

Francesca finally turned off the light in her office next to her bedroom. She started to head downstairs to the kitchen to make a cup of warm milk to help her sleep, and as she did, she heard a persistent dripping sound, and saw that there was a small leak coming from the skylight.

The water was hitting the banister and running slowly down it. It was a leak they'd had before, which Todd had tried to fix several times, but it had started again in the hard November rains, and he wasn't there that night to fix it. He kept telling her that she'd never be able to maintain the house by herself, and maybe he was right. But she wanted to try. She didn't care if the roof leaked, or the house came down around her. Whatever it took, whatever she had to do, Francesca wasn't ready to give up.

With a determined look, she headed down to the kitchen. On her way back up, she put a towel on the banister to absorb the leak. There was nothing else she could do until she told Todd about it in the morning. He was away for the weekend with friends, but he could deal with it when he got home. It was exactly why he wanted to sell the house. He was tired of coping with the problems, and if they weren't going to live there together, he didn't want to own it. He wanted out. And if she could find a way to pay him, the problems were going to be all hers, on her own. With a sigh, Francesca walked back upstairs to her bedroom, and promised herself she'd call her stepmother in the morning. Maybe she could think of something that Francesca hadn't. It was her only hope. She wanted her leaky house and her struggling gallery with its fifteen emerging artists. She had invested four years in both, and no matter what Todd and her mother thought, she refused to give up her dream or her home.

Chapter 2

The call to Avery was easier to make the next morning than Francesca had expected. Once she spoke to her, she felt better. They chatted for a few minutes and laughed about her father's latest antics. In many ways, he was charmingly adolescent, which Avery found lovable, and Francesca had learned to forgive his failings as a father. And after an easy exchange Francesca got down to business and told her what was going on. With a catch in her throat, she told her about the breakup with Todd, and her dilemma about the gallery and the house, and how upset she was.

'I'm so sorry to hear it,' Avery said immediately with compassion. 'I had a feeling something like that was going on. We haven't seen much of Todd in the last few months.' In fact, they hadn't seen him at all, and Francesca had visited them alone in Connecticut several times that summer. She had made excuses for him, but Avery had suspected there was more to it than that. And Henry had said as much himself, but didn't want to pry and intrude on his daughter, who was always extremely private. 'She'll tell us when she's ready, if something's going on,' he had commented to Avery, who agreed with him. So when she heard the news, she wasn't entirely surprised. 'And that's tough about the gallery and the business. Are you losing money at the gallery?' She wondered if Francesca could sell it.

'Not really. But we're barely breaking even. I don't think anyone would buy it with no profit. Todd thinks that if I raised prices, I'd be showing a profit in another two or three years, but he says that if I stick to emerging artists, it's never going to be a big money-maker, and I really don't want to start selling bigger artists. That's a whole different deal and not what I wanted to do when I opened.' She was very idealistic about art, which was one of Todd's complaints about their business. He wanted to get more commercial to increase what they made, and it was a compromise Francesca hadn't wanted to make, but she realized that now maybe she'd have to, although she would hate to do it. She loved serious artists, even if they were unknown, and commercial art wasn't her thing, even if it was Todd's. She had just acquired a new Japanese artist, who she felt had enormous talent. He had received great reviews on his first show, and she was selling his work for next to nothing. But she didn't feel she could charge more for an unknown. She was very ethical about what she sold, and how she sold it.

'You may have to compromise a little on your ideals, and sell a few midcareer artists,' Avery told her practically. She had learned a great deal about art from Francesca's father, and knew a lot about the business end of it. But his art was in a whole different league, and thanks to Avery, his work now sold for huge prices. 'Why don't we talk about the house first? Have you got anything you can sell to raise the money to pay Todd his half?' she asked practically, and Francesca felt miserable. She didn't. That was the whole problem.

'No, I don't. I put everything I had into the house. I can barely scrape up my share of the mortgage payments every month. I've figured out what I can do about that. I can take in roommates. I think with three, I can make it, which would solve that problem at least.'

'I can't see you living with strangers,' Avery said honestly. She knew her stepdaughter was an extremely private person, and as an only child she had always been something of a loner. But if she was willing to take in roommates, it would certainly help. It told Avery just how determined she was to keep the house, knowing that having roommates in her home would be a big sacrifice for her. 'But I guess if you can stand it, it solves the issue of the monthly payments. What about the rest that you'd owe Todd if you keep the house?' Avery sounded pensive as she asked her, and then suddenly out of the blue she had an idea. 'I don't know how you feel about it, but you have six paintings of your father's. They're some of his best early work, and they'd bring a lot at auction. Enough to pay your whole payment to Todd, I think, if you're willing to sell them. I can even call his principal gallery uptown. They'd go crazy to get their hands on his early work. There's always a market for it.'

Francesca winced as Avery said it. Just thinking about it made her feel guilty. She couldn't imagine selling her father's work, and she never had before. But she'd never been this desperate before either, and she had nothing else to sell. 'How do you think he'd feel about it?' Francesca asked, sounding worried. He was a little crazy, and a flake, but he was still her father and she loved him, and she had a deep respect for his work. She loved the six paintings she had.

'I think he'd understand,' Avery said gently. 'Before we

got married, he was always selling something to stay alive. He knows better than most people what that's like. He even sold a small Pollock once to pay your mother money he owed her. You do what you have to, Francesca.' She was a practical woman, which was why Francesca had wanted to talk to her, more than to her parents.

'Maybe I could get by with selling five. That way I could keep one. Daddy gave those to me. I feel like a real jerk selling them to buy a house.'

'It doesn't sound like you have any other options.'

'No, I don't.' And she hadn't thought of the paintings. She had absolutely nothing else with which to pay Todd. For a minute, she thought of agreeing to sell the house instead of the paintings. But she didn't want to do that either. 'Why don't you call his gallery and see what they say? If they can get a decent price for them, I guess I'll sell them. But only offer them five. I want to try and keep at least one.' She was extremely sentimental about them. This was going to be a big sacrifice for her, yet another one.

'I'll do that,' Avery assured her. 'They have a list of collectors for his work. I suspect they'll pounce on them pretty quickly, unless you want to wait and sell them at auction.'

'I can't wait,' Francesca said honestly. 'Todd has been

wanting to sell the house for months, and I promised him I'd pay him or let him sell the house by the end of the year. That's less than two months away. I don't have time to wait for an auction.'

'Then we'll see what the gallery says. I'll call them as soon as we hang up.' And she had another idea then too, although she wasn't sure what her husband would say about it. She shared her idea with Francesca. 'Your father's been very excited about what you're doing at the gallery ever since you opened. He loves emerging artists the way you do. I'm just wondering if he'd like to go into partnership with you, kind of as a silent partner, not that your father is silent about anything. But it might be exciting for him to help you with this, until the gallery starts to make a profit. From what you said, Todd wants a pretty small amount for his share.' He had been very fair about it. What he wanted was more of a token payment, barely more than what he had put into it in the first place. The house was a different story, and had appreciated considerably in four years, but he was being fair about that too. He was counting on getting more money out of the house, so he could buy an apartment. He had been very decent through the entire breakup and the untangling of their joint holdings. It was hard and a big disappointment for him too. They had never expected this to happen, but they were both sure now that it couldn't be worked out, and they both wanted to get it over with quickly. Francesca was moving as fast as she could, given the enormity of the problem for her.

'I never thought of asking my father to invest in the gallery,' Francesca said, sounding intrigued by the idea. 'Do you think he'd do it?'

'He might. It would be exciting for him, and I'm sure he'd like to help you. It's not a big investment. Why don't you have lunch with him and ask him?' Francesca liked the idea, and he was far more likely to help her than her mother, who had disapproved of both projects right from the beginning. She never had any interest whatsoever in art, although she had several of his now-very-valuable paintings too. She had hung on to them more out of sentiment than because of their value, but now they were a windfall for her. Thalia had at least a dozen of his early works, which were going for such high prices. She always said she would never sell them. Francesca never thought she would have to either.

'I'll call him and ask him to lunch tomorrow,' Francesca said, sounding hopeful for the first time in two months. 'You're a miracle worker, Avery, and a genius. My father is so damn lucky to have you.'

'No luckier than I am to have him. He's a good guy,

especially now that he's not a collector of women.' She had met several of his old girlfriends, and liked a lot of them, although some of them seemed pretty crazy to her. She was far more down to earth than any woman he had ever dated before her. And she had a fondness for Francesca's mother too. Thalia was so outrageous in her own way, that Avery found it hard not to love her, and be amused by her. But she could also understand Francesca's discomfort about her. Even Avery had to concede that Thalia would be embarrassing as a mother, particularly for a child who wanted a mother like everyone else's. Thalia was definitely not one of those. And Henry was fairly eccentric and freewheeling too. They were anything but traditional parents, and Francesca had become extremely self-effacing as a result. The one thing she didn't want when she grew up was to be like them, and she wasn't. She was much more like Avery than like either of her biological parents. And Avery was aware too of what an odd match Henry and Thalia must have been. They were entirely different people, and she was surprised the marriage had even lasted seven years. The only good thing to come out of it was their daughter, and Henry and Thalia were now casual friends. But Thalia liked Avery a great deal. They all did. One had to respect her, and everyone liked her easy, friendly, intelligent ways. She was a smart, wholesome, unassuming, real person. Everything Francesca's mother wasn't.

'I think you've solved all my problems,' Francesca said with a sigh of relief.

'Not really. I still have to call your father's dealer, and you have to talk to your father about the gallery. But I think we're off to a good start,' Avery said encouragingly, and she was hopeful it would work out for her. She loved Francesca, thought she was a good person, and she deserved some reward for her hard work. She hated to see her lose everything because of the breakup with Todd.

'I knew you'd help me figure out something,' Francesca said, sounding happy and hopeful for the first time in months. 'I just couldn't see where to go with all this. I couldn't find a solution.'

'You're too close to it,' Avery said simply. 'Sometimes it takes an outsider to come up with a plan. Let's hope this all works. I'll let you know what your dad's dealer says, as soon as I talk to him. Your timing is pretty good. They'll be going to Art Basel in Miami pretty soon, and if he doesn't have any collectors waiting for your dad's early work, he'll see a lot of other people there. You might just have your money by the end of the year.'

'That'll make Todd happy,' Francesca said sadly, thinking of him.

'It should make you happy too if you get to keep the house,' Avery said. With or without a marriage license, they had a lot to work out and split up. It was almost as bad as a divorce.

'I'll be happy with the house,' Francesca confirmed. 'I guess I'd better tell my parents about Todd. To be honest, I dread it. Dad will be okay about it, but my mother is going to remind me seven hundred times that she warned me of this in the beginning. She thought we were crazy to buy the house and start the business without being married.'

'That's what people do these days. A lot of people who live together make joint investments.'

'Tell her that,' Francesca said with a wry grin.

'I wouldn't want to try,' Avery said, and they both laughed. Thalia had a million of her own opinions, and it was impossible to sway her in any direction other than her own.

'I'll call Dad and set up lunch with him. And I'll call my mother about Todd. Let me know what the dealer says.'

'I will. I promise. And keep your chin up in the meantime. We'll work it out,' Avery reassured her, and a moment later they both hung up. It was what her mother should have said and never would have. Thalia was more an Auntie Mame than a mother. And Avery was more of a friend.

Francesca sat at her desk, thinking for a long moment before she picked up the phone again. She was feeling better after her conversation with her stepmother. Avery had helped her, just as Francesca hoped she would. She always came through, and had some truly good, solid ideas, which usually worked, just as they had for Francesca's father. He had been so impressed with her in the beginning, and still was. She had wrought miracles for him, and the proof was in their very comfortable lifestyle. Avery had money of her own too. She'd had a lucrative career and invested well. And the idea of being dependent on anyone other than herself would have made her laugh. As she put it, she hadn't worked her ass off all her life in order to be dependent on a man. She did what she wanted with her money – and always had. None of that had changed when she got married. Henry had benefited far more than she from their relationship. Financially, he had needed her, she didn't need him. But emotionally, they were dependent on each other, which seemed like the way it should be to Francesca. She thought she had had that with Todd, but she didn't. And now they were pulling everything apart, and it hurt. A lot.

Francesca's next call was to her mother. Thalia barely asked her how she was, and launched into a long conversation about herself, what she was doing, who she was annoyed at, what a terrible job her decorator was doing, what bad investments her stockbroker had made recently, and what a worry it was for her.

'It's not like I have a husband to support me,' she lamented.

'You don't need a husband,' Francesca reminded her practically. 'Don left you set forever.' Her two shopping malls had grown to ten over the years, and she had other investments as well. She wasn't the pauper she pretended to be, by any means. And her small, chic penthouse apartment on Fifth Avenue was ample testimony to that. It was a beautiful place with a splendid view of Central Park.

'I didn't say he didn't. But it's very unnerving not having a husband to protect me,' she said, sounding momentarily small, which she wasn't either. And Francesca didn't say that she should be used to it by now, sixteen years after her last husband had died in Rome. He had left her with the title of Contessa, which she enjoyed very much. Thalia was only sorry he hadn't been a prince, and she had admitted to Francesca years before that she would have loved to be a princess, but countess wasn't bad. She was the Contessa di San Giovane.

Francesca decided to dive in then at one gulp. 'Todd and I broke up,' she said quietly, waiting for her mother's reaction.

'When did that happen?' Her mother sounded startled, as though she had suspected nothing, unlike Avery and her father.

'It's been coming for the last several months. We tried to work it out, but we couldn't. He's going back to working at a law firm, and he wants me to buy him out of the gallery and the house.'

'Can you afford to?' her mother asked her bluntly. It wasn't sympathy, just a question.

'Not yet. But I'm hoping to work it out by the end of the year.' She didn't tell her mother that she had discussed it with Avery, and asked for her advice. She didn't want to hurt her mother's feelings. But Avery's advice was a lot more useful than her mother's, who relied on other people to manage her money. Avery made all the big decisions herself.

'I told you that you shouldn't have bought a house and started a business with him. That's a crazy thing to do if you're not married, and guaranteed to turn into a mess. Is he being difficult about it?' Thalia had liked him, but not the fact that neither of them wanted to get married. She strongly disapproved of that, and in some ways was very old-fashioned.

'Not at all, Mom. He's being very nice. But he wants to get his money out of the house, and a little bit out of the business.'

'Can you do all that?'

'Maybe. If not, I'll have to sell the house and close the gallery. I'm trying my best not to.'

'What a shame you got all enmeshed with him. I never thought it was a good idea.' She never let her daughter forget it.

'Yes, I know, Mother. But we thought we had a sure thing.'

'We all do, until it falls apart. And when it does, you're much better off with alimony and a settlement than just a broken heart.' It was the only thing she knew, and the only career she'd ever had.

'Alimony's not a job, Mom. Or at least not the one I want. Hopefully, I'll be able to work it out.' As usual, her mother annoyed her.

'Why don't you just sell the house? You can't handle it without him anyway. The place is always falling apart.' It was exactly what Todd had said to her, that she would never be able to manage it alone. She was determined to prove both of them wrong. 'Can you even cover the mortgage payments?' her mother asked her, without offering to help her. But Francesca wasn't surprised. So far the conversation had gone exactly as she had expected, starting with 'I told you so.' There were no surprises here. There never were with her mother.

'I'm planning to take in roommates to help cover the payments,' Francesca said in a tense tone.

Her mother responded instantly with horror. 'Are you insane? That's like having hitchhikers in your house. Are you serious? Rent to strangers?'

'I don't have any other choice, and I want to keep the house, Mom. I'll be careful who I rent to. I'm not going to put up signs on the street. And I'll check them out carefully first.'

'You'll end up with an ax murderer in your house,' her mother said, sounding distressed.

'I hope not. Hopefully, I'll find some good ones.'

'I think that's a terrible idea, and you'll regret it.'

'If I do, you can remind me that you told me so,' Francesca said wryly. She knew her mother too well. Thalia always reminded her of her mistakes and that she had warned her beforehand.

'I want you to rethink that,' Thalia persisted.

'I can't,' Francesca said honestly. 'I can't make the

mortgage payments otherwise without Todd. Once the gallery starts making money, I can give up the room-mates. But for now, I have no other choice. I'll have to bite the bullet on that one.' And all else. She was going to have to give up a lot to keep the gallery and the house, her privacy in taking in roommates to pay the mortgage, her father's paintings to buy Todd out, and if her father didn't want to invest in the gallery, she might lose it entirely. It was all upsetting to think about.

'I think it's utterly crazy. I won't sleep at night, worrying about who else is living at your house.'

'There's safety in numbers. With three of them, I should be fine.'

'Should, but maybe won't be. And if they sign a lease, you'll be stuck with them for the duration of the lease. You can't just throw them out if you don't like them after a while.'

'No, I can't. So I'd better pick good ones,' Francesca said practically.

She got off the phone as quickly as she could after that. She had told her mother all the pertinent information, that she and Todd were breaking up and she was trying to keep the gallery and the house. She didn't need to know more than that, nor the gory details. And her mother had done just as predicted. She had criticized her, and offered no help at all. Some things never changed.

Her call to her father was easier and quicker. All she did was invite him to lunch the next day, and he accepted. She was planning to tell him everything then and he was much more easygoing than her mother. They agreed to meet at La Goulue for lunch, which was his favorite restaurant uptown. It was close to his gallery and he went there often. He was part of the celebrity landscape there. He sounded happy to hear from her.

'Everything okay?' he asked her before they hung up. He wondered what it was about. She rarely invited him to lunch.

'Okay enough. We can talk about it tomorrow.'

'All right. I can't wait to see you,' he said pleasantly. He still had the voice of a young man on the phone although he was sixty-five. And he looked far younger than his years as well, as did his wife. Francesca thought her mother looked older than Avery, and being desperate to find a new man gave her a certain frantic look of desperation, and had for years. Her father was far more relaxed and free and easy. It was his nature, but he also had Avery at his side. Her mother hadn't had a serious relationship in years. Francesca had a theory that she wanted one too badly, and it showed. It was a good lesson for her to remember herself now, as she had to face the dating world again, for the first time in five years. The thought of it depressed her profoundly, and she wasn't even remotely ready to think about going out with other men yet. She couldn't help wishing that she would never have to face dating again. She wasn't looking-forward to it. As far as she was concerned, it was the worst of all possible worlds. She had to look for three room-mates to share her house if she found the money to keep it, and eventually she'd have to start dating again, if she didn't want to be alone for the rest of her life. It was a big decision, but not one she had to face in the immediate future. Todd hadn't even moved out yet.

Her lunch with her father the next day went smoothly. He hopped out of a cab in front of La Goulue, just as she was arriving, after a brisk walk from the subway. And as always, he was looking very dashing. He was wearing a black and white tweed coat he had bought in Paris years before, the collar raised against the wind, a battered Borsalino hat he had bought in Florence, boots, and jeans, and he looked half GQ and half artist. He had a lined, craggy face with a square chin with a deep cleft in it that had fascinated her as a child, and he instantly put an arm around her and hugged her. He was a much warmer person than her mother, and he looked delighted to see her.

It was easier to tell him about Todd than she had expected, and he admitted that he wasn't surprised, and told her that he had always thought they were too different. Francesca had never thought so. She thought they had everything in common. And in the beginning they had, but no more.

'He was just a tourist in the art world,' her father commented as their lunch arrived. He had ordered onion soup and a dish of haricots verts, which was how he kept his long, lean, slim figure, not unlike her own. And he thrived on Avery's good healthy cooking. Francesca was always more haphazard about what she ate, especially lately with Todd gone. Most nights she was too lazy to cook herself dinner and had been losing weight since the breakup. 'I always figured he'd go back to Wall Street eventually,' her father said as he started in on the onion soup. Francesca had ordered the crab salad.

'That's funny,' Francesca said pensively, 'I never thought that. I guess you were right. He says he's tired of being poor.'

Her father laughed at that. 'Yeah, so was I, until Avery saved me.'

She told her father then about trying to buy Todd out of the house, and with a guilty look, she told him that she might sell his paintings, and he was very nice about it. It was easy to see why women had always loved him. He was easygoing and charming, rarely critical, and all-forgiving. He made her feel better about it immediately, and assured her he wasn't upset about it at all. By the time their coffee arrived, she had gotten up the courage to ask him about the gallery, and he smiled at her across the table. Avery had warned him about it cryptically, and said she needed his help, and told him to be nice. But he would have been anyway. She was his only child, and however unreliable he had been as a father, he was essentially a kind man.

'I'm very flattered that you would ask me,' he said simply, as he sipped a café filtre. 'I'm not sure I know any more about running a gallery than you do, probably considerably less. But I would very much enjoy being your silent partner for now.' She told him how much money she needed to satisfy Todd, and it wasn't a great deal, but it was more than she had. 'You can always buy me out, when the gallery takes off,' he said confidently. 'You're not stuck with me forever.'

'Thank you, Dad,' she said, genuinely relieved. They looked very much alike as they sat smiling at each other. She was deeply grateful for his help and had tears in her eyes. He had just helped her save the gallery she had worked so hard on for four years.

She got a call from Avery after lunch that was the first

step to saving the house. Her father's dealer had been thrilled about the paintings she wanted to sell. He had buyers for three of them immediately and thought he could sell two more in Miami in December. But the money from the first three would keep Todd happy for now.

Her father had gone to see his dealer at his gallery, and as Francesca headed toward the subway to head back downtown, she felt as though she had gotten a reprieve from the guillotine. Thanks to her father, and the paintings he had given her over the years that had increased so much in value, she was going to be able to hang on to her gallery and the house she loved so much. It was better than she would ever have dared to dream. As she hurried down the stairs to the subway, Francesca broke into a broad smile. She was off to a good start, and the breakup with Todd didn't seem quite so bad now. There was hope. She still had a business and a home, and a very nice dad.

Chapter 3

Francesca called Todd at his office to tell him the news as soon as she got home. She told him she expected to have the money, or a good part of it for him, in the next few weeks. Her father had promised that Avery would write her a check for Todd's share of the gallery the next day. And Avery said that the gallery would give her a check for the first three paintings within the month. Todd was more than comfortable with that.

'I guess that means I'd better start looking for an apartment,' he said sadly at the other end of the phone. 'I'll check some out this weekend,' he promised, and it felt like a knife in her heart. Although they'd been talking about his moving out for months, and he was never there on the weekends now, it suddenly felt all too real. It was over.

'There's no rush,' she said softly. They had loved each other and thought they would be together forever, and they were both sad that it hadn't worked out. It was easier concentrating on the business details about the gallery and the house than talking about the loss to both of them. It was the death of a dream. They had both survived other failed relationships before, but neither of them had ever lived with anyone else. Suddenly, it really did feel like a divorce. She wondered what they would do about all the things they had bought together – the couch, the lamps, the dishes, the living room rug they both liked. It was painful to think about that now. But sooner or later they would have to face pulling their common life apart. She hated the thought. And he wasn't happy about it either.

'I'll let you know what I find,' he said, and had to hurry into a meeting, which was a mercy for them both. She wondered when he would start dating, and how soon he would meet someone else, or if he already had. She didn't ask him what he did on weekends, but she didn't think he was seeing anyone. They hardly saw each other at the house now. He came in late at night, and he was sleeping in a guest room on another floor.

Talking to him reminded her that she had to start looking for roommates, since she was going to be able to keep the house. In one sense, it was a huge weight off her shoulders, and in another sense, she was suddenly unbearably sad. They didn't hate each other, they just didn't get along anymore, and they wanted different lives. He had said something about moving uptown. That was more his world than hers. He had moved downtown for her, and now he was going back to his old familiar world. Maybe her father was right, and he had only been a tourist in her life, like moving to another country for a few years, and then deciding you wanted to go home again. She didn't blame him, she was just very sorry for both of them that it hadn't worked out.

She had a long talk about it with Avery that night. She was so wise.

'You can't make someone be something they're not,' Avery reminded her. 'He wants all the things you don't. Or he says he does. Marriage, kids right now before he gets any older, Wall Street, the law not art, and a much more traditional world and life. If he's calling you bohemian, that's not what he wants.'

'I know,' Francesca said quietly. 'I'm just sad. It's going to be hard when he moves out.' But it had been hard for the last year too, fighting all the time. They weren't arguing anymore, the way they had for months. They hardly talked to each other now, except about the details of burying the relationship they'd had. It felt like a death even more than a divorce. In the last five years, she had forgotten how hard it was to see a relationship end. Avery felt sorry for her, and she was glad that Henry had agreed to help her with the gallery. At least she had that, and the house. It wasn't a total loss.

Francesca had told her she wanted to look for new artists when she had time. There was so much she wanted to do to keep the gallery moving forward, and she felt as though she had her father to answer to now, although he had assured her he wasn't going to be too involved. He was busy, and currently preparing a show for the spring. She had his support, but he had no desire to interfere with her. She knew what she was doing, and they both understood that getting the gallery profitable was going to take time. He accepted that a lot better than Todd, who wanted to see results. Art galleries just didn't work like that. Her father was right, Todd had been a visitor in her world. And now he was going home.

She looked at ads in the newspaper that night, and on the Internet, for people who were looking for roommates and places to live, and none of the descriptions fit. And then she decided to place her own ad. She had already figured out that she was going to divide the house on Charles Street floor by floor. On the top floor there was a sunny little living room with an even smaller bedroom and a tiny bath, but it was big enough for someone to live. Todd was sleeping up there now. On the floor below it was her own bedroom, which she had shared with Todd. They had a dressing room, and a marble bathroom they had installed, and she had a small home office off their bedroom, where she worked when she was at home.

Below them was the dining room, which she was going to turn into a living room, and conveniently it had a guest bath, and a library she could turn into a bedroom for whoever rented that floor. And on the main floor was the main living room that she planned to keep for herself. The kitchen was one floor below, on the garden level. It was large and sunny with a comfortable dining area that she and her tenants could all use. And next to it there was a spacious storeroom where Todd had kept his gym equipment. It looked out over the garden, had a decent bathroom, and could be used as a studio unit for a third tenant. It was going to be tight, but there was enough space for four of them, as long as they were all respectful, considerate, and polite. She had the top floor and the floor below her bedroom to rent out, and the studio unit next to the kitchen. She was determined to make it work.

She wrote out a description of each area on her computer that night, and she described the house. She thought of only renting to females, but she didn't want to limit it, she needed all the eligible tenants she could find. So she made no mention of females only and decided to see what she would get in answer to her ad.

She was just editing it one last time when Todd knocked on the door of her office, and stood there with a serious expression.

'Are you okay?' He was worried about her. He still didn't think she could manage on her own, and thought she should sell the house. But he knew she wouldn't do that, and was stubbornly determined to make it work, even if it meant taking strangers into her home. It seemed foolhardy to him and concerned him for her.

'Yeah, I am,' she said, sounding tired. 'What about you?'

'I don't know. It feels weird, doesn't it? Pulling our lives apart. I didn't expect it to hurt so much.' He looked vulnerable and sad. It reminded her of everything she loved about him, which made it worse.

'Neither did I,' she said honestly. But neither of them could imagine putting it back together now either. It had gone too far, and all their differences were still there. Irreconcilable differences, as it said in a divorce. But it hurt anyway, no matter how bad it had been for the past year. 'I'm going to hate your leaving. Maybe I'll go to my father's in Connecticut, so I don't have to watch.' He nodded and said nothing. He was ready to move on, but sad to leave her behind. She was just as beautiful as she had been five years before, just as appealing and warm, but they seemed like different people now. They no longer belonged to each other and were already pieces of each other's pasts.

'If I can do anything to help after I move out, you can always call me. Mr Fix-It at your service. I'm going to be a plumber in my next life.' He smiled ruefully, and she smiled back. He was tired of doing their repairs, but he was willing to lend a hand. The best and worst of it was that they didn't hate each other, which made it that much sadder now. It would have been easier if they were both mad, but neither of them was. 'I'll leave you my tools,' he promised. He was happy to leave them behind and never have to use them again.

'Thank you,' she said, and laughed. 'I'd better learn to use them pretty quick.'

'What if one of your roommates turns out to be nuts, or a criminal or con artist, or ransacks the house?' he asked. But even as he worried, he knew Francesca was a strong woman, and she was aware of what she wanted. She had survived thirty years without him before he came along. He correctly assumed that she would manage without him once he left. But he would miss her anyway. As it turned out she wasn't the woman for him, but he loved her as the very special person she had been in his life. He would always care about her, and hoped she'd be okay. And she wished the same for him.

'If they're nuts, I'll tell them to leave,' she said firmly.

He went upstairs then to the room where he slept. And she finished the ad. She was planning to submit it to the paper, and put it on the Internet the next day. And then God knew who would turn up. It was hard to imagine living in the house with three strangers. It was going to be a whole new world. She was planning to check their references diligently, and they couldn't move in until Todd found an apartment, but it seemed like a good idea to start looking for roommates now. She had no idea how long it would take to find three people to live in the house with her.

It all felt very strange as she got into bed that night. She was anxious for Todd to go. It was too painful waiting for the other shoe to drop. And odder still to wonder about who would turn up to move into the house. 44 Charles Street was about to become a very different place, and so was her life without Todd.

Chapter 4

The responses to Francesca's ad were abundant, and most of them were pretty outrageous. She was stunned by what most people were willing to say about themselves. Some of them were fresh out of rehab and said they didn't feel ready to take on an apartment, and would be delighted to live with her. Everyone seemed to love the description of the house. Several couples answered the ad, and Francesca told them honestly that the spaces she was renting were too small for more than one person, and she didn't feel ready to live with more than three roommates. One couple had two kids and wanted to rent two of the three spaces, which didn't feel right to her either. They were three- and five-year-old boys and she was afraid they would destroy her house. Two people said they were recently out of prison, one said he was a sex offender, and the other said that he had been convicted of a white-collar crime he didn't commit. She didn't ask what it was. Four lesbian couples wanted to rent the house together and asked if she'd be willing to move out, which she wasn't. It defeated the whole purpose of what she was trying to do to keep the house. And at least a third to half of the applicants had dogs, many of them large. German shepherds, Labradors, two Irish wolfhounds, a Great Dane, a Rhodesian ridgeback, a Rottweiler, and a pit bull. She wasn't prepared to take that on either. And she was beginning to wonder if anyone normal and easy, without a partner, a child, a dog, a substance addiction, or a prison record would turn up. She was beginning to lose hope and wonder if Todd and her mother were right. Maybe they were all crazy, or she was for trying to find three sane, normal roommates. She was beginning to think that there was no such thing in New York.

It was two days before Thanksgiving when she got a call from a young woman who said her name was Eileen Flanders. She said she had just graduated from Loyola Marymount in L.A. in May, she was originally from San Diego, and had just gotten a job and arrived in New York. She was a special ed teacher for autistic children. She said nothing about having been to rehab, didn't mention doing time in prison, said she was alone, and had neither kids nor dogs. It was a hopeful start. Francesca couldn't help wondering if she was covered with tattoos, had countless body pierces, and wore a Mohawk, but the initial conversation over the phone went pretty well. She said she was hoping to move in quickly, but she was staying at the Y, and said she could stay there for a few more weeks, when Francesca explained that the place wouldn't be available until January first.

Todd had just found an apartment on East 81st Street, near the river. He was planning to pack between Christmas and New Year, and said he would be out on January first. She didn't want anyone moving in till then. It would be too painful for both of them to have strangers living in the house while they went through the emotional upheaval of his leaving. Eileen said she didn't mind, and she said she was going home to San Diego for the holidays anyway. It sounded good so far and Francesca made an appointment with Eileen to come to the house the following afternoon.

The next day Francesca was immensely relieved when she opened the door and saw Eileen standing on the front stoop. Eileen was wearing Nikes and jeans, and she had on a red car coat with toggles and a hood, white mittens, and earmuffs. She looked like a kid on a Christmas card. She was a redhead with freckles and blue eyes, and she had perfect white teeth when she smiled. She was wearing no makeup and looked about fifteen years old, and she looked nervous as she waited to come inside.

Francesca invited her in, and the two women chatted easily in the front hall. Eileen looked around and commented on how pretty the house was. There was a stained-glass window over the front door, and a narrow but handsome circular staircase leading upstairs. And she could glimpse a marble fireplace through the open door of the living room, which Francesca explained she was keeping for her own use. Eileen said she was fine with that, as Francesca explained that some of the furniture throughout the house would be going, when her current roommate moved out, but she would replace it as soon as she could. The room on the top floor was furnished with things Todd didn't want. And she was willing to furnish the other possible units if necessary.

She led Eileen upstairs to the top floor, where some of Todd's clothes were strewn around, since he was sleeping there. Eileen admired the view of the neighbors' gardens behind the house, and then peeked into the bathroom and the closets and seemed to like what she saw. And Francesca liked her. She appeared to be wholesome and clean, a small-town girl come to the big city. She said she was the oldest of six children, and asked if there was a Catholic church nearby. She was everything that Francesca could have wanted in a tenant. She was the epitome of a nice, friendly girl next door. There was nothing worrisome or unsavory about her. They both looked relieved.

Francesca showed her the floor below her own, and explained that the dining room would be turned into a living room and the den into a bedroom. It was bigger but darker than the top floor, and she and Todd had painted the walls a forest green, which worked as a dining room, but might be a little somber for a living room, or too masculine for her. And Eileen didn't like the garden unit. She said she was afraid that someone might come in through the sliding doors. She said she felt safer on the top floor. And she loved the cozy country kitchen that Francesca and Todd had installed themselves. Or he had, while Francesca watched, handed him tools, and made coffee. It was their favorite room in the house, and Eileen's.

'It looks like a lot of love went into this house,' Eileen said as Francesca nodded, not sure what to say, and not wanting her to see that there were tears in her eyes. A lot of love had gone into 44 Charles Street, and a lot of hope.

And now all those hopes were dashed, and she was standing here with this pixie of a girl from San Diego instead of Todd. It wasn't fair, but that was life. Francesca had made her peace with it over the past months, the transition was just hard. And talking to Eileen about moving in made it a reality that Francesca had to face. She was by far the most suitable candidate Francesca had seen so far. And if her credit and references checked out, Francesca was willing to rent her the top floor. She told her the price, and Eileen didn't flinch. It wasn't enormous, but it was enough to cover a quarter of the mortgage payment Francesca had to make.

'I think I can manage that. I thought I was going to be able to get my own apartment, maybe with a roommate. But everything I've seen so far has been way over my head. This is a lot for me, but it would work, and I like the idea of living with other people. It feels safer and less lonely that way.' Francesca thought so too. 'Do you know who the other tenants will be yet?'

'You're the first person I've seen so far who feels right to me,' Francesca told her honestly, and then told her that she was breaking up with someone who was moving out, and this was the first time she was going to be living with roommates in the house.

'I'm sorry,' Eileen said sympathetically, and looked like

she meant it. 'I broke up with someone in L.A. That's why I left. We started going out right after I graduated, and he turned out to be insane. He practically stalked me when I said I wanted some space. He climbed in my window one night and tried to strangle me. I quit my job and came to New York the next day. That was a month ago, and I was really lucky to find a job here.' She looked relieved as she said it and Francesca looked sorry for her. She looked so scrubbed and sweet and innocent, it was hard to imagine anyone wanting to strangle her or scare her.

'It's a good thing you got away,' Francesca said as they walked back up from the kitchen to the main hall. 'There are a lot of crazy people out there.' She had interviewed many of them as potential tenants. 'You have to be careful too in a city like New York. This neighborhood is very safe. I walk to and from work. I have an art gallery a few blocks away.'

'How exciting!' Eileen looked thrilled to hear it. 'I love going to galleries on weekends.'

She gave Francesca her credit details then and the phone number of her landlord in L.A. She had lived there for her last year of school at LMU and for five months after she graduated. She had worked in a children's shelter after school, and in a day care center for special needs kids after graduation. Everything about her was wholesome and nice. Francesca promised to call her as soon as she checked it all out. And with the Thanksgiving weekend ahead of them, she reminded her that she couldn't do it until Monday, but she would get on it immediately then. Eileen said that was fine, and that she hoped Francesca would let her move in. She liked Francesca and loved the house. She said it felt like home to her, and the house where she grew up. It seemed perfect for them both. She was exactly the kind of tenant Francesca wanted, one she didn't have to worry about. It was rare to find anyone as squeaky clean as that. She thought it a great stroke of good fortune that Eileen had responded to the ad.

Finding Eileen, the first of her tenants, put Francesca in better spirits for the Thanksgiving holiday. She knew it would be hard this year – it was the first holiday in five years that she hadn't spent with Todd. He was going to his own family in Baltimore, and she was going to her father's in Connecticut. Her mother had gone to Palm Beach to stay with friends.

Francesca ran into Todd that morning in the hall before they both left. There was a soundless look of sharp pain between them, and he gave her a hug.

'Have a nice turkey,' she said softly.

'You too,' he answered, gave her a quick kiss on the cheek, and hurried out. And she felt odd again as she sighed and went out to her car parked on Charles Street. Their breakup seemed to be taking forever, but it would be over soon. She wasn't sure if that would be better or worse.

She thought of Eileen again as she drove to Connecticut, and was so glad she'd found her. She seemed absolutely perfect to Fran cesca. She just hoped her credit checked out, and the references from her landlord.

When Francesca got to her father's house at noon, there were already a dozen people drinking champagne and standing around the fire, while Avery and a caterer organized things in the kitchen. The turkey looked fantastic and was golden brown. Francesca was planning to spend the night with them after dinner so she wouldn't have to rush back to the city. Most of the other guests were either locals or artists. Their neighbors, who had a handsome farm, were there, and Henry's art dealer from New York. It was an arty, intellectual, interesting, lively group. Francesca knew most of them, and always had fun with her father and Avery's friends. He had never been much of a father to her until recently, but he was good company, and treated her more like a cherished friend than his daughter. It didn't bother her anymore, but she had always felt cheated by it when she was young, and wanted a real dad, like everyone else, not an eccentric father with a revolving door of twenty-two-year-old girlfriends. Things had improved immeasurably when he married Avery, but Francesca was twenty-five by then. And at thirty-five, she accepted him for what he was, talented, kind-hearted, irresponsible, and fun to be with. And she was very grateful for his helping her out with the gallery recently.

He told everyone at lunch that he was now a partner in her gallery. And his dealer told her quietly after lunch that he had just sold another of her father's paintings for her, at an amazing price, so she was going to be able to make yet another payment to Todd for the house. Thanks to the sale of the four paintings, she had almost paid him the full amount. One more would do it. And that left her one that she could keep. Everything had worked out just right, and in a remarkably short time. All she had to do now was find two more tenants to make the mortgage payments with her.

She spent the night at her father and Avery's, and went back to the city on Friday afternoon. She had closed the gallery for two days for the holiday, but planned to reopen on Saturday. They got a lot of people just looking on Saturdays, but the occasional serious buyer as well. Much to her delight, they had a busy day and several young couples came in. They looked around nervously at first, afraid her prices would be too stiff for them, and were thrilled to discover that her prices were well within their range. It was the whole point of what she was doing. She wanted to bring young collectors together with artists starting out on their careers. She sold three very handsome paintings to two of the couples. The paintings were big, reasonably priced, and would make their décor. The prices were so low that it wasn't a major financial victory for her, but the three sales made her heart sing and she knew all three artists would be as excited as the people who had just bought their work. The art they sold was beautiful, and she was proud of it and each one of their artists. The people who bought paintings from her that weekend were so elated about their purchases that it touched her heart. It always did. She couldn't wait to tell the artists, all of whom desperately needed the sales. She felt like a mother hen with each one of them. And the day before, talking to her father's friends, some of them very well-known important artists, had invigorated her. She loved everything about her life in the art world, and being part of the process. She was the link between the creators, some of whom were very talented, and collectors of their work. It was exactly what she wanted to do, and what she knew best. She lived and breathed it. She had a keen eye for new artists, gave them good advice, and had a good sense for what would sell. It was why she was so convinced that given enough time, the gallery would do well. She often spent hours in the studio with her artists, talking about their process or guiding them toward a new phase of their work. They had a deep respect for her.

She spent Sunday cleaning out closets, and getting the upstairs ready for her tenant. And on Monday morning she called Eileen's landlord in L.A., and started the credit check on her. The landlord said she was a lovely young woman, had given him no problems, and paid her rent on time. And three days later, her credit check came back clean. She had no history of lawsuits, bankruptcy, bad credit, or unpaid bills. Francesca called her and told her she could move in on January 2, the day after Todd left, and Eileen was ecstatic. Now all Francesca had to do was find two more tenants. And from what she had seen in the past month, that wasn't going to be easy. Eileen was a rare gem as tenants went. But there had to be two more like her, or close enough, somewhere in New York. She was still running the ads, but for the next several weeks all she continued to get were freaks. Sometimes they were so bad that all she could do was laugh when she hung up the phone.

The weekend after Thanksgiving she had dinner with her mother at a small French bistro they both loved, and reported to her victoriously on having found Eileen. Her mother still thought she was crazy, but it was an opinion Francesca had harbored about her for years. She wouldn't have wanted her mother as a tenant either.

Thalia reported to her daughter about all the social events she had gone to in Palm Beach. She had always had an extremely active social life, and had a particular fondness for fancy watering holes, Palm Beach, Newport, St Tropez, Sardinia, and St Moritz, Gstaad, or St Bart's in winter. She had never had a job, and thanks to her ex-husbands, she could afford to do what she wanted. She was a totally self-indulgent person, and Francesca thought she was extremely spoiled. She thought of no one but herself. She had gone to a fabulous deb ball the previous weekend in Palm Beach, and was describing to Francesca what she had worn in minute detail. It sounded very pretty, but Francesca didn't care. She was used to making the right noises and wearing the right expression to feign interest. She couldn't even begin to imagine how her parents had ever gotten together, although her father had been sexy and young then, and her mother had gotten spoiled and snobbish later on.

She was a striking, still beautiful woman, tall, stately,

blond like her daughter, with big green eyes, and smooth creamy skin. She stayed in good shape with the help of a trainer, and she was rigorous about what she ate. She had worn a fur coat to lunch, and had sapphires on her ears, which matched a stylish navy wool dress by Dior. And she was wearing sexy high heels. Men had always flocked to her like bees to honey, and still did, but no one had taken her seriously in a long time. She was a little too fey, just a touch too eccentric, and she looked expensive and spoiled. And referring to her mother as 'colorful' had been Francesca's way of saying that she was a little nuts. She was going to a fat farm after the holidays to stay in shape, and wanted to have a tummy tuck by summer. She still looked great in a bikini. So did Francesca, but she rarely had time to wear one. And she couldn't help smiling at their feet under the table, when she retrieved her napkin when it slipped off her lap. Her mother was wearing the sexiest high-heeled black patent leather pumps she had ever seen. Francesca had delivered two paintings to clients before lunch and was wearing jeans and sneakers. The two women were nothing alike.

'And what are you doing for Christmas?' Thalia asked Francesca with a bright smile, as though she were someone else's daughter, or a niece she saw once a year. The question made it clear that Thalia wasn't planning to spend it with her. She never did. She usually went skiing in Switzerland, or to St Bart's in the Caribbean, particularly if someone invited her on a yacht, which happened often. Thalia's life was one long vacation all year round.

'Maybe I'll go to Dad's for Christmas,' Francesca said vaguely in answer to her mother's question.

'I thought he was going skiing in Aspen,' her mother said, frowning. 'I think that's what Avery said. It's been a while since we talked.'

'Then I'll stay home. I'm keeping the gallery open that week anyway, so I'll be busy, and Todd is moving out.'

'That's too bad. You two should have gotten married. It might have kept you together.'

'That never kept you with anyone when it stopped working,' Francesca said matter-of-factly.

'That's true.' Her mother smiled sweetly at her. 'I always seem to fall in love with someone else.' Francesca didn't remind her that that hadn't happened in a long time. 'Maybe I'll meet someone in St Bart's,' she said dreamily, with a hopeful expression. She was always hoping to fall in love again and get married. For Thalia, life without a husband was a wasteland. She was always on the hunt.

Francesca changed the subject and told her about her

tenant then, and her mother frowned in disapproval. 'I don't care if she's a Girl Scout and looks like Little Bo Peep. I still think you're crazy to live with strangers. You have no idea who these people are, or who they'll drag in.'

'I have no other choice, Mom, if I want to keep the house.'

'You'd be much better off in an apartment, by yourself.'

'I don't want an apartment. I love my house.'

'You can't live in a house without a man. It's just not safe.'

'Maybe one of my tenants will be a man,' Francesca said blandly, thinking of the people she had talked to, and how unsuitable most of them had been, which she did not share with her mother.

'You need a husband, Francesca,' Thalia said, and then laughed, 'and so do I.' Francesca disagreed on both counts but didn't say so. Her mother always said things like that and she no longer took the bait. There was no point.

'When are you leaving for St Bart's, Mom?' she asked her, to steer her onto neutral subjects.

'Two days before Christmas. I can hardly wait. I'm so tired of winter. I'm going skiing in Switzerland right after that. You should try to get away.' Her mother lived on a different planet, of parties and vacations, and never realized how hard Francesca worked. Whatever Francesca had, she had made on her own, and built from scratch. Her father had paid for her education, and she had supported herself ever since. And the money her mother had gotten in settlements from her ex-husbands she kept to herself. She felt she had earned it.

Francesca left their lunch feeling as she always did after seeing her mother, emotionally hungry. There was nothing satisfying about their exchanges, and never anything meaningful or deep. At least her encounters with her father were fun.

He stopped in at the gallery that week and bought a small painting for Avery that he thought she would like. Francesca gave him the partner's rate, which made it ridiculously cheap, but he loved the work she sold. He was impressed that she frequently went to art fairs in other cities to discover new artists and spent hours in her artists' studios, studying their new work with them. And he thought that most of what she had in the gallery was very good. He had a strong feeling that one or two of the artists she represented would have important careers one day. She told him that the artist he was buying had been selling well, and had sold several bigger pieces since Thanksgiving, although her father thought her prices were too low, and very fair. She commented that people seemed more willing to spend money right before the holidays. Her father was particularly pleased that he had just sold a very important piece himself. He was planning to buy Avery a new car, a Range Rover, with some of what he'd made. She had always wanted one, and despite her success, she still drove an ancient Toyota that Henry insisted wasn't safe, and she had refused to let him replace it until then. He said he was going to surprise her with the car for Christmas before they left for Aspen.

It struck Francesca as she closed the gallery on Christmas Eve that neither of her parents was worried about what she was going to do for Christmas. They always made their own plans. It had made holidays more meaningful with Todd, but not this year. He had plans of his own, and she had none. There were friends and artists she could have called, but she didn't feel like it. She had turned down two invitations. She felt melancholy this year and wanted to be alone. Todd was moving out in a few days, and his boxes were stacked in the hall when she got home. It was happening. She was ready for it now, but sad. It would have been hard not to be.

She watched movies and ate Chinese takeout on Christmas Eve. She hadn't set up a Christmas tree and didn't miss it. She wanted the holidays to pass as quickly as possible. And after the New Year, she could start a whole new life, alone again.

Both her parents called her on Christmas Day, and she saw Todd on his way out. He waved, smiled, and was talking to someone on his cell phone as he left. She noticed that he was wearing a suit, and wondered where he was going and with whom. It was hard to believe now that they had ever lived together, or had anything in common.

She took a long walk around the West Village that afternoon, and smiled at couples she saw, strolling with children. Some were carrying stacks of presents to someone's house, and she saw a Santa Claus in a red velvet suit get out of his car, put on his hat and beard, and hurry in to a party. It was a strange day to be alone, but in a funny way she didn't mind it. It was easier than pretending she was happy. She thought of her mother on the yacht in the Caribbean, hoping to meet a man, and her father and Avery in Aspen, and this year she was glad to be on her own. She went to bed early that night and was glad the day was over.

And then the day she had anticipated and dreaded for months came at last. She went to bed at nine o'clock on New Year's Eve, and was sound asleep by midnight, and in the morning she could hear Todd thundering up and down the stairs, moving his boxes. He had rented a truck, and had two friends helping him. Francesca wandered into the living room, in time to watch them pick up the couch. They had already agreed to what each of them was keeping and he had paid for the couch. It was a good-looking brown leather piece that went well with their décor, and she knew she'd have to buy a new one. He had agreed to let her keep the bed and most of the things in their bedroom, although he had paid for them too. But he wanted the couch and the two big chairs that went with it, for his new apartment. Francesca tried not to feel her stomach turning over as she saw them go. She felt as though her body parts had been sawn off and were packed in each box, and somewhere amid the bubble wrap and styrofoam popcorn, along with their wine-glasses that he had paid for too, was her heart.

It was over by midafternoon on New Year's Day. The truck was packed to the gills, and Todd came to find her, standing in the kitchen, with a devastated look, looking out at the wintry garden.

'I'm leaving,' he said softly, as she turned to face him, and he saw tears roll down her cheeks. He took her in his arms, and he was crying too. 'I know this sounds stupid now, but I love you. I'm sorry it worked out like this.'

'So am I. I love you too.' But no matter how much it

hurt and they cared about each other, they both knew it was for the best. It hadn't worked.

'Call me if you need me. I'll come and help, anytime.' She nodded, unable to say another word. And with that he kissed her on the forehead, turned, and walked up the stairs, as she stood in the kitchen and cried. She heard the front door close a few minutes later. He was gone. It felt as though someone had ripped out her heart, and she knew he felt no better. It was hard to believe, but it had finally happened. The house was hers, and his days at 44 Charles Street were over. All she could do now was move on. She could tell he already had.

Chapter 5

The day after Todd moved out, Francesca bought flowers for almost every room. She cleaned the kitchen, vacuumed the halls, and looked around the top floor to make sure that everything was in order, and by the time Eileen arrived at noon, the whole house looked terrific. She beamed as she walked in, and Francesca was ready for her. Eileen had four suitcases and several boxes, and three shopping bags of shoes. She pointed at them in embarrassment as Francesca helped her carry them up the stairs.

'Sorry. I went crazy over Christmas. I got so depressed that I went on a shoe binge. They didn't fit in my suitcase.'

'No worries.' Francesca smiled at her. 'I'm used to it. My mom has a shoe fetish too. I'm addicted to Nikes. My mother wears high heels that would give me a nosebleed.'

'I like them too,' Eileen admitted as they set her things down in the bedroom on the top floor, and Eileen went back downstairs for another load.

There was a whole different feeling in the house that afternoon. The day before she'd been in mourning, and today she had woken up with a sense of freedom. The other shoe had finally dropped. Todd was gone. She was sad about it, but not as devastated as she had felt watching him load his belongings into a truck and leave. The worst was over. His not being there wasn't going to make a lot of difference, since their lives had been so separate for months, except that now she wouldn't see him come and go anymore. But their lives had barely intersected for a year. And it was fun seeing a girl in the house when she saw Eileen in the kitchen later that afternoon. It was Sunday so the gallery was closed, and Francesca was hanging out at home.

Eileen smiled broadly when she saw her. She acted like a kid.

'I love my rooms. They're so pretty. And thank you for the flowers.' Francesca had put a vase of pink carnations and roses in her bedroom. Eileen looked ecstatic. 'I feel like I've finally come home. I've been living out of suitcases since I got here. It's going to be great having my own place.' And she didn't even mind the long hike up the stairs to the top floor. She noticed a computer on the kitchen table and looked hopeful. 'Mind if I check my e-mail? I don't have a laptop yet.'

'That's fine.' Francesca didn't mind. It was a laptop she always left sitting in the kitchen that she and Todd rarely used but it was convenient having one there. She had her own in her office.

'I'll just be a minute.' Eileen logged on, and smiled as she read her e-mails. She laughed out loud at one, and Francesca smiled as she left the kitchen and went back upstairs to her own room. It was kind of nice having someone around. The house already felt livelier and happier than it had for months. She was almost sorry that she had to find two more roommates. It might have been fun just sharing the house with Eileen, but she couldn't afford it. She had to find two more, and no one decent had turned up since Eileen. The freaks and crazies had come out in force again in answer to her ads before Christmas. There had been one decent-sounding woman who had just moved to New York from Atlanta, but she found another arrangement before she ever came to see the house on Charles Street. And Francesca had to find someone soon. She couldn't make the mortgage payments with just Eileen paying rent.

Francesca took a nap that afternoon, which she rarely did, but she was still tired after the emotional drain of saying goodbye to Todd the day before. He had promised to call, but she didn't know if he really would, or even if she wanted him to. She didn't want to lose touch with him, but she didn't want to be in constant contact with him either. They both had to go forward and make their own way now.

Francesca went back downstairs to the kitchen at dinnertime, and Eileen was there. She was eating a bowl of soup, and back on the computer. She apologized as soon as Francesca came into the room, poured herself a glass of milk, and grabbed an apple. The soup Eileen had made was her own – she had been careful not to help herself to Francesca's food. Francesca thought it was a good sign that she would be a respectful roommate.

She sat down at the table, and saw that Eileen had logged on to one of the online dating services, and was looking over the photographs on the screen.

'Do you ever try it?' she asked Francesca with a look of happy mischief and then giggled. 'I love it. It's kind of like ordering takeout guys instead of takeout food. I started doing it in college. I met some great guys in L.A. and San Diego. I went out with one of them for almost a year, until he got drunk and joined the Marines.'

'I didn't think people still did that, got drunk and enlisted I mean. And no, I've never met anyone online. It sounds too dangerous. I'd be afraid of who I'd meet. There's no screening process.' The idea of meeting men online really put her off. It seemed so desperate to her. She felt much safer meeting men through friends, although she knew many people who had met men, and even their husbands, online.

'You develop a pretty good sixth sense for who these guys are. I've only met one or two who were creepy.'

'Do you do it a lot?' Francesca asked with interest. It surprised her that a pretty, wholesome cheerleader type like Eileen would need or want to meet men online. She could have any man she wanted. But Francesca also knew that it wasn't easy to meet single eligible man, which was why online dating services existed.

'Not really. It's just a nice distraction when I have nothing else to do.' It made Francesca wonder if she needed to set some kind of guidelines about bringing people to the house, but realized she had no right to do that. She was her landlady, not the resident adviser in a girls' dorm, or her mother. They were both adults with their own lives, and who Eileen brought home was going to be her business, not Francesca's. So she didn't say anything. She just went back upstairs munching on her apple, and left Eileen alone to her pursuits. If she met men on the Internet, it was up to her, whether it seemed wise to Francesca or not. All she knew was that it wasn't for her.

Francesca hadn't even thought of dating till then, and didn't want to yet. She wasn't ready. Eileen was full of life, and trying to meet people in a new city. Francesca was older and more cautious. Online matchmaking services had no appeal to her whatsoever. If she met a man, it was going to have to be the old-fashioned way, through friends, or at some kind of social gathering, or at the gallery. But she didn't even want to meet a man right now, nor start dating. She didn't have time anyway, and the only thing she wanted to find online were two more tenants.

It finally happened two weeks later, in mid-January. She got a response from a man who sounded sane. He said he was a graphic designer who worked from home a lot of the time, traveled occasionally for business, said he was solvent, and was looking for a setup like the one she was offering. He said he was recently divorced, had no furniture, and needed a bedroom and a small study to set up his drafting table and his computer. Her currently unoccupied second floor, where the dining room had been, sounded adequate for him. They made an appointment for him to come and see the house. He mentioned that he was thirty-eight years old, and when he came to meet her, he explained that he had a seven-year-old son who spent alternate weekends with him.

'Will that be a problem?' he asked, looking worried. He had already come across several similar arrangements, but none was willing to include children. Francesca hesitated for a long moment before she answered and then nodded.

'I think that'll be okay, as long as he's not here all the time.' Two weekends a month didn't seem like a lot to her, and Chris Harley looked relieved. He was tall, thin, had sandy blond hair, gray eyes, and a serious expression. He was so pale he looked like he hadn't seen the sun in years. He would have been good-looking if he hadn't been so somber.

He said very little to her during their meeting, except his question about his son. He looked at the rooms, seemed satisfied, and said in a quiet subdued voice, 'I'll take it.' He didn't ooh and ahh the way Eileen had. He said almost nothing. He seemed extremely withdrawn to Francesca, but she didn't mind that either. This wasn't a date, they didn't need to like each other, get to know each other, and become friends. All she needed to know was if he was a responsible person and would pay the rent. This wasn't romance. And he didn't look interested in that either. After showing him his rooms, Francesca led him downstairs to look at the kitchen, and see the garden unit. But he said he liked the one on the second floor better. The garden studio seemed too small to him, and he didn't need or want to be that close to the kitchen. He offered to purchase furniture for the bedroom, which was fine with her.

Eileen was in the kitchen when they went down to see it, and she was on the computer again, as she was a lot of the time, not just looking for potential dates, but usually doing e-mail. She looked up and smiled when she saw Chris. As she told Francesca later, he was 'cute.' Eileen was beginning to seem a little boy crazy to Francesca. She went out a lot at night, but none of her potential suitors had come to the house or been a problem for Francesca. Chris Harley seemed like an excellent tenant, although she didn't know anything personal about him except that he was divorced and a graphic designer who thought he could pay the rent. That was all she needed to know, and if his credit was good.

She asked for the same details that she had asked of Eileen. Francesca took his credit information, and as she looked at him, he had a familiar look. She felt as though she had seen him sometime, somewhere. Or maybe that was just an impression. In any case, they shook hands on their deal, and Francesca said that after she checked his credit in the coming days, he could move in anytime if everything was fine, the sooner the better. So if all went well, they had their second roommate.

Chris Harley looked happy with the arrangement when he left the house on Charles Street that afternoon. And Francesca promised to call him as soon as she got the results of the credit check. But he didn't look as though he'd have a problem paying his rent or his bills. He seemed solid, and conservative and well-spoken. He said he designed industrial packaging and had given her his card. Francesca had a good feeling about him. She trusted her own instincts. He looked like a wholesome, decent guy, who would be pleasant to have around.

She said as much to Eileen while they tidied up the kitchen. 'He's nice-looking too,' Francesca said casually, and Eileen shrugged.

'He's too conventional, too boring. He's not for me.' Francesca wanted to ask her who was, other than the scores of men whose photographs she perused on the Internet. 'Besides, it would be stupid to get involved with someone living here. That's a little too close for comfort.' They both agreed on that.

'If things go wrong, one of us would have to move. I'd

rather go out with men I meet outside, or online.' She had half a dozen candidates going strong at the moment with whom she e-mailed, and Francesca had no idea which ones Eileen had met, and which she hadn't.

Much to Francesca's delight, Chris got an excellent credit rating when Francesca checked him out. He was good to go as her second tenant, although she hadn't met his son and felt she didn't need to. How bad could a seven-year-old be? And four days a month wasn't enough to worry about. She called Chris at the office number he gave her, and told him that he was welcome to move into the house as soon as he wanted.

'That's fantastic,' he said with pleasure. 'I could move in this weekend. I don't have much stuff. I'll get what I need for the bedroom tomorrow.'

She was mildly curious about why he didn't want an apartment of his own but she didn't ask him. She was glad he didn't. He made a comment after that that he had given everything he had to his ex-wife. He said all he had right now was his clothing, a stack of books, and two paintings. He had left everything else at his apartment with his wife and son, and was staying at a hotel. He said he'd been there for two months. And he liked the idea of being in a house and not an apartment.

When he moved in, Chris changed the whole feeling

of the house again. He added something solid. He was so serious and so calm that Francesca was certain he would cause her no problems, and even be easy to live with. He was exactly who and what Francesca wanted as a tenant or roommate. And Eileen looked unimpressed when Francesca commented on it.

'He's too quiet,' Eileen said without much interest. He was too old for her anyway. She said she liked boys her own age, most of whom were just graduating from college, as she had. Chris seemed very mature at thirty-eight, and in some ways even older than Todd. Francesca suspected that having a child had made him that way, or his divorce. Whatever it was, Francesca thought he seemed like a responsible adult, which was just what she wanted in a tenant.

He moved in the following weekend with his drafting table and art supplies. He set them up carefully, along with a set of barbells, a flat-screen TV, a sound system, and his clothes. His bedroom furniture had been delivered the day before, and she was startled to see he had bunk beds, which seemed a little odd. She assumed they were for his son.

He kept to himself once he moved in and Francesca didn't see him all day, since she was at the gallery. And by the time she came home, he had moved in, made himself something to eat, and was back on his floor, working. And Eileen was away for the weekend. The house was orderly and quiet. She didn't even see him until Sunday, when she met him in the kitchen, making a pot of coffee. She asked if everything was all right, and he said it was. He sat quietly at the kitchen table, drank his coffee, read the paper, poured himself a second cup, and went back upstairs. He didn't engage in conversation with her, and she noticed that there was something sad about his eyes. Whatever his story was, he had no desire to discuss it. Chris seemed to have no interest in making friends. He was pleasant and polite, and as cool as he had been with her when they first met. It suited Francesca just fine.

She told Avery about his moving in when she called that night.

'He sounds like the perfect tenant,' Avery commented. 'Good boundaries, good manners, good credit. Have you met his kid?'

'Not yet. I guess he'll be here next weekend.'

'Let's hope he's not a brat.'

'Chris doesn't look like the kind of guy who would tolerate that. He isn't a lot of fun. There's something sad about him. He's very quiet.'

'Maybe he's had a rough time. Or maybe he's just that

kind of guy. Not everyone is as charming and chatty as your father,' she said, and they both laughed. 'Any prospects for the unit downstairs?' Avery was impressed by how easily the other two had fallen into place, and it sounded like Francesca had lucked out with two ideal tenants. One was pleasant and sweet, and the other serious and quiet. It didn't get much better than that. 'Any news from Todd?'

'He called at the gallery a few days ago, but I was out, visiting an artist, and picking up some new work.' To save money and keep their overhead down, she did all the menial work herself. 'He left me a message saying that he hopes I'm okay. I hate to say it, but I miss him. I miss the way it was in the beginning, not the way it was for the last year. Life is pretty quiet. All I do is work, come home at night, eat, watch TV, and go to sleep.'

'Things will pick up again. You need to get out, go to some openings and some parties.' But Francesca wasn't in the mood. She told Avery about a new artist she had found through one of the gallery artists, in Brooklyn. They talked about her father for a few minutes, he was working hard on his upcoming show, and Avery said his newest work was fabulous. She was his biggest fan. And after they hung up, Francesca turned off the light and lay in bed in the dark. She could hear the sound of the

TV in Eileen's room, and Chris moving around downstairs. It was kind of reassuring not to be alone in the house. She liked the feeling, even though she hardly knew either of them, and maybe never would. And as she thought about it, she drifted off to sleep.

Francesca opened a show at the gallery the following week. Openings were always hectic and stressful. She had to make sure she had the work in the gallery in time, which often meant harassing the artists to get it ready, right down to the last minute, getting the invitations out to their clients, begging art critics to come to the show to review it, and hanging and lighting the show herself. By the time they opened their doors for the opening, she was exhausted.

The artist she was featuring this time was difficult, and kept insisting she move everything around. They sold four pieces the first night, and for several weeks she was too busy to check for new responses to her ad. She kept meaning to but forgot. She needed another tenant but she didn't have time to pursue it. And she never saw Chris or Eileen. The arrangement was working well. It was three weeks after Chris had moved in that she finally met his son. She was sitting in the kitchen checking her e-mail, when she heard a sound, startled, and looked up.

It was a little boy in a red sweater and jeans, who was staring at her with interest.

'I like your house' was the first thing he said, and then he smiled. He had dark hair, and big blue eyes, and looked nothing like his dad. 'I'm Ian,' he said politely, and held out his hand to shake hers. He was very cute and looked like a kid in an ad.

'I'm Francesca. Would you like something to eat?' It was eight in the morning, and there was no sign of his father. Ian had dressed and come downstairs on his own.

'Okay. Could I have a banana?' She had a bunch of them in a bowl on top of the fridge, reached for one, and handed it to him, and he thanked her.

'Would you like some cereal to go with it?' He nodded, and she poured some cornflakes into a bowl, with milk, and gave him a plate for the banana.

'I make my own breakfast every day,' he announced. 'My mom likes to sleep late. She goes out a lot at night,' he volunteered and Francesca didn't comment. She wasn't sure what to say. She wasn't used to kids his age.

'What grade are you in?' she asked as he took two bites of the banana, which puffed out his cheeks, and she smiled. It took him a minute to answer.

'Second. I changed schools this year. I liked my old one better, but my mom says it's too far away.' As he said it,

Chris walked into the room and took in the scene. He smiled as he looked at his son, and then at Francesca when he saw that she had fed him. She hadn't seen him look that happy since he moved in. Suddenly he looked relaxed, friendly, and warm. It was obvious that he was crazy about the boy, and very proud.

'Thank you for feeding him. He got away while I was in the shower.'

'We've been having a very nice time,' Francesca reassured him, and Ian looked pleased. He'd been having a good time too. He seemed very self-sufficient and totally at ease with adults.

'We're going to the zoo,' Ian told Francesca. 'They have a new polar bear, and a kangaroo.'

'That sounds like fun to me,' Francesca said easily, as Chris made some of the eggs he had bought, and he fried one for Ian too.

'Do you want to come?' Ian asked her happily, and she smiled.

'I'd love to, but I have to work.'

'What do you do?' Ian asked her.

'I have an art gallery a few blocks from here,' she explained to him. 'I sell paintings. You can come to see it if you like.'

'Maybe we will,' Chris said as he set the egg down in

front of Ian, and then sat down next to him with his own. And then Francesca went back to reading her e-mail while they ate. She'd had another response to the ad, from a woman in Vermont who said she was looking for a pied-à-terre in New York, and was interested in seeing the room that Francesca was renting. She had given her phone number, and said that she hoped it was still available and that Francesca would call. Francesca jotted it down along with another one, but the woman from Vermont sounded more appealing, and it didn't sound as though she would be there all the time, which might be good. It was very comfortable now the way things were. And Ian seemed like a pleasant addition to the group. He was obviously a nice kid.

She chatted with him again for a few minutes, wished them a fun time at the zoo, and went back upstairs. They had already left by the time she went out.

She had a busy day at the gallery after that and sold another painting. They had been selling well for months – the problem was that their prices weren't high enough to make much of a profit. She had been thinking of raising them again, and Avery insisted that she should.

It was mid-afternoon when Francesca remembered the woman in Vermont who had responded to her ad. She dialed the number, and a young woman answered. She sounded about Francesca's age, and she was cheery and pleasant on the phone. Francesca told her the unit was still available and described it as best she could, without glorifying it. She said that the room was small, and it was a studio, had a pretty view of the garden, and was next to the kitchen, and it had its own bath.

The woman's name was Marya Davis, and she said it sounded perfect for her. She didn't need a lot of space, and she said she liked to use the kitchen a lot, and would that be a problem?

'No, I work till seven every night, six days a week, so I'm not home much, and neither are the other tenants. One works at home some of the time, but he keeps to himself. And the other tenant just graduated from college, is a teacher, and goes out almost every night. The house is pretty quiet, and none of us use the kitchen much. I'm usually too tired to cook and just make a salad, or buy something at the deli on the way home. And the others do the same, so the kitchen is all yours.' Neither of her tenants had cooked dinner since they moved in, and she hardly saw them.

'That would be wonderful. I could come down from Vermont next week to see it, if that's all right with you. Do you think it can wait till then?' Marya asked, sounding worried, and Francesca laughed.

'No one's beating down my door. I have someone else to call today, but I spoke to you first, so I'll give you priority on it. When do you want to come?'

'Would Wednesday work for you?' she asked hopefully.

'That would be great.' They set a time, and Francesca jotted it down so she wouldn't forget if she got busy. And then they hung up. The woman had sounded very pleasant on the phone. And the person she called afterward had found something else. It was already early February, and it had taken her all this time to find two good tenants, and maybe now finally a third. She hadn't expected it to take this long. But she had been very cautious about who she showed it to, and no one else had suited her except Eileen and Chris, and now maybe this woman who wanted a pied-à-terre. She had mentioned that she was recently widowed and wanted to spend time in New York. And winters in Vermont were hard.

Francesca forgot about her then and remembered the appointment on Tuesday night. She had seen Chris's son briefly again before he left on Sunday night. She had brought a lollipop home from the gallery to give him. She kept a bowl of candy there for kids. She asked Chris's permission before giving it to him, and he didn't object. Apparently their visit to the polar bear had been a big hit, and there was a new tiger cub at the zoo too. Ian loved the lollipop and waved goodbye to her when he left. He was a really cute kid. Seeing children like him never made her want one of her own, she just enjoyed the ones she met. She had fifteen artists to worry about instead of kids. That was enough for her, for now anyway, and maybe forever. Particularly with no man in her life. Crossing paths with kids like Ian was all the kid fix she needed. She didn't need more. But she could easily see how crazy Chris was about his son. His eyes lit up whenever he looked at Ian.

Marya, the woman from Vermont, appeared at the house on Charles Street five minutes before the appointed hour the next day. She was wearing ski pants, snow boots, and a parka with a hood, and it was a cold day in New York too. She had gray hair cut in a stylish bob, and looked nothing like what Francesca had expected. And she was much older than she had sounded on the phone. She mentioned that she was fifty-nine, and had just lost her husband after a long illness. But she looked like a cheerful, happy person. She was lithe and had a youthful attitude and look, although Francesca was startled to realize she was nearly her mother's age, but an entirely different kind of person.

And she was much more interested in checking out the

kitchen than seeing her room, which she had glanced at rapidly and said seemed fine to her.

'I take it you like to cook,' Francesca said, smiling at her.

'Yes, I do. It's been my passion ever since I was a little girl. I'm very lucky to be able to do what I love. It never feels like work.' And then Francesca suddenly realized who she was, and how oblivious she had been. She was Marya Davis, the celebrated cook. She had written half a dozen famous cookbooks, and Francesca had two of them on a shelf. She was one of the most successful chefs, and specialized in French cuisine, made easy for the masses and people who were busy. She demystified some of the famous French dishes, and had written an entire book on soufflés. And here she was in Francesca's kitchen on Charles Street, examining the kitchen and sitting at the table. 'I'm working on a new book,' she explained. 'And I thought it might be fun to spend some time here while I do. It's too quiet where I live, particularly now that I'm alone.' She wasn't mournful about it, just a little wistful.

'Was your husband a chef too?' Francesca asked, curious about her. She had dancing eyes, and a huge smile, and seemed like one of the warmest, friendliest people Francesca had ever met. She was totally unassuming, and she looked completely at home in Francesca's kitchen. And if she moved in, Francesca realized instantly that there would be some wonderful things to eat.

She laughed in answer to Francesca's question about her late husband. 'He was a banker, not a cook, but he loved to eat, particularly French food. We used to spend a month in Provence every year, while I tried out new recipes. We had a lot of fun together. I miss him,' she said simply, 'so I thought it might be good to do something different and move here for a while. But I'll need to go back to Vermont occasionally to check on the house, and it's so pretty there in the late spring. But now that I don't ski anymore, I'd rather be here in the winter months.' Francesca's own mother still skied at sixty-two, and the two women were close to the same age, but they weren't even remotely alike. Marya Davis was a woman of talent, substance, humor, and depth. Thalia was none of those. And Francesca was thoroughly enjoying talking to Marya. She was a lovely woman, and Francesca was thrilled to meet her and at the prospect of having her live at the house. She had been lucky with all three of her tenants.

They talked about the details a few minutes later. Marya thought the price was fine, and the room was all she needed, and she was delighted to be near the kitchen. It was the perfect set-up for her.

'I hope you'll let me try some of my new recipes on you,' she said shyly, and Francesca looked delighted.

'It would be an honor, Mrs Davis.' Francesca smiled warmly at her. She was so sweet, she almost wanted to give her a hug.

'Please call me Marya, or you'll make me feel very old. I suppose I am, I'll be sixty next year.' She looked at least ten years younger than she was, and she was so simple and unassuming that it was endearing, and easy to feel close to her. Francesca could hardly wait for her to move in. She was planning to drive back to Vermont that afternoon, and promised to be back in a few days.

Marya hugged her in the doorway as she left, and Francesca was smiling as she walked upstairs and ran into Eileen.

'You look happy.'

'I am. Marya Davis, the famous chef and author of many cookbooks, just rented the downstairs room. I'm thrilled, and she said she'd cook for us whenever we want. We're going to be her guinea pigs for the next year.'

'How cool,' Eileen said, beaming. 'I hate to cook.'

'Yeah, me too,' Francesca agreed. It had never been her strong suit, and Todd had been a much better cook than she was. 'Well, that's it. We've got a full house now,' Francesca said, looking pleased and relieved. Her mortgage payments were fully covered now without Todd. And they were a good group. Eileen, Chris, and now Marya. She had been very lucky with the roommates she'd found, contrary to her mother's dire predictions, and even her own fears, and Todd's.

It was perfect. The house on Charles Street was alive and full. They were all nice people, and Marya was a wonderful addition. 44 Charles Street was teeming with life. They were even going to be eating great food as soon as Marya moved in. It didn't get better than that.

Chapter 6

Marya moved in on Valentine's Day, and had made delicate wafer-thin heart-shaped gingerbread cookies for all of them before she even unpacked. Chris had been designing a project at the house that day. It was for one of his demanding industrial clients, which was always challenging, and required concentration, and the baking odors drifted up to him, until he could no longer focus on his work, and had to go downstairs to check it out. He found Marya in the kitchen, wearing a plaid apron and humming to herself. Although he had known that she was moving in, he hadn't met her yet. She turned to him with a broad smile, put down a cookie tray, and shook his hand.

'I've never smelled anything so delicious in my entire

life!' he said, glancing at the stove. She held out a plate to him, and five of the irresistible cookies vanished instantly and melted in his mouth.

'It's just an old recipe I dusted off,' she said humbly, and once he was in the kitchen, Chris became aware of other delicious smells as well. She was trying out some new recipes, and making a tried and true one, and thought she'd set some food out for them in case any of them were planning to be home that night. Chris said he was. She invited him to come back later, and help himself to anything he wanted. 'It's so great having all of you to cook for,' she said. She had been so lonely since her husband had died. This was a perfect setup for her, and she was thrilled to be moving in. Her bags were still sitting unopened in her room. She hadn't been able to resist the lure of the kitchen as soon as she walked in, much to his delight. 'I hear you have an enchanting little boy,' Marya said as Chris poured himself a glass of milk from the fridge. He smiled at her words.

'He's a good boy. I have him every other weekend, and I usually take him out after school on Wednesday nights. He lives with his mom.'

'I can't wait to meet him.' Marya had no children of her own. It had never happened, and in her late fifties, she was of an era where the many options currently available to deal with infertility hadn't existed yet. So she and her husband had accepted their lot, and devoted themselves to each other. It made the void in her life that much bigger now that he was gone. Having three room-mates at the house on Charles Street was going to make her life a much happier place than the lonely home in Vermont that she still loved. But she wanted to be with people. She was ecstatic about the move to New York, and couldn't wait to visit museums, restaurants, and friends. She was excited about all of it, and had a cheer-ful, upbeat attitude about life.

Chris went back upstairs to finish his project, and moments later, Marya met Eileen when she came home from work and went to use the computer in the kitchen to check her e-mail. Eileen could smell Marya's cooking the moment she opened the front door.

'Wow!' Eileen said as she walked into the kitchen, and found herself looking at Marya. She was a pretty woman, and her slim athletic figure was noticeable even in the apron that she wore. 'What smells so good?' She couldn't tell if it was sweet or savory. Marya had put a chicken in the oven for all of them, was making asparagus, and planned to make a cheese soufflé when they all got home. She had baked a heart-shaped chocolate cake for dessert. It was a Valentine's Day feast.

'I didn't know if any of you were eating at home tonight, but I thought I'd take a chance. Valentine's Day is so much fun.' It was a good excuse for a great meal.

Eileen smiled as she checked her e-mail, and saw that she had a date for that night. It was a first date with a man she'd been e-mailing with for several days. So far she had met some really nice guys, and a few duds. She got rid of the duds very quickly, and had only brought two men home. Francesca was uneasy about it, but hadn't said anything to Eileen. She didn't think she had that right. Eileen was an adult, and this was her home, and Francesca couldn't screen her dates. But having strangers spend the night at the house seemed a little dicey to her. Nothing unpleasant had happened, but since Eileen was meeting them all on the Internet, Francesca was aware that she didn't know any of her dates well. They were strangers to her too, which seemed risky to Francesca. It was why Internet encounters with men didn't appeal to her at all. She had been lucky with her roommates, but had checked them carefully through references and credit checks. Screening dates would have been much harder, seemed more dangerous, and she still had no desire to date anyone yet anyway. Todd had moved out only six weeks before. She still missed him, and was trying to get used to the idea that he was gone forever out of her life.

And at times it was very hard. She had lost not only the man she loved, but her best friend and business partner, which made it a triple loss. The only other people in her life were the artists she represented. She had worked so hard on establishing her business for the past four years that the only people she saw were either artists or clients, and Todd.

Francesca was the last one to come home from work that night. She closed the gallery at seven, and walked the short distance home. She had sold two small pieces for Valentine's Day and had been feeling down all afternoon. She had forgotten that Marya was moving in that day, and when she got home, she found all three of her tenants chatting in the kitchen and sharing a bottle of Spanish wine Marya had opened for them. She had brought a few cases of French, Spanish, and Chilean wines with her from Vermont, and they were sampling one of them, and liked it very much.

'Welcome home,' she said to Francesca with a cheerful look. It suddenly boosted her spirits to see all of them. She was dreading coming back to an empty house, and trying to forget that it was Valentine's Day. Todd had always made a big deal of it, and took her out for a nice dinner every year. She hadn't heard from him all day, and knew it was just as well, but she was down about it anyway. She smiled happily as Marya handed her a glass of the Spanish wine. Dinner was ready by then. She hadn't planned to eat, and Eileen said she was going out, but the three of them sat down at the kitchen table, and devoured the delicious dinner that Marya served with ease. The asparagus and hollandaise were irresistible, the cheese soufflé for openers was beyond belief, and the chicken was roasted to perfection with a delicate mushroom stuffing. There was salad and French cheese, and the three of them finished off the chocolate cake as they talked animatedly around the table about food, travels, life experiences, friends. She had just arrived but Marya seemed to bring them all to life, and Francesca hadn't seen Chris as friendly or as talkative since he moved in. Marya had a magical gift with people and food. Francesca couldn't believe their luck that she was there, and Marya said that she felt fortunate to be living in Francesca's house, and greatly blessed. They had so much fun that Eileen nearly forgot her date, and rushed out without changing. She just put on high heels and perfume, waved goodbye, and disappeared, as Francesca, Chris, and Marya sat at the table over the last of the meal. She served coffee, the gingerbread cookies, and truffles afterward. Chris said with conviction that it was the best meal he had ever eaten, and Francesca readily agreed. It was the best Valentine's Day she had spent in years, even if it was without Todd.

She and Chris helped Marya clean up the kitchen, but Marya had tidied as she went along, and there was surprisingly little mess. Marya went to unpack then, and Chris and Francesca walked slowly up the stairs.

'I was dreading today,' Francesca admitted. 'It's my first Valentine's Day without the man I bought the house with. It turned out to be a lot of fun tonight, thanks to Marya.'

Chris nodded solemnly, a little more distant now that he was alone with her. He was always very guarded whenever he talked to Francesca or Eileen except when Ian was around. Marya had really brought him out of his shell. And Francesca couldn't help wondering what had happened to him to make him so withdrawn. She was beginning to think that it wasn't so much his personality as traumas that had occurred.

'Today was probably hard for Marya too, without her husband,' Francesca commented. 'She's a lovely woman. I'm glad she moved in. Her food is fantastic. We're all going to get fat if she cooks like that for us every night.' Chris smiled at what she said.

'I think this was just a special event. I haven't celebrated Valentine's Day, or even thought about it, for years. It's for lovers and kids,' and he was neither, although he had talked to Ian that afternoon and sent him a Valentine's Day card. Ian had a crush on his teacher and a girl in his class, and had sent them both cards, he had told his dad.

They said goodnight to each other outside Chris's door, which had once been her dining room and library and was now his home. She hadn't seen the rooms since he moved in and had no reason to, since he was renting them from her. And she walked slowly up the stairs to her bedroom, feeling lonely again. It was inevitable. There was so much hype about that day, if you didn't have a lover to share it with, it felt like a day of mourning. But Marya had made it a lot easier and happier for her, and she was grateful to her for that.

Francesca heard Eileen come in later that night, and she could tell that she had someone with her, and hoped she was all right. Her trust and innocence about the men she met on the Internet worried Francesca considerably, but they were whispering and laughing as they tiptoed past Francesca's door, and she saw him in the kitchen over breakfast the next day. Marya had left freshly baked rolls and croissants for them and gone out for a walk. And Eileen's date of the night before was happily gobbling the croissants and barely said hello to Francesca as she walked in. He looked a little rough around the edges, but Eileen was smiling and seemed happy and young as she giggled at him. Francesca was mildly annoyed to have to deal with him over breakfast, and Chris didn't look thrilled either as he poured himself a cup of the coffee Marya had made earlier. Mealtimes on Charles Street had become a lot more interesting since Marya moved in.

'How do you all know each other? Are you two a couple?' Eileen's date asked them as Chris shot him an evil look, poured himself a bowl of cornflakes, and didn't bother to answer. Fran cesca just said they were room-mates, and let it go at that. The man had several tattoos and had rolled up his sleeves, which exposed his arms. They were in vivid color, and his hair was long. He said he worked in TV, and then explained that he was a grip, and he fondled Eileen's buttocks openly just as she sat down. Chris almost laughed when he saw the look of disapproval on Francesca's face. She thought it was a bit much over breakfast among strangers, but Eileen didn't seem to mind and looked pleased. She kissed him passionately, and he looked like he had his tongue halfway down her throat. His name was Doug. And she had met him on the Internet, of course. It seemed to be her only resource for meeting men, which concerned Francesca. Other people seemed to meet decent men on the Internet, but Eileen appeared to be alarmingly naïve. Doug was still in the kitchen when the others left.

Francesca excused herself and said she had some calls to make from her room, and Chris said he had a client meeting at ten, to present the project he had been working on for weeks. It was finally complete. He had been designing new packaging for a well-known brand. He left the house with his portfolio a few minutes later, and so did Eileen. And by the time Francesca left for the gallery at eleven, she was alone in the house. Marya had gone out too after cleaning up the kitchen when she came back from her walk.

The house was beginning to feel full and busy.

Francesca had arranged for a cleaning service to come twice a week, and they were all sharing the expense, rather than having to clean the house themselves. She was thinking about Eileen as she walked to work in a light February rain, and wondered if they'd be seeing Doug again. She hoped not, and thought he was crude, and a lot less than Eileen deserved. She seemed to be much more interested in quantity and the number of men she could meet, than in quality and narrowing the field to some better guys who were worthy of her. Francesca reminded herself that she was young and still naïve. She would have worried about her a lot if she were a younger sister. As a tenant or roommate, it was none of her business. But her Internet hobby was a little unnerving. It was a whole new world to Francesca, and not one she wanted to explore, although a lot of people were enthused about it and claimed they met nice people that way. It seemed risky to Francesca and she hoped Eileen would slow down a little and be careful in the meantime.

Francesca had a new show to curate and hang at the gallery that afternoon. It was a group show she had been working on for months, for two abstract painters and a sculptor, and she thought their work enhanced one another. It was important to find work that didn't over-shadow or distract from the rest of the show. One of the artists did enormous canvases and it was going to be hard for her to hang them alone. Without Todd to help her hang the shows now, she had asked one of their artists to come in and do it with her if he had time. He worked as an installer for several galleries to make extra money, and he was pleasant and helpful, although vague about time. He had been one of the first artists she signed up and his paintings sold fairly well. And he worked hard and was serious about his art and well trained. For once, he arrived on time, and Francesca figured out where she wanted him to hang the paintings, and he got up on a tall ladder for several hours to adjust the lights once they hung the work. It was after six when they were finished, and they both were tired but pleased with the result. He was ten years younger than she was and a cute guy.

'So where's Todd these days?' he asked her casually. She had told most of their artists verbally that she had bought him out, but hadn't sent an official letter to them yet. She hadn't had the heart. And most of them could figure out that he was no longer around. A few asked her, but most of them had guessed that he was gone when they didn't see him.

'I bought him out,' Francesca said equally off-handedly. 'My father is my business partner now. Todd is practicing law again.' She thought it was all he needed to know, and the artist nodded.

'You two still together?' he asked over his shoulder, as he put the ladder away.

'No, we're not,' Francesca said, and turned away, embarrassed and saddened by the question. She didn't know why, but it made her feel like a failure, as though she had been unable to keep him or make it work. She hated feeling that way and wondered if Todd did too.

'I wondered about it. I haven't seen him around in a long time. Did you sell your house?'

'No, it's mine now, with three roommates.' It was more information than he needed.

'I'm happy to hear it,' the young artist said with a broad smile. 'I've been waiting for him to get out of the way for years. How about dinner some night?' He looked hopeful as he asked. He admired Francesca for how hard she worked and how good she was at what she did. She was fiercely dedicated to her artists, and did everything she could to promote their careers.

Francesca took a breath before she answered his invitation to dinner. 'I don't think so, Bob. I'm not so keen on mixing business with pleasure. I've never gone out with any of my artists, and I don't think I should start now.' She tried to look businesslike as she said it, and Bob seemed undaunted.

'There's always a first time,' he said hopefully.

'Yeah, maybe, but I don't think so. But thanks anyway. I'm really not ready to start dating yet. It's kind of a big adjustment after five years.'

'Yeah . . . I'm sorry . . .' He looked disappointed and left a few minutes later, and Francesca locked up the gallery and walked home. It was raining harder than it had been that morning, which matched her spirits.

It depressed her to think of dating anyone, or sleeping with anyone except Todd, although they had stopped sleeping with each other months before. It was going to be hard getting used to someone new. She just didn't want to yet. And she walked up the steps of 44 Charles Street, soaked to the skin, and with a heavy heart.

She went straight to her room, without dinner, and cried herself to sleep that night. It told her that she wasn't over Todd yet, and she wondered how long it would take. Maybe forever.

Francesca felt better in the morning, and she smiled when she walked into the kitchen. It was early, and she thought she'd be alone, but instead she found Marya making pancakes for Ian. They looked like Mickey Mouse, had a cherry for a nose, and raisins for eyes when she put them on his plate. They had just met. It was Saturday, and one of Ian's weekends with his father.

'Hi, Ian,' Francesca said easily, as though they were old friends. 'Pretty cool pancakes, huh?' she asked him, and he nodded with a grin as she smiled at Marya over his head. He was an irresistible child with a big happy smile and wise old eyes.

'Marya's going to make cookies with me later. Chocolate chip. My mom used to make those with me,' he said carefully. 'She doesn't anymore. She gets sick a lot, and she sleeps all the time. Sometimes she's still asleep when I get home from school.' The two women exchanged a look but said nothing. Francesca wondered if she had an illness, but she didn't want to ask.

'I like chocolate chip cookies too,' Francesca added to lighten the moment.

'You can make some with us if you want,' Ian said generously as Chris walked in. 'Or we'll save you some if you have to go to work.'

'I'd love that,' Francesca said warmly, as Eileen walked in with the unattractive Doug, who asked for pancakes too. Francesca was quick to step in. Marya hadn't been hired as a cook, she was a world-class chef who was doing them a favor and making them a gift by cooking anything for them. She wasn't a short-order cook there to prepare them breakfast. 'We're doing self-service,' Francesca said quietly, 'except for Ian.' Doug looked annoyed, shrugged, and helped himself to a cup of coffee as Marya looked at Francesca gratefully. Chris had taken due note of the scene, and didn't like Doug either. He was crass and rude, and made it clear to everyone in the room that he and Eileen were sleeping together and when Ian left the room for a few minutes, Doug even intimated that they had had some pretty hot sex the night before. Eileen didn't seem to mind his saying it, but the others did on her behalf. It was a lack of respect for her that she appeared not to notice or object to.

Oblivious to the scene, Ian happily finished his pancakes and politely thanked Marya when he was through. He then carefully rinsed his dish and put it in the dishwasher. Francesca noticed and wondered if he had to take care of himself if his mother was sick or sleeping all the time. He seemed unusually capable for a child of seven.

They were all still milling around the kitchen when the doorbell rang. Francesca went upstairs to answer, and was horrified to see her mother standing outside, waiting to come in. She was wearing a Chanel running suit and Dior sneakers, her hair was in a ponytail, and she looked beautiful even without makeup, but she was the last person Francesca wanted to see that morning. She had no desire to introduce her to her roommates or listen to her mother's comments about them after.

'Hi, Mom,' she said hesitantly, not sure what to do. 'What are you doing here?' She was hoping she would leave without coming in, but doubted she would. Her mother was too persistent and curious for that.

'I'm trying a new skin doctor in SoHo. I hear she's fabulous, so I thought I'd drop over before I see her. May

113

I come in?' She looked expectant and imperious, and Francesca stepped aside, feeling like a kid in trouble. She knew her mother would not like the scene in the kitchen.

'Of course,' Francesca said, as her heart sank, thinking of the odd melee of people in her kitchen, and suspected her mother would be shocked, particularly by Doug and his tattoos.

'Something smells delicious,' Thalia commented as Francesca debated between taking her upstairs to her bedroom, with the unmade bed, the living room where there was no place to sit, since she hadn't gotten around to replacing the couch and chairs Todd had taken, or the kitchen, where all of her roommates were having breakfast. She hated to introduce them to her mother. But Marya had just taken a fresh tray of croissants out of the oven, which provided an irresistible lure toward the kitchen.

'One of my roommates is a famous chef,' Francesca explained as her mother headed down the stairs toward the kitchen without her. Reluctantly, Francesca followed.

Chris was at the kitchen table with his son doing a drawing, Marya was at the stove in her apron holding the fresh batch of croissants, and Doug with all his tattoos visible was wrapped around Eileen like a snake, while she giggled and was still wearing a slightly indiscreet nightgown with her robe hanging open. It was not the scene she wanted to present to her mother. She introduced her to all of them simply as her mother, as Thalia pursed her lips and stared over all of them to Marya. She seemed to be the only civilized person there, in Thalia's opinion.

'You must be the chef,' Thalia said, looking slightly daunted. The idea of her daughter living with all these people still upset her. And she had instantly noticed Doug and his tattoos and thought him dreadful.

'I am. Would you like breakfast, Mrs Thayer?' Marya asked kindly. She was slightly startled by the grandeur of Francesca's mother. Even in a sweatsuit, she looked as though she should be wearing a ball gown.

'I'm *not* Mrs Thayer,' Thalia said quickly. 'Countess di San Giovane,' she corrected in the accent her late husband had taught her. She only used the Italian pronounciation of her name for state occasions, which this wasn't. But it was her way of letting them all know that she was much more important than they were. They got the message. Chris glanced at her over Ian's head, said nothing, and went back to talking to his son. Doug was nuzzling Eileen's neck, and she couldn't stop laughing. It was not the dignified welcome Thalia thought worthy of her. Francesca was cringing.

'Of course, Countess,' Marya said politely without batting an eye. 'May I offer you some croissants and a cup of coffee?'

'I'd like that very much,' Thalia said, and sat down next to Ian. He looked up at her with interest, and went back to his drawing. And a moment later Marya set the plate of warm croissants and a steaming cup of coffee in front of her. Francesca sat down in the only spare seat at the table, across from her mother, silently dying, wishing she hadn't come.

The scene went on as it had been when she entered, for a few minutes, and then everyone went about their business. Marya cleaned up the kitchen, Chris went upstairs with Ian, and Doug and Eileen went back to her room, as Doug let them all know on the way out that they were going back to bed. Eileen's girl-next-door halo was definitely slipping. A moment later only Francesca and her mother were left at the kitchen table as Marya buzzed around.

'I can't believe you're living with those people,' Thalia said in horror, and looked as though she were about to burst into tears. 'What are you thinking?' she said, ignoring Marya.

'I'm thinking that I need to make my mortgage payments, and they're all very nice,' Francesca said sternly, as Marya pretended not to hear them and finished the dishes.

'That man with the tattoos?'

'He doesn't live here. He's dating the girl who lives upstairs. She teaches autistic children.'

'You'd never know it to look at her,' her mother said with a disapproving look. She wasn't wrong. Her look had gotten racier as she got comfortable, and her skirts shorter.

'She's young,' Francesca said, trying to defend her, although she couldn't stand Doug herself, and was also bothered that Eileen had come downstairs in a night-gown and robe. It was poor judgment and bad taste, but not a crime.

'Everyone gets along very well,' Marya interjected, as she refilled Thalia's cup with the delicious brew she had brought with her from Vermont. 'They're all very decent,' Marya reassured her, and Thalia looked at her mourn-fully, relieved to have found a friend and ally among them.

'Doesn't it upset you too?' Thalia asked her.

'Not at all,' Marya answered. 'I'm happy to be here. They're all very kind young people. I lost my husband a few months ago, and I'm so glad to be here with them, and not alone at home in Vermont.'

'What did he die of?' Thalia's mother asked with interest.

'A brain tumor. He was sick for a long time. The end was pretty rough. It's a relief to get away now, and it will be good for me to be in New York.'

'This is a hard town to find a man,' Francesca's mother said bluntly, and Francesca was shocked and embarrassed, and then laughed. It was all Thalia ever thought of. That and herself. 'Especially at our age,' she added, and Marya laughed. Thalia didn't bother her at all. She had dealt with colleagues with far more imperious ways than Thalia. Many of the chefs she had worked with were notorious divas, and some had been downright nasty to her over the years, mostly out of jealousy or just because they were rotten people.

'I'm not looking for a man,' Marya told her. 'I don't want one. I had the best one there ever was, for thirty-six years. No one else could ever measure up. I just want to have a nice time, do my work, and make some new friends.' Thalia looked as though Marya were speaking in tongues. She was a very attractive woman. Why on earth wouldn't she want a man? She assumed that she was probably lying. In Thalia's opinion, every woman wanted a man.

'You'll probably feel differently about it in a few

months,' Thalia said knowingly, and then complimented her on the excellent coffee.

'No, I won't,' Marya said firmly. 'I don't need a man to be happy. I had a great one, that was good enough. I don't expect to find another one like him, and why settle for anything less? I'm going to be perfectly content alone.' She looked certain of it, and Thalia stared at her as though she thought she was crazy.

Francesca looked at her watch then. She was meeting a client at the gallery at ten, before they opened, so they would have time to look at paintings in the racks without being disturbed. 'I hate to say it, but I have to go, Mom.'

'That's all right, dear,' her mother said, planted firmly in her chair with no intention of moving. 'I can stay and chat with Marya. I still have time before my appointment.'

Marya nodded at Francesca reassuringly, who was looking panicked, and then Marya turned to Thalia. 'Countess, would you like another cup of coffee?' She said it as though she were calling her Your Highness, and Thalia smiled.

'Please call me Thalia. I wouldn't want the young people calling me that, but there's no reason for you to use my title.' She had decided they were equals, in stature as well as age. 'You know, I have two of your cookbooks.

I particularly like your recipe for hollandaise. It's so easy, even I can do it.'

'Thank you, Thalia,' Marya said, beaming, and handed her another plate of croissants.

'I hate to leave you, Mom,' Francesca said uncomfortably, but it was more that she didn't trust her. She had no idea what she'd say to Marya, or how she would behave. And she didn't want to offend Marya, who looked totally at ease with her mother.

'Don't be silly, dear. I'll call you later.' Thalia had stopped complaining about the other tenants, and Francesca really had to leave. The client she was meeting had been referred to her by a satisfied client. She had never met him before, and she didn't want to be late.

Francesca gave a last anxious glance at Marya as she left, and hurried up the stairs to get her purse, and a moment later, she was hurrying down the street, thinking about her mother. She was sure she was going to get an earful about all of them at some point, except maybe Marya, whom her mother seemed to like.

At that very moment, the two older women were bonding in the kitchen. Marya was amused by her, but it didn't show. She could hold her own with people like the countess, and had with people who were infinitely worse.

'You have no idea how I worry about her, especially with this insane arrangement,' Thalia was confiding to Marya. 'She should have married Todd instead of buying real estate with him. He would have had to pay her a decent alimony, and she'd own the house free and clear. Living with all these people is just a crazy thing to do.' Thalia looked distressed, and Marya was very calm.

'It seems to be working out very well. Chris is respectable, he seems well educated, and his son is very sweet. And I think the little girl upstairs is just young and a little silly. She's fresh out of school. She's all excited about being in the city and meeting men. She'll calm down.'

'Her friend looks like he's fresh out of prison,' Thalia said, near tears. For the next hour, Marya reassured her, and by the time Thalia left to see her new skin doctor, she was feeling better. Marya sat in the kitchen for a few minutes, smiling to herself after she left. The Countess di San Giovane was definitely a handful. She couldn't help wondering how Francesca had managed to be so normal and down to earth with a mother like that. But more than anything, Thalia seemed foolish to her, and most of what they'd talked about was her desperation about finding a man and getting married again. She had confessed shamelessly that without a husband, she didn't even feel like a woman. Her entire identity was wrapped up in who she was married to. And without that she felt like no one at all. She was the exact opposite of Marya, who was self-respecting, confident, knew exactly who she was, and didn't depend on anyone for her identity. The two women were as different as black and white. And in Francesca's opinion, her mother's obvious obsession with finding another husband had been scaring men away for years.

And at the gallery, Francesca had taken out nearly every painting she had in the racks. She kept a good selection of her artists' work in stock. The client she was wooing wanted to buy a large painting, he said he had a fondness for emerging artists, but didn't seem sure of what he liked. And whatever direction Francesca steered him, it didn't feel right to him. He said he was divorced, and his wife had always selected all their art. He wanted to make a statement of his own now, but had no idea what it should be. He was a fifty-year-old dentist from New Jersey, and Francesca was utterly fed up with him by noon. He seemed to be incapable of making up his mind. He finally promised that he would think about it, and call her the following week if he made a decision. He said he liked everything she had showed him, but he was nervous about buying the wrong thing. It was always frustrating dealing with clients like him.

She handed him photographs and information on all the artists he was interested in, and he looked even more confused, and then he looked up at her.

'You wouldn't like to talk about it over dinner, would you?' he asked, looking far more interested in her than in her art. But nothing about him appealed to her, she didn't like him, and she wasn't in the mood.

'I'm sorry,' she said pleasantly, smiling at him, 'I don't go out with clients.' It was the perfect excuse.

'I haven't bought anything from you yet. I'm not a client,' he said cleverly. And she'd have much preferred to sell him something than go out with him. She was beginning to wonder if he had looked at the art as a ruse. And if so, he had wasted her time, and his own.

'I'm sorry, I can't.' She shook her head.

'You have a boyfriend?' he asked, and she hesitated, and decided that a lie was better than the truth. Particularly if it got her out of an awkward spot with him.

'Yes, I do,' she said with a look of innocence.

'That's too bad,' he said, looking disappointed, and finally made it out the door, much to her relief. She sank down into the chair behind her desk, exhausted by the day halfway through it. Breakfast with her mother, and two hours with an indecisive client who asked her out to dinner was more than she wanted to deal with on any day of the week.

She called Marya to see if she had survived her mother's grilling, and Marya assured her that she was fine.

'I had a very nice time with your mother. She's certainly nothing like you.' Marya chuckled. She liked Thalia's style, despite the fact that she was obviously spoiled, and somewhat eccentric.

'That's the nicest thing you could have said,' Francesca commented, smiling. 'All my life I've been terrified I'd wind up like her.'

'Not a chance,' Marya reassured her. 'Have a nice day. I'll see you tonight.' And as Francesca hung up and went to work at her desk, she had the comforting sensation that she had a new friend in Marya.

Chapter 7

The following week Francesca was insanely busy. She went to three artists' studios, reorganized the racks where she stocked the paintings, returned old work that hadn't sold to several artists, in order to make room for new pieces. And she made a list of the group shows that she wanted to do for the next year. It was always a challenge trying to figure out which artists to show together so that their work would enhance one another and not conflict. And in the midst of everything else she was doing, four of her artists dropped by that week just to hang out and visit. She always tried to be welcoming, as she was with her clients, but she was pressed for time and had a lot to do. And in the midst of all the activity in the gallery that week, she made several sales. Much to her amazement, the dentist of the weekend before called her and bought three paintings. New clients appeared, referred by other clients, two art consultants called her with big jobs, and a well-known interior designer stopped by and liked what she saw. Francesca was pleased. She got home late every night, and scarcely saw her roommates. And she was touched to find little notes in the kitchen from Marya, telling her what was in the fridge. It was Friday night before Francesca had time to breathe. Her mother had called her several times during the week, to comment about her roommates, but Francesca didn't have time to talk to her, which was a relief.

She lay on her bed on Friday night, grateful that she had to work only one more day, and was thinking about spending Sunday in bed with a good book. There was nothing she wanted to do, and no one she wanted to see. And most unusually, that weekend, she knew that all of her tenants would be gone. Chris had said he was going away. Eileen announced on Friday morning that she was going skiing with a new man, and Marya had decided to go to Vermont for the weekend to check on things at her home. On Saturday night when she got home, Francesca was entirely alone. At first it felt wonderful, but she was startled to find on Sunday morning that she was lonely and depressed. Their presence on a daily basis was a shield from the ghosts in her past, the most alive of which was Todd. She hadn't heard from him in more than a month, which told her that he had made the adjustment better than she had. In quiet moments, she still missed him. She was beginning to wonder if she always would. When she thought about it, she didn't want their life back, but she missed him anyway.

And by Sunday afternoon she was feeling seriously sorry for herself, and missed her roommates. She couldn't help wondering if Chris had had a date, although it was none of her business. He never brought women home and was extremely private.

By seven o'clock Sunday night, she was still alone. It made her realize what a blessing it was to have them there. She would have been miserable in the house on her own, with no one to talk to, and no sign of life.

She was making herself scrambled eggs for dinner, thinking about Marya's delicious cooking, when she suddenly noticed a steady drip. She wasn't sure where it was coming from, and looked around the kitchen. It was coming through the ceiling at a rapid rate. There was a powder room above the kitchen, and when she went upstairs to check, she saw that there was a torrent coming through the ceiling from the floor above, where Chris's bathroom was. They had had leaks from there before. She ran up the stairs, and there was water everywhere, it was coming right through the wall, probably from a broken pipe. She ran downstairs at full speed to grab a wrench and Todd's tools, and panicking, she grabbed her cell phone and called him. He answered on the second ring.

'What do I do?' she shouted into the phone, and he tried to tell her. She put the phone down, tried what he had suggested, and nothing worked. The water was gushing harder than ever.

'Turn off the water!' Todd was shouting at her. He told her where the valve was, and she was soaked from head to foot as she tried to get to it, just as Chris walked in, and looked startled by the scene in his bathroom. Francesca was soaked to the skin, they were up to their ankles in water, and there was a geyser coming from the broken pipe in the wall. She looked at him frantically, and he gently pushed her aside, grabbed the wrench from her, and turned off the water. Instantly, the shooting spray stopped, as she stared at him.

'I'm sorry. Thank you,' she said, pushing her hair out of her eyes. He was smiling at her, and looked amused.

'Have you been in here all weekend?' he teased her, and she shook her head.

'I just discovered it. The water was coming through the kitchen ceiling,' and as she said it, she shrieked, 'Oh my

God, I left my eggs on the stove.' She raced downstairs, and her eggs had been incinerated to ash. Marya had come in, and she was quietly scrubbing the pan. 'I'm so sorry,' Francesca apologized. She was totally unnerved by the runaway leak, and then remembered Todd on the phone. She had left it on Chris's sink. Todd had hung up by then, but answered immediately when she called him back.

'Do you want me to come over?' he asked helpfully.

'No, I'm fine. My tenant turned the water off. I'll have to get the plumber here tomorrow.'

'Where was it?'

'Same one you could never get right either. The library bath.' It was Chris's bathroom now.

'One of these days you'll have to replumb that house, and it will cost you a fortune. You should sell it before that happens.' She was annoyed by what he said. He might not love the house anymore, but she did. She thanked him for his willingness to help and hung up. Chris helped her dry the floor. He was pleasant and calm despite the mess, unlike Todd who complained bitterly every time something went wrong in the house, particularly in the last year. He had been totally fed up with it. Chris had a more tranquil nature.

'Old houses do this kind of thing. I had an old house

too a long time ago, when Ian was born. I loved it, even if it was a pain in the neck, but it was fun to work on. I did most of the work myself.' It was the most he had ever said about his previous life, and he never talked about Ian's mother. He was an incredibly private person, and Francesca liked that about him. He was infinitely discreet, often to the point of seeming taciturn.

'We did the same thing here,' she said. 'The place was a mess when we bought it. I loved it. The man I lived with didn't.'

'It gets old, but I still think it's fun. When I was younger, I used to restore old houses for a living. It was terrific, but the real estate market got too high to turn a profit. I still miss it.'

'Well, you can play with this house anytime you want,' she said, as they stood barefoot in two inches of water, and he laughed.

'I'll keep it in mind,' he said kindly.

She wanted to ask him how his weekend was, but didn't dare. She didn't want him to think she was prying. His weekend was none of her business. He was her tenant, not her friend. She reminded herself of that as she went upstairs to her own room and heard Eileen come in a few minutes later. She stuck her head in Francesca's door and said she'd had a fantastic weekend with a great guy. She said that Doug was history, now that she'd met this one. Francesca thought it was a little quick to run off with him for a weekend, but who was she to judge? Eileen was young, and with a dozen years between them, Eileen was of a different generation. She was essentially a nice girl, even if she was more liberal than Francesca had been at her age. But she considered herself a slow starter. Todd had been her first real love, at thirty, although she'd had relationships before.

Francesca was just happy to hear that Doug was gone and wouldn't be back. She wondered what the new one was like, and didn't have long to wait. She didn't hear Eileen let him in late that night, but he was at breakfast with them the next morning. He looked preppy and pretty square, and slightly embarrassed to be there. Francesca approved, and then laughed at herself, feeling like her mother, passing judgment on everyone around her.

She had another busy week. She went to two events at other galleries, and the opening of a major show at MOMA, which was very exciting. She met a photographer at the museum event. His name was Clay Washington, and much to her own surprise, when he asked her out to dinner, she accepted. She was trying to make an effort, and Avery was right, she couldn't stay locked up on Charles Street forever. He took her to a Chinese restaurant on Mott Street and they had a good time. He was interesting to talk to. He had traveled extensively in Asia and lived in India and Pakistan for several years. He was intelligent and attractive, and she tried not to be put off by how different he was from Todd. Clay, the photographer, was much more like her. He would have qualified as bohemian to Todd. He was just new and different. He dropped her off at her house in a cab after dinner, and she didn't invite him in. He promised to call her. She hadn't been swept off her feet by him, but it had been a pleasant evening, and for now that was enough.

He called her three days later, as promised, and invited her to lunch. He came by the gallery, admired the show that was up, and was impressed when he realized her father was Henry Thayer. Everything about him seemed right, except that she wasn't attracted to him, but maybe that would come in time. He kissed her on the lips after lunch at a restaurant called Bread, and she let him, but she felt nothing. She felt dead inside, or numb. Maybe Todd had taken her heart with him.

She tried to explain it to Marya in a quiet moment that night.

'It was so weird. I felt like I was cheating on Todd.'

'It takes time to disengage from someone. It was a long time ago, but I was engaged to someone else before I met my husband. He was killed in a boating accident. I didn't look at anyone else for two years. I just couldn't. I even thought about going into a convent.' She smiled as she said it. 'I was very young. And then I met John and fell madly in love, and I came alive again, more so than ever. We got married a year later. Give yourself time. And even because someone is a good person, that doesn't make him right for you. You'll know it when you find it. Maybe you and the photographer can be just friends.' It sounded like a better idea to Francesca, and she was grateful for Marya's wisdom and perspective. She was sure that she was right.

The next time Clay called her, she told him she was busy. She was planning to go to an art auction at Christie's and had thought of asking him, but realized she didn't want to. So she went alone. It was easier than going out with the wrong man. She had a fairly decent time talking to assorted people after the auction, which had been lively, and was just leaving when she saw a familiar form in the distance. She recognized the way he walked and moved, and she saw him lean over and talk to someone as her heart took a leap. It was Todd, talking to a very pretty young woman. She had her arm linked into his, and he was smiling as he spoke to her, just the way he had looked in the beginning with her. Francesca wanted to drop to the floor and hide or crawl out of the room before he saw her. She felt like she was spying on him. She wasn't, but she was mesmerized by what she saw, and she felt her heart sink to her feet. She was unable to feel anything for another man, and he was with this very pretty woman, looking completely enamored. There were tears in her eyes as she ran out of the gallery and lunged into a cab, and gave the driver her address on Charles Street. She cried all the way home, and wanted to hide when she got in. She didn't want to see anyone. She just wanted to climb into bed and die.

It was a wake-up call for her. She was mourning a man with whom she had been profoundly unhappy for a year, a man she had loved but who was wrong for her. They had been wrong for each other, even if they loved each other. They had broken up, he had moved on, and she was still hanging on to something – memories, the ghost of him, the relationship they wanted and couldn't pull off. His reaction was much healthier. He was living his life – she wasn't. She suddenly felt as though someone had thrown cold water on her. She wondered if he was in love with the girl she'd seen him with, but whether he was or not was irrelevant. He no longer belonged to her, and never would again, nor should he. She didn't want the agony they'd shared in the end any more than he did. The message of that night was clear: she had to move on. It was over.

She still didn't want Clay Washington, the photographer she had met at MOMA, but somewhere out there was a man for her, and she had the right to find him. No matter how sweet it had been for a while, Todd wasn't it. She was going to have to find her dream somewhere else. Maybe he had already found it. But whether or not he had, she knew she had to start living again, and not just between the gallery and 44 Charles Street. She needed a new life and a broader world. But seeing him with another woman had definitely smarted. It had been excruciatingly painful. She thought about it for a long time that night, and was haunted by the look on his face when he turned to the woman he was with. She was still shaken by it when she went downstairs the next morning and sat at the kitchen table, staring into space. She didn't even hear Chris come in.

'That bad, huh?' he said, teasing her, as he started a pot of coffee. No one else was up yet.

'Hm? . . . What? . . . sorry . . .' She looked ragged and exhausted. She had slept badly and looked it.

'You look hungover,' he said honestly, and handed her

a mug of coffee a few minutes later. They were developing a casual camaraderie as roommates.

'Just haunted by the ghost of Christmas past. I saw my old boyfriend last night, with a new woman. I guess it shook me up more than it should have. It was a reality check for me.'

'Who sets the rules for that? About how long things take,' Chris said as he sat down across from her. 'Who decides how upset you're going to get? If it shook you up, so be it. You have a right to your feelings. That's a pretty upsetting thing to see.' She had the impression he'd been there, from what he said, but she didn't ask him. She was grateful for his kind words and thanked him as Marya walked in, looking bright and cheerful as usual. She always seemed to be in a good mood. It was a sharp contrast to the way Francesca was feeling, as she reached for the computer that was sitting on the table. Chris never touched it, Marya had no idea how to use it, and the one who used it most of the time was Eileen, who still didn't have her own.

Francesca had just turned it on when it sprang to life, and the next thing she knew, there was an incredible scene on the screen. Two women having sex with three men, and the intricate combinations were stunning as they all watched in disbelief, and Francesca realized what had happened. Eileen had been watching porn, probably with her new boyfriend, and Francesca had never even imagined the things they were doing, as she finally came to life and switched it off, still looking shocked. Chris was laughing loudly, and Marya gave a little giggle. They were all adults, Francesca knew they shouldn't have been horrified, but it was pretty amazing to see it. Chris looked vastly amused, although he didn't look like the type to watch porn, but he thought the incongruity of it on their breakfast table was very funny.

'I guess Little Bo Peep is not quite as innocent as she looks,' he commented. He thought it was harmless, and it didn't bother him, although he wouldn't have thought it so funny if Ian had been in the room. That would have upset him deeply.

'I'll ask her not to watch that stuff on the house computer,' Francesca said quietly, thinking of Ian too. He liked playing with the computer and was good at it. She didn't want him happening on any scenes like that, and she didn't want to see them either. She liked Eileen, but she felt like a house mother in a college dorm a lot of the time. Some of the men Eileen went out with looked worrisome to Francesca. But Eileen breezed right through it, went out with them a few times, and then moved on to the next one. The one she was seeing for the moment seemed like a good guy, and he had lasted longer than the others, but some of the previous ones had seemed unsuitable and downright crude. Eileen didn't always notice the difference. She was a small-town girl in the big city, excited by everything.

Chris was still chuckling over the porn incident when he went back upstairs to work. And Francesca mentioned to Eileen discreetly that evening not to watch things like that on the house computer, in case Ian came across it on the weekends.

'Oh, I would never do that!' Eileen said, looking horrified. 'We just watched it because we thought it was funny. I guess I forgot to turn it off when we went to bed. I had kind of a lot to drink last night. I'm really sorry, Francesca.' She looked so contrite and like such an innocent child as she said it that Francesca felt sorry for her. It made her suddenly grateful that she didn't have children. She hated telling anyone what to do, or scolding them for their behavior. It wasn't her place to tell Eileen how to behave. But she didn't want porn on the kitchen computer. Eileen hugged her after she apologized, and Francesca sighed as she watched her bound up the stairs. Francesca was beginning to feel like her older sister, and wasn't sure she wanted the role. But Eileen's sweetness was hard to resist.

Chris was still chuckling about it the next night when he, Francesca, and Marya ate dinner in the kitchen. Marya had made them a wonderful roast beef, with vegetables and Yorkshire pudding. Eileen was out on a date with her new friend. 'Maybe we should buy them porn DVDs instead,' he teased. He was in a good mood and chatted more than usual as they reached dessert. Marya had shared one of her better wines with them, and it had been a delicious meal.

Marya had made baked Alaska and had just lit the flames when Chris's cell phone rang, and he took it out of his pocket and answered as he admired the spectacular dessert. It was like living in a four-star restaurant having Marya there, and she loved cooking for them. She alternated old favorites with new recipes.

The two women were chatting as Chris got up from the table with a suddenly serious face. He walked into the hallway, still holding his cell phone, and Francesca could hear him asking questions in a terse voice, and a moment later he rushed into the room and grabbed his jacket with a panicked look.

'Are you okay?' Francesca asked him, looking worried. Even though they weren't close friends, their lives had become intertwined from living under the same roof.

139

'No, I'm not,' he said as he struggled into his jacket and headed for the stairs.

'Is it Ian?' Francesca asked as she hurried after him.

'No . . . yes – I don't have time to explain it. That was the police. I have to go get him.'

'Oh my God . . .' She didn't waste his time with any more questions, and just prayed the boy wasn't hurt. She and Marya sat staring at each other at the table, and no one touched the beautiful dessert. All they could think about was the little boy they had come to love.

Marya quietly cleaned up the remains of dinner and Francesca helped her. Neither of them knew what to say or do. Chris's face had been sheet white as he ran out of the kitchen. He was obviously terrified for his son, and the two women were desperately hoping the child would be okay. They had no idea what had happened to him. Francesca had sensed for a long time that there were frightening things in the boy's life that Chris worried about, probably related to his ex-wife's illness, which Ian occasionally referred to, or something even worse.

They both went to their rooms after dinner, and were thinking about Chris and the boy. All they could do was wait. At midnight, Chris still hadn't come home, and he hadn't called either of them. Francesca knew that he owed them no explanations. He rented rooms from her, and he owed her nothing except rent. The details of his private agonies were none of her business, but it explained a lot about him, why he was so quiet and introverted, shared nothing about his past, and said very little. She suspected Chris had a great deal on his mind.

She fell asleep at two A.M. and had left her door open so she could hear him come in, in case he needed moral support or help of any kind. But she heard nothing. All she knew was that his door was closed the next morning, and he hadn't come downstairs when she left for the gallery at ten-thirty. She had no idea what had happened to Ian, or how the crisis had resolved itself, or even if. She thought about him as she walked softly past his door and hurried down the stairs. Whatever had happened to panic him the night before was a mystery. They each had their private griefs and traumas to deal with that had nothing to do with the others, and belonged only to each of them.

Chapter 8

When Francesca came home from the gallery that night, she found Ian sitting quietly at the kitchen table with Marya, eating a bowl of soup. His father was nowhere in the room, and Francesca was instantly aware that it was Thursday, a day when Chris didn't normally see Ian. And he only came to the house on weekends. Something was clearly out of step.

Francesca set down her bag, and slipped into a chair next to Ian and smiled at him. She wasn't sure what to say. She wanted to hug him but didn't want to overwhelm him. Marya had been reading him a story.

'I'm happy to see you, Ian,' Francesca said softly, and ran a gentle hand across his hair. He looked up at her with sad eyes, with the weight of the world on his shoulders, and when he looked at her it nearly broke her heart.

'My mom got sick last night,' he said quietly. 'She fell asleep and wouldn't wake up. I tried to wake her but I couldn't. There was a lot of blood. I thought she was dead. I called nine-one-one.' Francesca tried not to look as shocked as she was as she listened and nodded.

'That must have been so scary for you.' He nodded, and Francesca didn't want to ask if his mother was still alive or had died the night before. It would have explained the expression of shock and sorrow on his face. He looked like an orphan sitting there, and she wanted to put her arms around him, but he seemed so fragile she didn't dare.

'She's in the hospital now, but she's very sick. I'm going to stay here with Dad.'

'I'm glad you're here,' she said softly.

'So am I,' Marya added. 'You can help me bake lots of cookies. You can take some with you to school.' He nodded again, as his father came into the room, and Chris looked as traumatized as his son. There were dark circles under his eyes from the night before.

Chris took a seat at the table and smiled at Ian, as though they had come through the wars together. Francesca suspected they had, given what she had just heard.

'How are you doing, Champ?'

'Okay,' Ian said quietly. He had eaten very little of the soup.

'I think we both need to go to bed early and get some sleep. How does that sound to you?' Chris looked utterly worn out.

'Okay,' Ian said again. He wasn't the bouncy, happy child he normally was on weekends, but if he had watched his mother nearly die in a pool of blood, it was easy to understand why he was so subdued.

Marya touched his arm sympathetically, as Chris picked the boy up and carried him upstairs. He looked gratefully at Marya, who had been wonderful to Ian all that afternoon. Francesca stayed and talked to Marya for a while. Neither of them knew exactly what had happened, but it sounded bad, and the horror of it was written all over the child's face.

Francesca was watching TV in her room when Chris came upstairs to see her after Ian fell asleep.

'Sorry for all the drama,' he said, looking acutely unhappy, as she motioned him to a chair in her bedroom and he sat down. She was wearing a sweatshirt and jeans, and so was he. 'This isn't new for us, but it's always shocking anyway. Ian's mother is a heroin addict. She OD'd last night. She told me she was clean, but she never is. I don't know what happened, I think she's been involved with some bad guy recently. She shot up, slashed her wrists, and proceeded to nearly bleed to death in front of Ian. He saved her life and called nine-one-one. He was keeping pressure on her arteries with his fingers when they showed up. He was covered with blood, and so was she, but he saved her. She's going to rehab again after she gets out of the hospital. I'm sorry to tell you all this, Francesca. It's pretty nasty stuff, and it's really tough on him. I got out, but she's his mother and we have joint custody.

'As long as she stays clean, we share him, and as soon as she gets better after this, he'll probably go back to her. I hate it, but that's the way it is. She's very convincing whenever she cleans up. And judges don't like taking kids away from their mothers, so they always give her another chance, at least so far. She gets drug-tested weekly, so they give us shared custody until she blows it, like now. And Ian's very loyal to her. She's his mother, and he loves her. Every time something like this happens, it tears him apart, and me for his having to go through it. I used to want to kill her for this. Now I just want to get him through it without having it destroy his life. She did a pretty good job on me. I'd love to get sole custody, but she talks a good game and sounds like Mother Teresa in court when she's clean. The judges fall for it every time.' Francesca could see how ravaged he was by what was happening to his son, and she could only imagine what their married life together must have been like. He was the last person she would have suspected of being involved with a drug addict. He was so square and sensible. But clearly, she wasn't. It struck Francesca that you never knew what people's private lives were like. His had obviously been a nightmare, and now Ian was living it. Chris looked near tears as he talked to her about it.

'I came up to talk to you because I don't know how long Ian will be with me. She's supposed to go to rehab when she gets out of the hospital. If she's willing. She says she is now, but she could change her mind when she gets there. Ian won't go back to live with her unless she's drug-tested and clean. She could get her shit together in a month, or two or three. Or she could kill herself with it one of these days. I told you Ian would only be here two weekends a month, but that's not going to be the case right now for a while. I wanted to ask you if you want me to move out. You weren't expecting to have a child here full time, so I'll look for an apartment for me and Ian, if you prefer. I didn't think I needed an apartment when I moved in here, but apparently I do right now. It's up to you, Francesca, and I understand perfectly if you don't want us here. Just tell me what you want me to do, and I'll take care of it as fast as I can.' He looked utterly washed out as he volunteered to move, and she looked at him in horror.

'Are you kidding? Do you think I would ask you to leave with all of that going on and happening to Ian? He's welcome to stay here, and so are you. I wouldn't think of asking you to move out, and I don't want you to. We love Ian, and I'd like to be there for him too. This has to be a really hard time for him, and for you both. I'm sorry you have to go through it.' She was truly sorry for him.

'So am I,' he said, with the vision of his child covered in blood when he picked him up at the hospital the night before. 'No kid should have to live with this. If she had half a heart, or a brain, she'd give up custody, but she won't do that. She's afraid of how it will look to her parents, and they'll stop giving her money, so she hangs on to him. She can't take care of him. But they don't want her to give him up, which stinks. I have to go to a temporary custody hearing tomorrow. They'll give him to me now, but as soon as she's back on her feet and can bullshit a judge and look halfway clean, they'll give Ian to her for our custody arrangement. It makes me sick to send him back. This is the third time this has happened, and they keep giving him to her when she looks okay.

Her father is a very powerful man. That holds a lot of sway with the judge.'

'What does Ian want?' Francesca asked him softly.

'He's afraid that if he's not there to save her, she'll die. This is the second time he has. But one of these days it won't work, and she'll die right in front of him with a needle sticking out of her arm.' There were tears rolling down his cheeks as he said it, and Francesca got off her bed and gave him a hug.

'Do you want me to go to the hearing with you tomorrow? No one should have to go through that alone.' He shook his head.

'I've been there before. And thank you, but I wouldn't do that to you. This is my problem, not yours. But thanks for offering and being a good friend. At least the judge said Ian doesn't have to be there. This should be pretty quick, and it's only temporary custody till she gets out of rehab. Her lawyer can't say much after everything that happened last night.' It was agony for him and Ian, and Francesca could see it in his eyes. She understood now why he spent his time alone. He was obviously still traumatized by everything he'd lived through with his ex-wife. He said all he wanted now was to be with Ian and enjoy a peaceful life. He had lived through hell when he was with her, and Ian still was. But Chris knew that if he tried to take him away from her permanently, the child would blame himself forever for not being there for her. It was a nightmare for him. Ian had become the caretaker, and his mother the child.

They talked for a few more minutes, and Francesca reassured him again about not moving out. He was very grateful, and then went back to his room to be with Ian. They had hardly slept the night before, and Ian had terrible nightmares that night. She could hear him screaming through the floor of her room, and the deep rumble of Chris's soothing voice. She felt desperately sorry for them both.

Marya baby-sat for Ian when Chris left for the temporary custody hearing early the next morning. Chris was wearing a dark suit and a tie. He looked more serious than Francesca had ever seen him, and her heart went out to him as he left in a cab to meet his lawyer at the courthouse. He'd been through it before, too many times. Ian knew all about it too. He explained it to Marya and Francesca as they sat with him in the kitchen and tried unsuccessfully to distract him. He explained that he would live with his dad now until his mother got out of the hospital, and then he had to go back to her to take care of her, otherwise she might die. He said it with the saddest eyes Francesca had ever seen. Chris had confided to her the night before that Ian saw a therapist twice a week just to get through the trauma he lived with on a daily basis. Francesca thought it was criminal to put a child through it, and an agonizing blackmail for the child.

Ian had spoken to his mother early that morning on the phone, when Chris let him talk to her. But they both knew that once she got to rehab, she wouldn't be able to call him until she was clean and got out. It could be months before Ian would talk to her again, and a grieving process for him every time. He looked like he was in mourning as he sat on Marya's lap and she held him, and then he cuddled up next to Francesca and fell asleep. He was still dozing when Chris got home at eleven. The judge had given him temporary custody of Ian, as he expected. He whispered his thanks to Francesca and Marya, scooped the child up in his arms, and took him back to their room to sleep and try to recover from everything he'd been through. Francesca was still shaken by it when she left for the gallery, and she thought about both of them all day. She wished that she could do something to help them, but there was so little anyone could do, except be there for them. They were rapidly becoming friends and taking care of each other. It was better than Francesca had ever hoped when she decided to take in roommates. It felt like the residents of 44 Charles Street were a family now.

Chapter 9

Once Ian moved into the house full time, the atmosphere at 44 Charles Street changed totally, just as it had when each of them moved in. It became a family and a real home, with a child in their midst. Marya cooked and baby-sat for Ian when Chris was too busy to take care of him after school. Francesca took him to the gallery with her and went on outings with him on weekends. He loved hanging out at the gallery, meeting the artists who dropped by regularly, and was fascinated by the paintings. And Eileen demonstrated her teaching skills and played wonderful games with him, and taught him to make origami birds. With Eileen directing them, they all made puppets in papier-mâché one weekend and turned the kitchen into a total mess but the results were beautiful and Ian was thrilled. Eileen had an amazing knack with kids, and Ian followed her like the Pied Piper. He'd go up to her room, and she would read him his favorite books for hours. Chris was always grateful to her. Ian loved it.

And they all dyed Easter eggs with him, and put them in little baskets with brightly colored shredded cellophane 'grass.' Eileen provided the supplies. Ian suddenly had a grandmother and two aunts whom he'd never had before. And Francesca's father and Avery came to Easter dinner, where Marya prepared a splendid ham and decorated the table with Easter eggs, with a gigantic chocolate egg in the center of the table, which she allowed Ian to eat for dessert. He went to see his maternal grandmother several times, and Chris was good about getting him there, but it was in the house on Charles Street where Ian felt the most loved and had the most fun. The women in the house were devoted to him, each in her own way, and Ian loved them.

Chris beamed as he watched the child blossom, and it was an agonizing day when he had to go back to court in May when Ian's mother claimed to be back on her feet, and was out of rehab again. She wanted Ian to come home. Chris looked gray when he left for court, and worse when he got back. She had done it again with her father's help, and convinced the judge. Chris had to take

Ian back to her the next day, and return to the visitation schedule they'd had before she OD'd. It was his worst nightmare come true again. She had appeared angelic and remorseful in court.

Ian looked painfully subdued when he said goodbye to all of them.

'You'll be back next weekend,' Marya reminded him. 'We'll make almond cookies then. See you soon, Ian,' she said as she kissed him goodbye, and Francesca had a lump in her throat the size of a fist when she hugged him. Eileen gave him her own teddy bear to take with him. All three women were crying when they walked back into the house after he and Chris left in a cab. And Chris looked devastated when he got home after dropping Ian off. He looked sick, and Francesca knew he was. He went upstairs and went to bed, and stayed there for two days, while Marya brought him comfort food on trays and he refused to eat. He was morbidly depressed that weekend and worried sick. What if something happened to Ian? Or she used and put him at risk? Chris could hardly function until Ian came back for the weekend the following week. The child had been sorely missed, and the house felt like a tomb once he left on Sunday night.

Without Ian, the house took up its old more adult rhythm again. Marya went to Vermont to check on things there. Eileen started dating more again, and was out almost every night. She had slowed down for a while. During Ian's time there she had stayed home more than usual, and enjoyed being with him. She had been through several boyfriends in the past few months, and she got involved with someone new in June. And Francesca was trying to force herself to think about dating too. Everything had been on hold in all their lives while Ian lived with them. Without him, they became single adults again with lives of their own to lead. But on the weekends he was there, they all concentrated on him. It touched Chris's heart. They had acquired a new family at the house on Charles Street. And he had three good friends to help him through tough times. And at least for now, his ex-wife was clean according to the tests, and being responsible with Ian. But judging from past history Chris knew it wouldn't last.

June was a busy month for all of them. Marya was working hard on her new book. They had new dishes to try every night. Chris loved to tease Marya about it. As time passed, he seemed more relaxed and less anxious about Ian, although still skeptical about his ex-wife's ability to stay sober long term.

'If I don't come home to a five-star meal every night, I

feel deprived. I think I've gained ten pounds since I moved in,' he complained to Marya with a grin.

'You needed it.' Marya smiled at him. And she was teaching Ian to cook when he was with them on alternate weekends. So far his mother was behaving, but Chris knew it was only a matter of time before she screwed up again. He had been through it with her for ten years. He had discovered her addiction to drugs before Ian was conceived. He had seen her through two rounds of rehab and then she got pregnant. The only time she had been totally off drugs was while she was expecting him. She fell off the wagon again three months after he was born. He no longer believed that she could clean up for a reasonable amount of time. He was sure she'd start using again any day. He just hoped that when it happened Ian would somehow be spared the agony of it. Chris was waiting for the other shoe to drop and he knew it would. The only question in his mind was when.

Eileen showed up with her new boyfriend, and Francesca was discouraged to see that he was one of the ones with pierces and tattoos. She seemed to ricochet between preppy young men who worked in ad agencies or banks, were school teachers, or had other traditional jobs, and wilder ones who worked on the fringes of the arts or related fields. This time she had gone a little further off the beaten path, and her new man was a motorcycle mechanic. Francesca couldn't stand him and thought he was intolerably rude. He was handsome, there was no denying it, and sexy, she could see his physical appeal, but there was an underlying current that made everyone uncomfortable, and he wanted to control everything that Eileen did. It infuriated Francesca whenever Eileen talked about it. It seemed as though his wanting to control her flattered her, and she mistook it for love. It reminded Francesca more of abuse. And he didn't hesitate to put Eileen down in front of them and belittle her. He had just done it one morning, after Marya had made breakfast for all of them, and Brad, the new boyfriend, made a nasty comment to and about Eileen. Francesca bristled immediately, but didn't say anything. And then he did it again. This time she called him on it, while Eileen looked mortified and stared into her plate. She didn't like to upset him.

'Why do you say things like that about her?' Francesca challenged him. She had only seen him a few times, but she didn't like anything about him.

'What's it to you?' He glared at Francesca across the table, intending to intimidate her. He didn't. It just made her angrier at him.

'It's mean. She's a wonderful woman, and she's nice to

you. We're her friends. Why would you say something like that about her?' He had called Eileen a dummy, repeatedly, which she certainly wasn't, except maybe about him. And he hadn't said it affectionately.

Francesca and Brad had an encounter at the coffeepot a few minutes afterward, when he grabbed it away from her, still angry about what she had said to him. He felt humiliated. And a little bit of the hot coffee splashed onto Francesca's hand, which he had intended. She gave a sharp shout as it burned her, and gave the coffee pot up to him.

'Oh, did it burn you?' he asked sarcastically with a grin. 'Sorry, dear,' he said as he poured it into a cup and started back to the table, and walked right into Chris, who stood looking at him with murder in his eyes.

'Don't ever do anything like that again. Don't even think about it,' Chris said to him. 'This is a family. We stick up for each other, and you're lucky to be here. So you'd better be nice to everybody while you're here, and that includes Eileen. Got that, mister?' Francesca was stunned when she saw the look that passed between the two men. Chris was shaking with anger, and Brad took one look at him, threw his napkin down, and stormed out of the kitchen. Eileen stayed just long enough to apologize to everyone, and then ran after him. They could hear him shouting at her at the front door, and a moment later his motorcycle roared off.

'I don't like that guy,' Chris said through clenched teeth. 'He's dangerous. I don't know what she's doing with a guy like that.' No one did, but he was sexy and she was young, and so was he. The bad-boy syndrome. Maybe she was going out with him just because she could, and she figured she could handle it. Francesca was thinking about asking her not to bring him to the house again, but it was Eileen's home too. She wondered if Chris's outburst might keep him in line, or maybe he wouldn't want to come back either. She was touched by what Chris had said, and she loved the family feeling they now shared.

Francesca started dating someone too that month. She had only been out with him three times, and he seemed nice enough, although she wasn't in love with him. But he was nice to go out with.

He was an artist, but not one she represented. She had a good time with him, although she wasn't serious about him. He had very left-wing ideas, and he thought her father was a sellout for becoming successful and charging big prices. He thought artists should do their work for the people, which was a little too out there for her. But he was intelligent and fun, and slightly irresponsible. In some ways he reminded her a little of her father when he was younger. He had something of his looks and charm, and he was a little vague the way her father had been in his youth. There was something very familiar about him. She knew the type, although she didn't have Avery's patience with it. She had no desire to reform him. Dinner with him was enough. More than that would have been too much. But he was really the first person she had dated since Todd. It was good practice, but she knew she'd never be serious about him. He made her laugh, which was nice, and feel like a woman again, which wasn't bad either. But she had no chemistry for him whatsoever. He was naïve and unrealistic and seemed like a child to her. She didn't want to date a boy, she wanted to go out with a man, if she took that step again with anyone. She knew the type, a lot of the artists she knew and represented acted like children. She didn't want to mother him.

The day after Chris's run-in with Eileen's new boyfriend in the kitchen, Marya was going to try out a new recipe on them. They had all promised to be home for dinner, and they were looking forward to it. And just before they sat down, Eileen called Francesca on her cell phone and said she had a terrible cold and a fever. She hadn't come down that day at all, and Marya was concerned.

'Poor thing, I'll send up some soup,' Marya said. She put together a nice tray for her, which Francesca carried up to her room. She knocked on the door and was surprised to find it locked, and Eileen wouldn't let her in.

'Marya made you some food,' Francesca explained through the door, and Eileen said she was too sick to eat. 'I can't take it back downstairs, it'll hurt her feelings,' Francesca said through the locked door.

'Just leave it outside,' Eileen said from the distance. 'I don't want to make you sick.'

'You won't. I'm as healthy as a horse.' But Eileen still wouldn't open it. 'Hey . . . are you okay?' Francesca persisted. 'You're worrying me. Let me in. I've got some Tylenol for you too, for the fever.'

'Just leave it outside on the tray. I'll get it in a minute.' Francesca could hear that she was crying, and she was panicked.

'I want you to let me in,' she said, sounding stern, and feeling like an intruder, but she had the feeling that something was wrong. And Eileen didn't sound like she had a cold. There was a long pause where neither of them moved on either side of the door, but Francesca wasn't leaving. She could hear the bolt turn in the lock, but Eileen still didn't open the door, and setting the tray down, Francesca gently turned the knob. Eileen was on the other side of the door, crying silently, in her night-gown, with the worst black eye and bruises on her face that Francesca had ever seen. And there were bruises on her body too, her arms and her breasts. Someone had beaten her to a pulp, and Francesca suspected who it was. 'Did Brad do that to you?' Eileen didn't answer, and then she nodded and began to sob.

'Don't tell anyone . . . please promise you won't . . . he said I humiliated him in front of all of you . . . and I didn't stick up for him.'

'I want you to call the police,' Francesca said, shaking as she looked at her. Seeing the condition she was in made her want to cry too. She put her arms around her and held her as Eileen sobbed.

'He said he'd kill me if I call the cops on him, and I think he will. Promise you won't do anything, Francesca. I won't see him again. I promise.'

'I don't want him back in this house.' Francesca didn't say it, but if Eileen had him there again, she would have to ask her to leave. Brad was clearly dangerous, to all of them, not just to her. He had burned Francesca's hand intentionally, and God only knew what he would have liked to do to Chris, and would if he got the opportunity. She really wanted to call the police but didn't want to put Eileen at greater risk. 'Do you want me to take you to the ER?'

'No,' she said miserably. 'They might report it to the cops. I'm okay, I've been through it before. My father used to beat me and my mom up all the time when I was a kid. He's a drunk. That's why I left home.'

'I'm so sorry,' Francesca said, wishing they could do something to Brad, like put him in jail where he belonged. 'Eileen, you can't keep meeting guys like this. You don't know who they are. It may be fun and exciting to meet them online, but some of them are dangerous. And you can't bring anyone here again.'

'I won't. I swear,' she sobbed as she clung to Francesca. 'Please don't make me leave. I love it here. It's the only real home I've ever had.' What she said tore at Francesca's heart.

'Then I want you to be careful from now on.'

'I promise . . . I will . . .' And then she looked at Francesca guiltily. 'He took my key. I tried to stop him, but he took it and ran after he beat me up. He said he'd come back and do it again if I told anyone.'

'I'll change the locks,' Francesca said grimly. She kissed her gently on the forehead then, promised to come back after dinner, and ran back downstairs. She had been gone for half an hour.

'What took so long?' Chris asked her when she got back. They were halfway through the main course, but

Marya hadn't wanted it to get cold. 'She must be really sick.'

'Sick as a dog,' Francesca confirmed, not wanting to upset either of them, and not sure what to say. She said almost not a word through dinner, and Chris could see she was upset. They had all gotten to know each other well. He spoke to her in an undervoice when Marya was getting a chocolate soufflé out of the oven, and then made crème Chantilly and sauce anglaise to go with it. It was yet another feast.

'What's wrong?' Chris asked in a whisper. Francesca hesitated for a minute and then decided to tell him. She wanted his advice.

'Brad beat her up. Badly. She's got bruises all over her face and body and a black eye.'

'Jesus.' Chris looked furious. 'Did she call the police?'

Francesca shook her head. 'She said he told her he'd kill her if she told anyone. She can't even go to work. She looks a mess.'

'Do you think she should move out?' he asked practically, as Marya worked on the whipped cream and made so much noise she couldn't hear what they were saying.

'She begged me not to. I told her she can't have him

here again. He took her key. I'll get the locks changed tomorrow. We can put the chain on tonight.'

Chris sighed and leaned back in his chair. 'I hope she's not addicted to the guy, or getting beaten up. Physical abuse is a tough addiction to break, one of the worst.' But as far as they knew, it had never happened before. Francesca was encouraged by that.

'I think he's just a random bad guy she met on the Internet. I wish she'd give that up. She doesn't mean to, and she's a sweet kid, but she's putting all of us at risk along with herself.' Chris nodded, and Marya arrived with the dessert. Francesca picked at it, and Chris ate most of it. It had been a delicious meal. Marya's recipe was flawless, but what was happening upstairs was upsetting to Francesca and Chris. They didn't tell Marya, and agreed that she didn't need to know.

After helping Marya clean up the kitchen, Francesca went back upstairs to see Eileen. She looked terrible, but she had eaten some of the food Marya sent her and felt better. She made a thousand promises to Francesca, who went back downstairs to talk to Chris. They were uneasy about Brad, but they hoped he'd leave Eileen alone after this. She had sworn to Francesca that she'd never see him again.

Francesca put the chain on that night, and Chris said

he'd call the locksmith the next day and get the locks changed while she was at work. There wasn't much else they could do, except keep an eye out for him. And Francesca had told Eileen that she would call the police if he showed up at the house again. Francesca could hardly sleep that night, thinking about the bruises on Eileen's face, and she wondered what Chris had meant about physical abuse being a hard addiction to break. Who could possibly be addicted to abuse? It made no sense. She was sure Eileen had learned a lesson, and would stay well away from Brad from now on. After seeing what he'd done to her, Francesca had no doubt about that.

Chapter 10

Chris arranged to have the locks changed, and Eileen took a week off from work. She told them she'd had a car accident, and eventually she admitted what had happened to Marya, who was shocked. She was relieved that Francesca had changed the locks, and she felt desperately sorry for Eileen, who was such an innocent, harmless young girl. And even if she was foolish about her Internet encounters, she didn't deserve to be beaten up. No one does. It crossed Francesca's mind that Eileen's problems weren't with the Internet, which was just a venue for her to meet men, like a bar, or any other place. Her real problem was the poor judgment she exercised about the men she met, and her attraction to the wrong ones.

It took them all some time to settle down after that.

Francesca went out with her artist again, and was even less impressed. He was a nice man, but they had nothing in common and were just too different. She didn't want to make that mistake again and decided not to pursue it. He acted like an irresponsible kid, unlike Todd, who was a man. There was no point forcing things, and she told him she couldn't go out with him anymore. She was content to be alone, although her mother was nagging her about it. She couldn't understand Francesca's willingness to be without a man, and suggested she go back to her shrink. Francesca laughed and said she was feeling fine. She was in no hurry to get involved again – she had been with Todd for a long time.

The next shocking piece of news she got was from Todd. He called her at the gallery, asked her how she was doing, chatted for a few minutes, and told her he was engaged.

'Already?' She was stunned. 'You just moved out five months ago. What's the rush?'

'I'm forty-one years old. I want to get married and have kids.' She was thirty-five and still felt none of that.

'Is that the woman I saw you with a few months ago? She's tall and blond, you were at Christie's together.' Francesca sounded sad. It was hard to get used to the idea of his being with someone else.

'Probably. I've been seeing her since February. We're getting married early next year. I thought you should know before we announce it or tell anyone else.'

'Thank you,' she said softly. She was happy for him if that was what he wanted. But hearing it still hurt. He knew it would. They were different people with different needs. It was what had driven them apart. And now he was engaged. It left her feeling dazed all day after she thanked him for telling her and wished him luck.

She was still feeling down about it when she went home that night. Chris was getting out of a cab as she walked up the front steps. He had delivered a design project to an art director uptown, this time for a New Age-looking capsule designed to contain laundry detergent. He looked happy to see her.

'How was your day?' he asked as she unlocked the front door. It was nice for both of them to have someone to come home to. Neither of them would have otherwise.

'Not so good. Todd called to tell me he's engaged.' They had few secrets from each other now, if any, except for their hopes and dreams, which they kept to themselves. But after the drama with Ian's mother, and Eileen getting beaten up, they talked about everything that happened to them on a daily basis, and considered each other friends, as they did Marya and Eileen.

'Wow, that's heavy,' Chris commented as he followed her into the front hall. There were the usual fabulous smells coming from the kitchen. They were used to it by now, they loved it but were less impressed, although the smells wafting up to them were particularly good that night. All of them offered to chip in for the food, but most of the time, Marya insisted on providing it herself. It was her generous and greatly appreciated gift to them. They all gave her little gifts whenever they could, and Chris bought her some very good wine. 'Are you upset?' Francesca looked shaken as she turned to look at him. She hadn't expected this from Todd, not this soon anyway.

'Yes, I am,' she said honestly. 'I guess I should be gracious about it and say I'm happy for him, but I'm not sure I am. I'm still sad for me that it didn't work out with us.'

'At least you both admitted it and cut your losses. It took me ten years to do that, and by the time I did, I was a mess and never wanted a relationship again. You did it in half the time, and you were decent to each other. I waited till she nearly destroyed my life along with her own. I kept thinking Kim would get clean and stay off drugs for good. The relationship we had was totally sick. I was addicted to her, and thought I could help her fix herself. No one can do that. She's a mess. You and Todd are whole people, but you wanted different things. You figured that out and moved on. He found someone, so will you. You didn't destroy each other on the way out.' She felt sorry for him when he talked about Ian's mother. She could barely imagine what a nightmare that must have been, and it still was, at their child's expense, which was even worse.

'You're not too old to find someone too, you know,' she reminded him gently.

'Not too old,' he admitted. He was thirty-eight. 'But possibly too damaged and too badly burned. I'm not sure I could ever trust anyone again, in a relationship. She lied to me constantly and I believed her. She slept with her dealer. It took me three years to figure out she couldn't stay off drugs. Addicts are incredibly convincing and amazing liars. She's a piece of work. I feel sorry for her now, but I hate what she does to Ian.' Francesca nodded. He had been essentially out of the marriage for two years, ever since he gave up on her, although he had only left her six months before. He had stayed with friends in the beginning, then a hotel, and had finally come here. Francesca was sure he'd find someone again, and he was equally sure of it about her. They were both too young to give up on love forever.

'Let's go see what Marya is cooking up for us tonight,' he said, to distract them both. They had been trying out recipes for her almost every night. She'd been cooking up a storm, and all of them were gaining weight.

Francesca followed Chris down the stairs to the kitchen, expecting to see Marya, and both of them looked startled when they saw a tall white-haired man instead. He had fierce blue eyes and a mane of shoulder-length white hair. He looked at them with suspicion for an instant and then burst into a broad smile.

'Francesca and Chris?' he asked in a heavy French accent. He seemed to know who they were. He introduced himself as Charles-Edouard, and suddenly Francesca realized who he was. His last name was Prunier, and he was one of the most famous chefs in France and obviously one of Marya's friends. She appeared a moment later and explained that he was in town from Paris and was cooking for them that night. She promised that it would be an unforgettable experience, and he looked at her with eyes that sparkled. He was a very handsome man.

They shared a bottle of champagne he had brought with him, and everyone in the house was excited about dinner. Eileen came home a few minutes later with flowers she had bought for Francesca and Marya and a bottle of wine for Chris. They were a lively bunch talking about France as she walked in. Charles-Edouard said that he and Marya had known each other for thirty years. It was easy to see that he had a crush on her, and he flirted with her as they cooked together. She was playing sous-chef that night and chopping things for him, as he juggled half a dozen pans, and twice as many bowls. She looked at him with affectionate smiles from time to time, and they seemed very comfortable with each other.

The result when they sat down to dinner was stupefying. Everyone agreed that they had never had a dinner like it in their lives. He was modest and funny and outrageous, and he constantly looked at Marya with loving glances, which she happily ignored. She loved cooking with him, and they were thinking of writing a book together about the delicacies and herbs of Provence and how to use them. But the handsome Frenchman obviously wanted to collaborate with her on more than that.

'He's adorable,' Francesca whispered to Marya as they did the dishes together. 'And he's crazy about you.' It was easy for anyone to see and they all had, while eating his astoundingly good dinner. He and Chris were smoking cigars in the garden, while the three women washed up.

And after that, Eileen went upstairs. 'What about him?' Francesca asked. She thought they made a very handsome pair, and he was about Marya's age.

'Don't be silly,' Marya said shyly, and then laughed. 'And what about his wife? He's very French. He's married to a very sweet woman who used to be one of his sous-chefs. He's cheated on her for years.' She said it as though talking about a badly behaved brother.

'Would he ever get divorced?' Francesca asked with interest. She was feeling better about Todd's engagement after a very pleasant evening, an exquisite meal with good friends, and a bevy of fine wines.

'Of course not. He's French. French men don't get divorced. They cheat until they die, usually in someone else's bed, like their mistress's. I'm not sure she's any more faithful to him, and he claims they've never been happy. But he sleeps with everyone in every kitchen he works in. I don't want to get in the middle of a mess like that. I like him better as a friend.'

'That's too bad. He's cute. He's very good-looking. Keep him away from my mother, or she'll be chasing him and dragging him to the nearest divorce lawyer. Maybe you should think about that.' Marya shook her head and laughed. 'Your mother might just be a match for him. I'm not. I can't deal with men like that. John and I were faithful to each other all our lives. I prefer men like that. Charles-Edouard is handsome and exciting, but he's a very, very bad boy.' Marya had no doubt about it.

'He sounds like my father before he married Avery. Sometimes men like that do reform.'

'Yeah, one in a hundred million. I don't like those kinds of odds. I'd rather work with him and keep him as a friend,' Marya said firmly with a smile. 'This way he's someone else's problem, not mine.'

Chris and Charles-Edouard wandered back into the kitchen then with what was left of the Cuban cigars the famous chef had smuggled in. He poured each of them a brandy then, and halfway through it he said he had been in love with Marya for thirty years. He looked at her adoringly, and she laughed at him. She took his declarations of love for her with a grain of salt.

'Yeah, me and ten thousand other women. That's a long list, Charles-Edouard,' she teased him as he smiled.

'But you were always top of that list.' He twinkled as he teased her.

'That's because you couldn't have me, and you still can't. Besides, I like your wife.'

'So do I,' he said matter-of-factly with a mischievous smile. 'I'm just not in love with her. I don't think I ever was. We're very good friends now. She went after me once with a butcher knife,' he said, pointing to his lower parts with the stub of his cigar, and they all laughed. 'I've been very nice to her ever since.' He said he had no children either, like Marya, and had never wanted any. 'I'm too much of a child myself,' he confessed. He was totally charming and easy to be with. It had been a magical evening for all of them, and he promised to cook dinner for them again before he left. Francesca really liked him and wished he were available for Marya. It was obvious that they had a deep respect for each other, and a lot of fun together, and he loved flirting with her. She had opened up that night like a flower in spring. It was nice to see her that way and admired by a man. She was such a pretty woman, so kind and so talented, it made Francesca sad to think of her alone. She didn't seem to mind it, but Francesca was sure she must get lonely at times. Marya didn't have the strident quality of her mother, who was desperate for a man, but it made her all the more appealing. She was very feminine, and there was no question about it, Charles-Edouard was crazy about her. It really was too bad he had a wife. And she could sense that Marya was right and knew him well. He spoke of his wife with affection and fondness, and he would never get divorced. He was *very* French.

Francesca walked Chris to the landing outside his

room that night, after they said goodnight to Marya. They talked about Charles-Edouard for a few minutes. He was definitely a character, and had enormous talent as a chef. Neither of them mentioned Todd again. Chris didn't want to upset her, and Francesca was still digesting it but felt better after tonight. And then she went upstairs, and Chris went to his room. He had spoken to Ian during dinner, and everything seemed fine.

The house was quiet after everyone went to their rooms. They'd all had a lot to drink. The wines had been important and delicious. He had served Château d'Yquem with dessert, and the brandy finished them all off. They were all happily asleep in their beds, as Eileen tiptoed quietly down the stairs with her stilettos in her hand. She was quiet as a mouse as she opened the front door and closed it softly behind her. Brad was waiting for her outside. He had his motorcycle parked around the corner, and he looked annoyed.

'What took you so long? I've been waiting for an hour.'

'I'm sorry.' She looked at him nervously. She could cover what was left of the bruises with makeup now. He had convinced her that his punishment was her fault, because she hadn't defended him as she should have and had pissed him off. Her father had always told her it was her fault too when he threw her or her mother down the stairs. He had broken her arm twice. 'I had to wait until everyone went to bed,' she explained to Brad, and he looked furious as they walked around the corner to where his bike was parked.

'What are you? Twelve? You pay rent in that place. That bitch can't tell you what to do.'

'Yes, she can. It's her house. She can throw me out.'

'Fuck her,' Brad said angrily, and handed her a helmet, and a minute later they took off, with Eileen on the back of his motorcycle, holding on for dear life. He was pissed about it, but Eileen had been adamant that he couldn't come upstairs. They were going back to his place. She wanted to make it up to him for upsetting him before. He was right. She hadn't defended him to the others. And he had convinced her, just as her father had, that she was bad, and wrong. She was going to prove otherwise to him tonight.

Chapter 11

Eileen sneaked back in the next morning before anyone got up. She felt like a kid again, and no one knew she had gone out. Brad hadn't brought her home, and she didn't want them to hear the motorcycle anyway, so she took a cab. She was home in plenty of time to shower and dress for work. Brad had been incredible to her, gentle, loving, kind, and it was the best sex she'd ever had. She thought it was a shame her roommates didn't know him better. He was a very decent man. They had just gotten off to a bad start. She hoped that Francesca would relax about him in time and forgive him. Eileen already had. She was seeing him again that night. The relationship with him was heady stuff.

They all had a quiet evening at home that night.

Marya was studying recipes, while Francesca did her laundry, and Chris was reading in bed. Eileen said she was going out with friends from work. They had had such an exciting evening with Charles-Edouard cooking the night before, that all of them took a night off. Marya had left some soup on the stove, and Francesca was on her way upstairs with her laundry, when Chris shot out of his room with a look of panic.

'She did it again!' he said, looking both furious and scared. 'She OD'd again. She's in a coma. Ian was with her, and they said he was frantic when they found her. Now he can't speak. He's in shock. She had a guy with her. He's dead. They think she might not make it this time.' And somewhere in his heart, Chris hoped she wouldn't. It would be simpler for Ian. He was desperate to get to his child. He flew down the stairs and out the front door as Francesca stared after him, praying Ian was all right.

She waited up for them to come back. It was four in the morning when they finally did. Chris was carrying Ian, who was sound asleep. She opened her door and came down the stairs when she heard the front door close.

'How is he? Is he okay? Can he talk?' She looked as worried as Chris, and he looked as though he had been hit by a bus. It had been a long night.

'He said a few words before he fell asleep. They said I could bring him home. He watched the guy die when he OD'd, talk about trauma for a kid. They're holding Kimberly responsible for it. That's what happens when someone OD's, the survivors are charged with their death. That's why no one ever calls the cops when some-one OD's. She'll probably go to jail for this, or prison, unless her father's lawyers can get her off again.'

'How is she?'

'Alive unfortunately,' he said angrily. 'She was coming around when I left. I can't let Ian go through this again,' he said with a look of desperation as she followed him into his room and he set his son down on the bed. Ian never stirred. 'They sedated him. He was hysterical at the hospital. He thought his mother was dead. I'm going to fight for custody this time, and win. No sane judge can give him back to her now. I won't let this happen to him again. She's too sick.' Francesca nodded, and wondered who her father was, that his lawyers were so powerful. Chris had mentioned it before. But of course she didn't ask. It was irrelevant. Ian was all that mattered now.

Francesca went down to the kitchen and brought Chris a cup of warm milk. She was just on her way back with it when she saw Eileen slip in. It was very late for an evening with friends from work. And Francesca guessed correctly from what Eileen was wearing that she'd had a date, but she had no idea with whom. At least she hadn't brought him back to the house. All Francesca hoped was that she'd been out with a nice guy. Eileen looked happy as she ran quickly up the stairs to her own room, and Francesca delivered the cup of warm milk to Chris. He was sitting in a chair, watching Ian sound asleep on the top bunk.

'It's going to make a huge stink if his mother goes to jail,' Chris said as he sipped the milk. But he had no regrets for her if it got him sole custody of Ian. He only cared about his son. He had stopped caring about her years before, except for her effect on Ian.

'Don't worry about it,' Francesca said softly in the dimly lit room. 'Get some sleep. You can deal with all that tomorrow.' And she knew he'd have to face another temporary custody hearing in the next few days. That was how it worked. Custody cases got priority and went ahead of everything else.

'Thank you,' he said to Francesca, and she slipped quietly out of the room and went back to her own.

The mystery of who Ian's mother was was solved for all of them on the front page of the newspaper the next day. Chris had been married to Kimberly Archibald, of one of the most powerful families on the East Coast. Her father was an important venture capitalist who had made a vast fortune with the one he already had. The article told Francesca essentially what Chris already had the night before. It said that she was being charged with manslaughter for the death of a fellow addict in her apartment. The article claimed that she had bought and paid for the drugs. Francesca felt sorry for Chris and Ian as she read it, and then stopped as she saw the second paragraph that mentioned his name. She realized then what an innocent she was. It said that she had been married to and divorced from Christopher Harley of the Boston political family of the same name. More important, his mother was a Calverson. They were related to senators, governors, and two presidents. Chris's marriage to Kimberly had been a merger of two of the most powerful families in the country, one financial and the other political. And Chris wasn't just a graphic designer quietly making a living and renting a room from her on Charles Street. He was the heir of an important family, which he seemed to have divorced himself from to lead a quiet, simple life, until his ex-wife splashed him all over the front pages of every paper in New York. He was totally unassuming. Francesca put the paper in a drawer so Ian wouldn't see it when they came down to breakfast a few minutes later. Marya still didn't know what had happened the night before. She looked surprised to see Ian, but didn't comment on how pale he was, or how shaken he looked. He didn't smile, and hardly said a word at breakfast, even when she gave him his favorite Mickey Mouse pancakes. He still looked sleepy from the sedation they'd given him the night before and he hardly ate.

'What happened?' Marya whispered to Francesca when Chris thanked her for breakfast and took Ian back upstairs. Chris looked worried and exhausted, and he hadn't seen the paper either. Francesca handed it to Marya, who read the article and gasped as she read it. 'Oh my God, how awful. I hope Chris gets custody of him now for good.'

'He should, particularly if she goes to prison. Chris thinks her father won't let that happen.'

'He may not have a choice,' Marya said wisely. 'Ian looks awful.'

'He saw the man die, and his mother OD.'

'No child should have to go through that.' She felt terrible for both Chris and Ian, as did Francesca. Chris came back downstairs then without Ian. He had left him upstairs, he wanted to see the paper. His mouth was a thin line when he did.

'Nice, huh?' he commented to both women with a grim look. The story was bad enough, but he hated it when they traced his family back through all the generations. At least most people who knew him never made the connection with him. And they hadn't mentioned Ian being on the scene, which was a blessing. They had had some respect for the fact that he was seven years old. 'Burn this, will you?' he said as he handed Francesca the paper and went back upstairs. Eileen had come in by then, and Francesca explained it to her after Chris left. She felt deeply sorry for him. Neither she nor Francesca mentioned the hour she got home the night before or where she had been. Francesca staunchly believed it was none of her business, as long as Eileen didn't put the rest of them at risk with who she brought home. Francesca hoped she was using good judgment.

Chris kept Ian home from school that day, and he was still very quiet when Francesca and Eileen came home from work. Charles-Edouard was there that night. He had been with Marya all afternoon going over recipes and talking about their joint book. He offered to make them a light meal, and a special pizza for Ian. He had bought soft-shell crab, and a few lobsters, and in a short time he and Marya had whipped up another feast. She had told him about what had happened to Chris's son, and he felt terrible for him. When the boy came into the kitchen that afternoon, Charles-Edouard introduced himself and asked if Ian would mind helping him for a few minutes. They hadn't met yet until then. Charles-Edouard asked Ian to hold an egg in his hand and stand very still. Ian was expressionless as he stood there holding the egg, and Charles-Edouard looked extremely serious as he suddenly pulled the egg out of Ian's ear.

'Why did you do that?' Charles-Edouard asked him solemnly. 'I told you to hold the egg, not put it in your ear.' In spite of himself and the trauma he'd been through, Ian grinned. 'Now, this is very serious. Hold the egg please. And this time don't move. Ah, so, and a carrot in this hand. Excellent. Please listen to instructions, I'm a very important chef.' Ian was smiling by then. And this time the egg appeared to come out of his nose, and the carrot from the neck of his shirt. Ian guffawed as Charles-Edouard did his tricks. Within five minutes, he had Ian giggling, and then squealing with laughter, as another egg came out of his sweatshirt, and a lemon from his jeans. 'I can't trust you at all, can I?' Charles-Edouard said, suddenly doing a juggling act with three eggs, several vegetables, and two spoons. It was executed flawlessly until one of the eggs fell and broke on the floor, and Ian screamed with laughter at the mess. Charles-Edouard pretended to be embarrassed and then dropped the other eggs on the floor and made an even bigger mess.

Everyone was grinning by then, and Ian looked up at the tall man with the white mane and told him he was really silly. But Ian was talking again and even laughing. It brought tears to Francesca's eyes as she watched them. He was wonderful with the boy. He was as good a clown as he was a cook.

Marya cleaned up the mess before they made a bigger one, and Charles-Edouard sat down and put Ian on his knee. 'Would you like to help me make dinner?' he asked him, and Ian nodded, and a few minutes later he had a chef's hat on the boy and was showing him how to cook lobster and crab and he demanded a round of applause for his young sous-chef when he served it. And he had taught Ian how to make pizza, and tossed the dough high in the air while he did. And once again the dinner was delicious. But better than that, Ian was talking a blue streak. Chris thanked him when they shared more Cuban cigars in the garden, and Charles-Edouard acted as though it were nothing. But it meant the world to Chris. The world-famous chef had won his heart forever for what he had done with Ian. He was better than any social worker or shrink.

It was a quiet night after Charles-Edouard left. He had promised to come back and cook dinner for them over the weekend, and Marya had suggested that Francesca invite her mother, which she dreaded, but she knew that she would love it.

She called her mother the next day and invited her, and she accepted. And the following day Chris had the custody hearing, which was a media circus. His ex-wife's lawyers made no attempt to fight it. They had their hands full trying to get Kimberly's manslaughter charges dropped. Chris's lawyer had already warned them that he would be seeking permanent custody of Ian, with a vengeance this time. He had no mercy left for Kim after what she'd done, and exposed Ian to again and again. And he was awarded temporary custody at the hearing. It was on the news that night, and Francesca's mother happened to see it and called her immediately when she did.

'Do you know who that man is?' She was enormously impressed by who he was related to. Francesca was more so by his humility and discretion.

'Yes, I do.'

'He's related to some of the most powerful people in this country.'

'I guess he is. He doesn't talk about it. And this whole thing with his ex-wife is really hard on him, and his son.'

'She sounds like a complete mess. I feel sorry for her parents.'

'I feel sorry for her son. He's seven years old, and he's

187

been through a lot of trauma thanks to her.' Her mother didn't comment.

'I can't believe you have Charles-Edouard Prunier cooking dinner tomorrow night. I'm looking forward to it,' she said, switching to pleasanter subjects. 'How did you pull that off?'

'He's a friend of Marya's.'

'You certainly got yourself some interesting room-mates,' her mother said, sounding amused, as though it had been her idea. That was usually how things worked with her. If things turned out badly, it was someone else's fault. If they turned out well, she was responsible for it and took full credit. Francesca would have liked to have her father and Avery too, but she enjoyed her parents more separately than together. Her mother got competitive with Avery sometimes, which was stressful for Francesca.

Her mother arrived for dinner on Saturday night, dressed to the nines, in a short sexy black dress and very high heels. Francesca saw Charles-Edouard's eyes open wide when he saw her, and Marya looked amused. She was wearing loafers, a black sweater, and jeans, with her chef's jacket. Ian was wearing his chef's hat again, and looked pleased.

They had capellini with caviar, and Chateaubriand

with foie gras and black truffles. It was an exquisite meal, and her mother got a little giddy on the wines, and predictably, she flirted mercilessly with Charles-Edouard, and Marya didn't seem to mind at all.

'He is divine, isn't he,' Thalia commented to her daughter when the men went outside to smoke cigars, and Ian went with them. He was wearing both rings from the cigars.

'Don't get too worked up, Mom,' Francesca teased her. 'He's married. And French. That means he won't get divorced for you.'

'You never know, stranger things have happened,' she said confidently.

'Not in France,' she and Marya said in unison, and then they laughed. Eileen had gone out. She said she had a date with a new man. She was the busiest girl in town, and the happiest these days. Things seemed to be going well for her. Francesca was pleased. She loved her job and her roommates, and she was having fun again after the incident with Brad. He was history.

'He's certainly a very handsome, charming man,' Thalia said admiringly about Charles-Edouard, and Francesca brought her to earth and told her he had been in love with Marya for years.

'That's not fair,' Thalia complained directly to Marya.

189

'You don't even want a man. You said so. I do, and he's in love with you.'

'He's not in love with anyone,' Marya said easily. 'He just likes women. In quantity. We've been good friends for years.'

'What a waste,' Thalia said mournfully, as they walked back in, and she tried her charms on the famous chef again. And even though she had always embarrassed her, Francesca had to admit that her mother was beautiful. She looked sensational in the black dress and high heels, and she had the legs of a twenty-year-old as she crossed them enticingly, but Charles-Edouard only had eyes for Marya, and was unimpressed. Her mother looked a little deflated when she left. For once, her beauty and charm hadn't worked, although he thought her a very beautiful woman, but not for him. And besides, Francesca thought to herself, he had a wife. There were a few too many women floating in his soup.

It was another perfect evening thanks to him, with lots of interesting conversation and great food. He had a passion for history and literature, as well as food. And it was a lazy Sunday the next day. Charles-Edouard came to pick up Marya, and wanted to try a new Chinese restaurant with her. He knew the chef, and had met him in Beijing. Chris and Ian were going to the model boat pond. Francesca had things to do in the house, and Eileen hadn't come home the night before.

Francesca was looking at slides of new artists on a light box that afternoon when she heard Eileen come in. She called out to her but couldn't see her from where she was sitting, and Eileen headed up the stairs. Francesca got up to get more slides then, and she caught a glimpse of Eileen hunched over and barely able to move. She turned to look at Francesca with a look of devastation, as Francesca caught her breath. She had been beaten up again.

'Who did that to you?' Francesca asked her as she put an arm around her to help her. Eileen was crying, and she refused to say. 'Did you see Brad again?' And slowly Eileen nodded.

'He was so nice to me. He's so loving, and then I upset him again. He thought I was making fun of him. He said I humilated him in front of his friends.'

'Eileen, swear to me you'll get help. You can't see him again.'

'I know. He said he never wants to see me again. He says he's through with me, and never to call him again. He's gone.' Francesca knew now that he wasn't and never would be. He'd be back. To do it to her again. She had to be the one to walk away. And Francesca's worst fear was that Eileen didn't have the courage or the strength.

She helped Eileen upstairs to bed and left her there. Francesca felt sick, thinking about her, as she went back down the stairs. Chris's fears for her had been well founded. Eileen was hooked on the man and the abuse.

Chapter 12

The residents of 44 Charles Street were less sympathetic to Eileen this time. Marya gave her a motherly lecture, after bringing her soup and soft foods for five days. This time Brad had not only blackened her eyes, and made mincemeat of her face, he had loosened her teeth. She had to see the dentist twice in three days. Marya told her that she couldn't allow herself to see him again. Francesca was being firm with her and begging her to get help. And Chris wanted nothing to do with her.

'I'm tired of lunatics and addicts and self-destructive people,' he said harshly to Francesca. 'She's addicted to the guy, and even if you chain her to the wall in her room, she'll sneak out to see him, and he'll beat her up again. She's too sick. I went through the same thing with Kim and drugs. You can't fight people's addictions, and I've gotten smart enough not to try. She'll do anything to protect her addiction. It's no different than drugs. You can't fix them, or stop them, and you'll break your heart trying.'

'I can't just sit there and not say anything to her about it,' Francesca insisted. She thought Chris sounded very cold.

'You're wasting your time. She has to want to get help, and until she does, nothing you do or say will have any effect on her.'

It was heartbreaking to watch, and Francesca hated to see the condition she was in. She was such a sweet girl, with no self-esteem whatsoever. That was clear now. Her father had pummeled it out of her. Abuse was what she expected and thought she deserved.

Her employers were equally fed up with her. She had to take a week off, until she could cover the bruises with makeup. And when she went back to work, they fired her. She came back to the house in shock that afternoon. She was out of a job. Brad was no longer speaking to her and had told her he wanted nothing more to do with her. He had shut her out, and she kept asking Francesca if she thought he would ever call again. It was sick.

'I hope not' was all Francesca would say to her, but she was beginning to realize that Chris was right, and the abuse was an addiction. She was having withdrawal from not seeing Brad even if he abused her. And she refused to get help. Francesca just hoped he would stay away long enough for Eileen to come to her senses and to detox from him.

And Ian's mother was demanding to see her son in jail. Chris flatly refused, and claimed it would destroy him. Two psychiatrists who spoke to Ian agreed. He was happy with his father and leading a normal life with him. He and Chris were doing healthy, normal things.

Charles-Edouard was spending a lot of time at the house these days to see Marya, and do the preliminary work on their book together, and Ian was his shadow whenever he was there. He was teaching him French and to cook simple things. He loved the boy, and was wonderful with children, although he had never wanted any of his own. But he felt sorry for Ian and all he'd been through. Ian particularly loved it when Charles-Edouard pretended to pull an egg out of his ear, and sometimes two, and begged him to do it again, and the flamboyant chef did.

'He's around quite a bit these days, isn't he?' Francesca mentioned casually one day when she was alone in the kitchen with Marya.

'We're working on the book,' she said innocently.

'Are you sure he's so devoted to his wife?' Francesca asked, hoping he wasn't. They were so cute together. She would have loved to see Marya with him, who always insisted that would never happen and believed it. And she had no intention of having an affair with a married man, and Charles-Edouard knew it, although he still tried to convince her, as he had for thirty years. Marya just laughed at him, and reminded him regularly of his marriage and wife at home.

He was leaving for Paris shortly, at the end of the month, and to the South after that. Marya was planning to meet him in July to work on their book there. And then she was going to Spain on her own, and Italy after that, all to visit chefs she knew and restaurants she wanted to explore. And she wanted to spend August in Vermont, before she came back to New York in September. She was going to be away for more than two months, and Francesca knew she would miss her. Francesca was trying to figure out her own summer plans. Marya invited her to Europe with her, as did her mother, but Francesca wanted to go sailing in Maine with friends as she did every summer, and had for four years with Todd. They were friends of his, but she loved them dearly and they had become her friends as well. Todd was planning to visit them too with his fiancée, but at a different time.

'That's not healthy,' her mother pointed out to her. 'You're doing the same things you did with him. You need to do something new.' Her mother was going to St Tropez and Sardinia, as she did every year. She was a creature of habit too. But Chris commented on it to Francesca as well.

'Are you sure you want to go to the same place he is, even if you go on different weeks? That sounds a little dicey to me.' They both knew Todd was going with his fiancée.

'I love sailing in Maine,' she said stubbornly.

'You can come and visit me and Ian in Martha's Vineyard. We'd love to have you.' Chris would be in Martha's Vineyard with Ian for all of July and most of August. He was planning to do work while he was at the Vineyard. His family had an enormous compound there, but she felt odd doing that. She and Chris were just friends, and now that she knew who his family was, she thought they were too high-powered for her. She would have been scared to death. She had thought about going to a ranch in Montana or Wyoming to see the Grand Tetons, but she didn't want to go alone. Her father and Avery were going to Aspen, but she didn't want to go there either, nor to Europe with her mother or Marya. She didn't know where to go, and she couldn't afford an expensive vacation. It was easier to go sailing in Maine again, on her friends' boat. She resisted the idea that she was running the gallery she had started with Todd, living in the house they had bought together, and spending the same summer vacation she had shared with him for years.

'Maybe you need to let go of some of that,' Chris suggested gently. She was stuck in a rut. She couldn't seem to think of anything to do that she hadn't done with Todd. But she didn't want to admit it, even to herself. At least sailing in Maine would be a change of scenery, relaxing, and fresh air. She had always had fun there. She was going for the first three weeks of August.

The only one who had no summer plans was Eileen, and she couldn't afford to go anywhere now, since she was out of a job. She had enough money put aside to keep her afloat for two months, and she figured she'd have a job by then. Francesca suggested she go home to San Diego to see her family, but she didn't want to. And after her stories about her father, Francesca didn't insist. She felt sorry for her, she had nowhere to go. But every day was a vacation for Eileen now that she wasn't working. She had started to send her résumé around to various special ed schools, but no one had offered her anything so far. Her references from her previous job were not good, from taking too much time off work, thanks to Brad. It wasn't helping her find a new one. Brad had not only injured her, he had cost her her livelihood. She still hadn't heard from him, and Francesca was relieved. Maybe he was gone for good. Chris knew better and doubted it.

'An abuser never loses sight of his prey. He'll be back.'

'Maybe he's found someone else to beat up,' Francesca said cynically.

'He'll be back anyway,' Chris said. He was barely speaking to Eileen now. Her addiction reminded him too much of his wife, and he had suffered too much from it, to want another addict in his life, even as a friend. As far as he was concerned, their pathology was all the same, and he thought that Eileen's addiction to abuse was pathological, which made it so hard for her to give up. And with no job, she spent most of her time now in bed, crying and missing Brad, and not looking for a job as she should. Francesca could see that she was spiraling down and had no way to stop it.

Charles-Edouard was the first of the group to leave, when he went back to France, and it created a real void. It had been a lot more exciting when the flamboyant Frenchman was around, and Marya admitted she missed him too, but she was meeting him in Provence in a few weeks, to work with him on the book.

'Maybe he'll leave his wife this summer,' Francesca said

hopefully, and Marya just laughed. She wasn't expecting him to and said she wouldn't know what to do with him if he did.

'There's no room in my life for a man,' she said to Francesca practically. 'I like my life the way it is. I'm comfortable like this. Besides, I'm too old to find a man, and I don't want one.' Francesca couldn't help thinking again how different she was from her mother. Thalia's only hope was that she was going to meet a man in St Tropez or Porto Cervo. She was meeting friends everywhere, and planned to be away for two months, as she did every year. She was even meeting friends in Venice for an enormous party. Her summer was always much more glamorous than her daughter's, or anyone else's that Francesca knew.

Chris and Ian left for Martha's Vineyard for the Fourth of July weekend. Chris's family were planning picnics and barbecues, and family football games, and Ian would be spending the summer with his cousins, far from the agonies he'd been through with his mother. It was going to be good for him, and for Chris. And there were always lots of parties at the Vineyard and all of his old friends. It was a life that Chris assiduously avoided all year, but always gave in to in the summer. His parents would be there, although he wasn't close to them, and they wanted to see Ian. Ian was going to visit his mother's family too, in Newport, on the way home. Chris hated it there, it was too social, but he had promised to take Ian to see them for a long weekend. It was all he was willing to do. They were still staunchly defending their daughter, blamed Chris for leaving her, and had denial about her problems, although that was harder to do now, with manslaughter charges pending. She was still in jail, and despite all of her father's manipulations, the judge had refused to set bail. She was detoxing in jail.

Marya left for France on the tenth of July, so she could spend Bastille Day there. She was stopping in Paris for a few days before Provence, to visit her cooking buddies, some of whom ran the best restaurants in Paris. She had trained there in her youth, and still had friends she loved there. And then she was planning to wend her way to Provence and get to work with Charles-Edouard.

The house was deathly quiet after the others had left. Francesca used the time to get some repairs done, and unwind. She closed early every day – the gallery was dead in the summer. They never sold anything in July, and she closed for most of August. She used the time to clean out her files, and go through slides of new artists. And it was tomblike when she went back to the house. She made the mistake of going out with one of her artists out of pure boredom. They got blind drunk together, and he wound up crying over the girlfriend he'd just broken up with. And all the evening did was depress Francesca. He called her to apologize the next day. The evening had been a total bust and reminded her not to go out with her artists. It was always a bad idea.

Eileen was seeming a little more cheerful, although she didn't have a job. She was still mourning Brad, which Francesca refused to discuss with her. She didn't want to feed her sickness. They had a few quiet dinners, before Francesca left. They always seemed to connect at a deep level, and Eileen's innate innocence and sweetness always tore at her heart. She was so trusting and loving and open. She seemed to have none of the defenses she needed to protect herself in the world. Francesca wished she would harden herself a little and be less vulnerable, but that just wasn't Eileen. Francesca was feeling guilty about leaving her alone for three weeks, and even offered to take her to Maine with her, but Eileen insisted she'd be fine. She was making friends on the Internet again, which made Francesca uneasy, but she didn't feel it was her place to say so. The Internet was the epicenter of Eileen's life and how she made all her friends. Meeting men was just part of that. She was part of a generation that was linked to their computers by an umbilical cord. She was either online or sending texts, something Francesca rarely did. She'd rather pick up the phone and call people, and hear their voice. But Eileen's generation communicated by e-mails and texts. For most it worked, as did the Internet. For Eileen, it seemed to make her a magnet to the wrong guys.

Francesca took her out to dinner on her last night in New York. They went to the Waverly Inn, and it was fun. There were still plenty of people in New York. And Eileen's mood seemed lighter and brighter than it had for a while. Francesca commented to her that their house felt like a boarding school where everyone went home for the summer. It reminded her that only Eileen had nowhere to go. The others all had family, friends, or other homes. Eileen said she was planning to go to the beach when she wasn't job hunting and she'd be fine. She was looking forward to some time alone. And Francesca felt a tug at her heart again when she left her the next day. Eileen looked like a little kid as she stood on the top step and waved with a big smile as the cab drove away to take Francesca to the airport to fly to Bangor to meet her friends. Eileen was wearing pigtails and shorts, and after Francesca left, Eileen walked back inside. Her cell phone was ringing, and she answered it. It was Brad.

Chapter 13

The summer flew by for all of them. Marya covered the most ground. She drove from Paris to Provence, then down to St Paul de Vence, and spent a weekend with friends in Antibes. She flew from Nice to Spain to visit her friend Ferran Adria, at elBulli in Roses with all his innovative creations. He had invented 'molecular' cooking, where he broke the food down and reconstituted it. He had closed the restaurant for a while, and was planning to open again after doing more research. Marya was always fascinated by his ideas and creative genius. And from there she went to Florence, Bologna, Venice, Padua, down to Rome, and back to Paris again for a few days, before she flew to Boston, and then home to Vermont. Marya had friends everywhere, and everyone welcomed her visits. She had a fabulous time, and was happy to be in Vermont again, in her own bed, and cooking in her own kitchen, although she felt her husband's absence more there. He'd been gone for a year. She still missed him, but she was busy and had a full life.

She and Charles-Edouard had traveled extensively in Provence, and discovered new recipes for their book. They were ready to submit the outline to the publisher, and were planning to write it in September. She added two new chapters while she was in Vermont, and then left for New Hampshire. It was already chilly at night, and fall was in the air. Some of the leaves were already turning as she drove through the countryside. She stayed longer than she intended with her friends in North Conway, and then she slowly drove back home. She'd had a good time all summer, and was starting to think about going back to New York after Labor Day, as she drove up to her house, and was startled to see Charles-Edouard standing on her porch. He looked impatient and relieved as she got out of her car.

'What are you doing here?' she asked him in amazement. His hair looked longer and wilder than ever, and his eyes were the same blue as the Vermont sky. 'I thought you were in St Tropez.' He had a house in Ramatuelle, which was just behind it, and had planned to spend

August there. She hadn't heard from him since Provence, and didn't expect to. They had agreed to call each other when she got back to New York. And she had no idea what he was doing in Vermont.

He started talking the moment she stepped onto the porch. 'She left me for one of my sous-chefs. Can you believe that? Just walked out, packed everything.'

'Who did?' She was sure he was talking about the chef who ran his restaurant in Paris. They'd had a stormy relationship for years, and she threatened to quit every three weeks.

'Arielle. My wife,' he responded with a look of outrage, and then he burst into a broad smile as he looked at Marya. He was happy to see her, and it showed.

'Your wife left you for the sous-chef?' Marya looked stunned.

'She's divorcing me. I got a letter from her lawyer five days ago. He filed the papers. I got on the first plane here, but you were away.'

'Why didn't you call me if you wanted to talk to me?' She looked totally mystified about why he was there.

'I wanted to talk to you in person,' he said insistently as she fished her house keys out of her bag and unlocked the door.

'What about? Our publisher is still on vacation. I

added two more chapters last week, by the way. I think you'll like them. One is entirely on spices, and how to use them, and the other is fish.'

'I didn't come here to talk to you about fish,' he said, looking annoyed.

'Then why did you come here?' She looked vague as he followed her around the house, and she finally sat down on the couch, and he sat down next to her and looked her in the eye.

'I came to tell you in person that I'm a free man. For thirty years, you refused to take me seriously because I was married, and so were you' – a mere detail to him in the scheme of things, but neither of them was married now. 'I'm not married anymore, or I won't be. She wants to marry that idiot, but I don't care. I haven't loved her in years. I've been in love with you since the first time I laid eyes on you, Marya. I'm not going to let you brush me off anymore. I love you. You're a great woman, a great chef. You're the only woman I've ever met that I would be faithful to. I'm not leaving here until you agree to marry me. That's what I came to say.' And with that he kissed her, totally stunned her, and took her breath away. For a moment she didn't know what to say, and then she laughed.

'Charles-Edouard Prunier, you are completely crazy.

You're insane. I don't want to get married. I adore you too. But I don't want to get married again at my age. I'm going to be sixty years old. Sixty-year-old people don't get married. I'd be a laughingstock, and so would you.' She felt a flutter over what he was saying, and she had always loved him as a friend, but had never let herself be attracted to him. Now suddenly everything was different, and all obstacles had been removed.

'I don't care,' he said firmly with a ferocious look in his eye. '*L'amour n'a pas d'âge*. Love has no age. I don't care if you're turning a hundred. I'm sixty-five, and I've been in love with you since you were thirty. And I'm not going to wait another thirty years.' And with that, he kissed her again, and much to her amazement, she kissed him back, and felt all the feelings she had ignored for years. And she had been deeply in love with her husband while he was alive.

She looked at him with a horrified expression then. 'Oh my God, now what are we going to do?'

'You're going to do the right thing after all these years, and marry me,' he said firmly, and she laughed at him again.

'No, I'm not.'

'Yes, you are,' he insisted. 'I won't relent until you do.'

'You're crazy. We're too old to get married,' she insisted.

'We are not. Besides, I want to have a baby with you.'
She laughed even harder at that. 'Or write books together.
Or do whatever you want to do. I'm giving her the house
in Ramatuelle, by the way, and the flat in Paris. I think
we should get our own. I've never liked the neighborhood. I'll buy a flat for you.'

'Wait a minute,' Marya said seriously. 'Let's slow
down. Are you serious about all this?' She looked utterly
amazed. She had no idea if he was kidding or not.

'Do you think I sat on your porch every day for a week
for no reason? I've waited a lifetime for this, Marya.' She
loved him too, as a friend. He was one of her closest
friends, and she loved working with him and spending
time with him, but she had never allowed herself to think
of him as more than that. She had loved her husband
deeply, and they had a wonderful marriage. But Charles-
Edouard was certainly crazy and a joy to be with, and
they got along wonderfully, and always had.

'I need time to think about this, if you're serious. And
I don't know if I want to get married.'

'Why not? And don't tell me you're too old. That is not
a reason I will accept.'

'I don't know if we need to get married. You're French.
Frenchmen have affairs. We can have an affair for the
next thirty years. Maybe that's enough.'

'You're not that kind of woman,' he said, pretending to be shocked.

'Maybe I am at this point in my life. I don't know.' She had never intended to be with another man, and now she was talking marriage and affairs with Charles-Edouard. 'Can we try this out for a while, and see how it works?' And then she looked at him seriously. 'I don't want to be married to a man who cheats on me, and I know you've done that all your life. You were never faithful to Arielle.'

'My parents made me marry her. She didn't love me either. And I solemnly promise that I would be faithful to you.' He looked as though he meant it, but she wasn't sure if he was capable of it.

'Prove it to me. If you're faithful to me and don't cheat on me, I'll marry you. Maybe,' she added, and then laughed. She was being coy. This was suddenly a delicious moment in her life. At nearly sixty, a handsome Frenchman was in love with her, and proposing to her. She was beginning to like the idea. 'Who'll do the cooking if we get married?' she asked with interest, and he thought about it. It was an intriguing question.

'We both will. Together.'

'Who will be the sous-chef? Me or you?'

'You will. You're the girl.'

'You're a chauvinist,' she said, looking delighted. She

was having a great time, and so was he. She suddenly felt very young.

He took her out to dinner that night, and they talked about their plans, about whether to live in Paris or New York. They both thought they'd prefer Paris. Marya had wanted to live there all her life. He thought they should find a flat on the Left Bank, in either the sixth or seventh arrondissement.

By the time they got back to her house, they still hadn't settled the matter of whether to get married. But she was serious about wanting to see if he could be faithful. He certainly never had been in his entire life. She wanted to give it a few months to find out. She was talking about moving to Paris with him, if he behaved, by the end of the year. They could decide whether to get married after that. And in the meantime, they could enjoy each other. He offered to stay in New York for the next few months, where they could work on the book together.

He walked her into the house, and everything happened naturally after that. They wandered into her bedroom, their clothes seemed to disappear, and they wound up in bed in each other's arms. And as he reached out to her, they felt as though they had been together all their life, and would be for the next hundred years. She felt like a girl again in his arms.

* * *

Chris's time with his family was just what Ian needed, and it did Chris a great deal of good too, especially this year. Ian got to be a child again, playing with his cousins, and swimming every day. He learned to water-ski, and he made lots of new friends. It was so easy and carefree and normal that he almost forgot his mother was in jail. She called him once a week. And Chris dreaded the calls. They brought Ian back to reality and reminded him of all the pain he'd been through, all of it because of his mother. Chris was still furious with her for dragging Ian through it. But at the Vineyard, their wounds seemed to heal, although Chris's conversations with his parents about Ian's mother were always difficult for him. They thought Ian should be entirely removed from his mother, even if that meant sending him to boarding school, which Chris refused to even consider. Ian was far too young and Chris wanted his son with him. His parents didn't agree.

'You're not providing a proper home for him,' his mother said sternly one afternoon after lunch, after Ian scampered off. 'I don't understand why, but you're not. You're living in a house full of people, with "roommates," or a commune of some kind, like a student. You have a child, Chris, and if you can't provide a proper home for him, you should send him away to school. Or at least get your own apartment and a nanny to take care of him. And the farther away you get him from his mother, the better off he'll be. He should see as little of her as possible.' Chris didn't disagree with that, but he was violently opposed to all the rest, and Ian was his son, not theirs. It was easy for them to sit on the sidelines and criticize him. They weren't the kind of grandparents to want hands-on involvement, but they felt they had every right to comment on how Chris was bringing Ian up, and they didn't approve.

'I don't live in a commune,' Chris said hotly, 'and my housemates are wonderful, intelligent people, who add a whole other dimension to Ian's life, much more than any nanny. I moved in for convenience before Ian came to live with me, because I wasn't ready to set up an apartment, but now I see what these people add to Ian's life. It would be a real loss to both of us if we moved.' He believed it profoundly, but his mother wasn't convinced.

'It's all a bit too modern for me,' his mother said bluntly. 'Children need a mother and a father and a proper home. In a case like yours, with a mother like Kimberly, Ian is certainly better off alone with you, but only if you can give him a sane, normal life in a real home, not living in a room in someone else's house. I'm sorry, but I just don't understand that, Chris. It's not like you can't afford to get your own place. This is sheer laziness on your part. And Ian will pay the price for it later on. What does he tell his friends at school? Who does he say those people are? You're too old to live with roommates, Chris, and you have a child.'

'I'm well aware of that, Mother,' Chris said coldly. His father had made similar comments to him several times. He referred to Chris's 'alternate lifestyle' as unsuitable for a child. They were both very conservative people, and Chris renting a room in a house in the West Village, and having Ian live there with him, seemed like a very bad idea to them. His father said it was irresponsible, and his mother was saying much the same thing. It was impossible to explain to either of them the kindness of Francesca, Marya, and Eileen to his son. Ian lived in a very special world, with four adults who doted on him, and even Charles-Edouard, the French chef, had been kind to him. Ian wasn't living alone with a single father, he was living in a tribe, and in some ways Chris felt it was the best possible antidote to the agonies his mother put him through. The fact that Kim was entirely unsuitable, no one could deny. But Ian loved her, and she was his mother, so he had a right to some contact with her too, as long as it was in a safe setting for him. Chris knew that his parents were sorry Kim hadn't died when she OD'd, and thought Ian would be better off just putting all that behind him and moving on. But the reality of their life wasn't as simple as that, and Kimberly was still alive.

'I hope you'll reconsider about boarding school,' his mother reiterated as Chris frowned. He hated having conversations like this with either of his parents. Their ideas were rigid and old-fashioned, and they were more concerned about what was 'proper' and traditional than about what was good for the child. They had brought him up that way too, and all it had done was give him a profound dislike for their lifestyle and everything it represented. He had a deep respect for family traditions, and summers at the Vineyard that brought all the gener-ations together, which was why he came here every year, but he couldn't tolerate their clinging to traditions out of habit, or old-fashioned ideas that didn't work in the com-plicated situation he was in. He never would have sent Ian away to school. At least this way, Ian had one loving parent with him, and for the moment, a house full of people who genuinely cared about him, and spent time with him. Chris's parents never did. They enjoyed their grandchildren, and liked having them around, as long as their parents or a nanny were present, but his parents stayed at a distance, and observed them without ever really connecting with them, or finding out who they were. He never saw his mother with her arms around a grandchild, and the only thing his father ever asked any of them was how school was, and what sports they played.

Chris had never gotten much more than that from them either, which was why ultimately he had fled Boston and moved to New York. He couldn't have existed on a daily basis in the rigid confines of their world. He knew they cared about him, and loved him, but the ways they chose to express it and demonstrate it had never worked for him. He had realized long since that he had been starved of emotional contact and connection as a child, and he didn't want that for Ian, and he wanted even less to dump him in a school and leave him there. Whatever mistakes he was making, at least he had Ian with him, and could give him all the love and attention he'd never had as a child himself. The dignity and stand-ing of their family had always been more important to his parents than the happiness of their children. It wasn't out of meanness or even indifference, it was simply a concept they didn't understand and never would. They had grown up and lived with so many restrictions and social rules and obligations that they could never break out of it themselves. But in Chris's generation, the world had changed, for him and Ian anyway, but not for them. They still lived as the family had for generations, governed by rules that were meaningless to Chris now. All he had wanted as an adult was to get away from all that, which had always made him something of a rebel and a misfit in their midst. He still came home for summer vacation and holidays, but rarely for anything else. And it was particularly hard for him being there this summer. They felt free to comment on his life and Ian's, about which they understood nothing. But his ongoing problems with Kimberly made him an easy target for their disapproval and concern, and their opinions, which he didn't share.

There were times when Chris thought about Francesca, and found himself missing the house. If he got custody of Ian, he had also thought that he should get an apartment, but he worried that it might be lonely for them there, and his roommates were so kind to Ian. With Marya and Francesca, he had built-in baby-sitters, and the benefit of two women who cared about him and were almost like aunts. And Eileen was an additional loving friend to Ian. There was a lot to be said for all of them living in one house. Chris missed his conversations with Marya and Francesca during the summer. He hadn't heard from either of them, but he was sure they were having a relaxing time too, and he hoped they were having fun. He wasn't as fond of Eileen, despite her kindness to Ian. She reminded him too much of his ex-wife with her addiction to self-destructive behaviors and bad men. And in Kim's case, Ian had paid the price. And before that, Chris had too.

He managed to avoid further serious discussion with his parents, and the only part of his vacation that Chris didn't enjoy was visiting Kim's parents in Newport. He hated hearing them wail about what had happened to her, as though it had been done to her by someone else. And her father was doing everything he could to get her out of jail, thus far with no success. And they talked to Ian about her as though she were a martyr and a saint. She was the devil in Chris's eyes, particularly to their son.

Ian had sensed correctly that Chris didn't like his grandparents, and he knew that his parents didn't get along. He knew that his father's parents didn't like Kimberly either. He hated that everyone was mad at someone else. He talked about Francesca and Marya a lot, and occasionally Eileen, and when people asked him who they were, he said they were his friends. He told Chris he couldn't wait for Marya's Mickey Mouse pancakes when he got back. And they laughed about Charles-Edouard and the trick he did with the eggs. Ian loved it when he dropped them on the floor and made a mess.

In the end, they had a great summer. Ian grew two inches, and Chris finally relaxed. Chris enjoyed seeing his brother and sister, and their children, although he and his siblings were no longer close. They had turned out to be too much like his parents and remained in the mold they had grown up in. But he was happy to see them and Ian loved playing with his cousins at the family compound. They were both tan and happy, and the younger generations spent a lot of time on Chris's parents' boat. It was a handsome sailboat with four cabins and a teak deck, not unlike the one they'd had when Chris was a child. Ian loved that best of all. They were both going to miss it when they went back to New York. And when they got back, Chris was going to begin the permanent custody battle. He was determined to win. He was never going to give Ian up again.

Francesca's time on the sailboat in Maine was easy and freewheeling. Todd's friends were wonderful to her, and they said nothing to her about Todd and his fiancée, although they had been there the week before, and they'd had a good time with them. But they had a good time with Francesca too. She relaxed and had fun and stopped worrying about the gallery. For once, she didn't think about anything except the wind and the sails, what time dinner was, and if she wanted lobster or steak. It was a totally self-indulgent time.

She didn't have a single call while she was away, not a text message or an e-mail. Her BlackBerry was silent for three weeks. It was exactly what she needed, but she decided that her mother was right. Next year she needed to do something new. It was a slightly odd sensation spending her vacation with Todd's friends, and following in his footsteps like a shadow. She thought about going to Europe next year, or somewhere alone. She almost felt ready for that.

At the end of the vacation, Francesca thanked her hosts profusely for their hospitality. She flew from Bangor to Boston, changed planes, and from there she flew back to New York. And as they landed at La Guardia, she was thinking about Ian and Chris. They had been gone for a long time, and she missed them. She missed seeing Ian's funny little face and talking to Chris. She wondered how Ian's mother was doing in jail.

Francesca looked happy and relaxed as a cab took her into the city. She had a deep tan, and her hair was blonder than ever. She felt as though she had been gone for months. And the house looked cozy and familiar when she saw it. As she turned her key in the lock, she wondered if Eileen had found a job. She hoped she had, that things had gone well for her, and that she had stayed away from Brad. She could hardly wait to find out. She hadn't heard from her either in the past few weeks. She had left her a few messages, but Eileen didn't return her calls.

As Francesca walked in, she had a suddenly eerie sensation. Everything in the house seemed to be in order, and she had no idea why, but the hair suddenly stood up on her arms, and she felt a chill run down her spine. She felt stupid for feeling that way. Nothing was out of place, but she almost sensed that someone was there. She called out Eileen's name, but there was no sound. And then as she turned she saw the door to her living room standing open, and saw that a chair had been splintered against the wall. She stopped dead in her tracks. She knew instantly that something was wrong. Her instinct was to run. She had closed the front door, and feeling like a fool, she dashed back outside, stood on the front steps, and took big gulps of air. She was shaking from head to foot, and she didn't know why.

She thought about calling Todd, but she felt awkward doing that now, and not knowing what else to do, she called Chris on his cell phone to steady her nerves and ask his advice. She walked back down the stairs, and sat on the first step outside. There was lots of noise around him when he answered. She could hardly hear him, and it sounded as though he was in a playground surrounded by children, which was fairly accurate. He was at the family compound, with his many cousins' children around him. He sounded happy to hear her.

'Hi, Francesca. How've you been?' He smiled at the sound of her voice.

'I've been great,' she said, her voice shaking a little. She felt silly for calling him now. Everything was probably fine in the house. But she couldn't explain the shattered chair in her living room, or the hair standing up on her arms. She wondered if they had been robbed. But if there had been a burglary, why hadn't Eileen called her? The pieces of the puzzle didn't quite fit together. 'I had a great vacation. How's yours?'

'Wonderful. We went down to Newport a few days ago, and this is our last weekend here. You won't recognize Ian. He's ten feet tall.' She smiled at his description, and took a breath to steady her nerves.

'I'm sorry to bother you, and I feel really stupid calling you. But I just got back to the house about five minutes ago, and I got a really strange feeling when I walked in. And this sounds even crazier, but my living room door was open, and it looks like someone smashed one of my chairs. Nothing else looks disturbed. But it was eerie, and

I ran back outside. I'm sitting on the front steps, feeling like a moron, but I'm scared to go into the house. What if someone is in there? Like intruders, or burglars. I called Eileen's name, but she's not home.' The alarm hadn't been on. And Francesca hadn't even thought to call her, and felt stupid for that now too. And it seemed pretty wimpy to be calling him, like a damsel in distress, or a coward sitting on the front steps of her own house. But she was scared.

Chris didn't hesitate for a minute, and he frowned as he answered her. 'Trust your instincts. Whatever you do, don't go back in. Call the police. There may be someone in there. There are a lot of burglaries in the summer, when they figure people are away. I'd call the police right now.'

'They'll think I'm crazy,' she said, feeling foolish, but she wondered if he was right.

'Better foolish than injured, or shot by a burglar in your own house. Call the cops. And call me back once they check it out.'

'Okay.' She hung up then and called the police. She told them she had just gotten back from vacation, and she thought there might have been a burglary or might be someone in the house. She couldn't explain the shattered chair to herself, unless one of Eileen's Internet boyfriends had gotten drunk and gone nuts.

The police told her it wasn't a problem, instructed her not to go back in, and promised to be there in ten minutes. They were there in five, they had a car with two patrolmen nearby. She described the feeling she'd gotten and what she'd seen, and they told her to wait outside. They asked her if anyone else lived in the house. She described the other occupants and said that all of them were still away, except one who had stayed in town, and she might be at work, or asleep upstairs. She described the layout of the house and who lived where. She said Eileen lived on the top floor, and everyone else was gone. Both patrolmen walked in, looking alert, with their hands resting loosely on their guns. It told her that they had taken her seriously. She thought of calling Chris while she waited, but she didn't want to bother him again, and more than likely they would find nothing more than the broken chair. She didn't want to sound like a hysteric, and she started to relax after they'd been inside for a while. Obviously nothing was wrong, nothing had happened, there had been no gunshots, no burglars had come running out. She had moved slightly away from the direct line of the door, but it was fully twenty minutes later when one of them came out. They had made a thorough search. The officer came slowly down the stairs and looked at Francesca with an unreadable expression.

'Everything okay?' Francesca smiled at him, feeling foolish again. His partner was still inside.

He spoke to her in a quiet, calm voice. 'Your instincts were right. Your tenant on the top floor is dead.' Eileen. Oh my God. That couldn't be. It wasn't possible. Francesca felt like she was going to faint. He led her back to the steps and helped her to sit down. She looked so pale that he told her to put her head between her legs. It took Francesca a minute to catch her breath.

'She can't be dead,' Francesca said in a choked voice. 'She's twenty-three years old.' As though that made it impossible. Francesca's mind was a blur. She couldn't think.

'She was severely beaten, and strangled. We're not sure, but she may have been raped. She's naked in her bed. She's been dead for about three days. Do you have any idea who might have done this? Did she have a boyfriend? An ex-husband? It doesn't look like it was done by an intruder. Very little is disturbed in the house. A couple of chairs, and that's about it.'

Francesca was staring at him with wide eyes. 'She had a very nasty boyfriend, but when I last saw her, she hadn't seen him in a while. He beat her up twice. I left three weeks ago, and I don't think she'd been with him since June. I don't know. She wasn't always honest with me

about it. But I think it must have been him . . . or someone new she met on the Internet . . . she did a lot of
that . . .' He had taken out a notepad, and the other
patrolman had called for backup. As they were talking,
three squad cars and an ambulance arrived.

'Do you know his name?' the officer asked her, taking
notes, as everyone else ran inside.

'Brad. Brad Turner, I think. He was a really nasty guy.'

'Do you know where he works?'

'No, I don't. He's a motorcycle mechanic, but that's all
I know. He has a lot of tattoos.'

'Do you remember what they look like?'

She closed her eyes as she answered, trying to see them
again in her mind. She was shaking even more violently
by then, and she felt like she was going to be sick. 'An
eagle. . . a rose . . . a big snake down one arm . . . some
kind of Chinese thing . . . I can't remember the rest of
them.' She opened her eyes again, and all she could think
of now was Eileen, dead upstairs in her room, probably
killed by Brad. The officer looked at her apologetically
then.

'I'm sorry to ask you this, but we're going to need
someone to identify the body, to make sure it's her. Do
you think you can do that?' Francesca didn't answer and
looked at him with terrified eyes.

'Do I have to?' She didn't want to see Eileen that way. Francesca had never seen anyone dead before.

'You're all we've got. We don't want to ID the wrong person. For all we know, that's a stranger up there in her bed.' Francesca nodded, as another squad car arrived. Her house had become a crime scene, and it was crawling with cops. The patrolman went back inside for a minute then, and with a shaking hand on the phone, she called Chris.

He saw her number come up on his phone and answered immediately. 'Hi, Francesca. What did they say? Coast clear?' He was hopeful.

There was an endless silence at her end before she spoke. 'Eileen's dead. Someone beat her up and strangled her, and may have raped her. She must have seen Brad again after I left. Or someone else just as bad.'

He was silent for a moment, absorbing what she'd said. 'I'm so sorry.'

'She was just a kid. They want me to identify the body. I don't know if I can. They said it might not even be her. But she's naked in her bed.' She was clutching at straws. Chris had no doubt that it was Eileen, and neither did she. She didn't want it to be, but she was sure it was.

'Do you want me to come back right now?' Chris offered. 'I can be back in a few hours.'

'It's okay. It'll just scare Ian. When were you planning to come back?'

'In three days. I can shorten the trip and come back tomorrow. I don't think you should be there alone.'

'I won't stay at the house.' There was no way she could now. 'I'll go to a hotel.'

'I'm so sorry you have to identify the body. If they'll wait, I'll do it when I get back.' He didn't want to either, but he would have done it for her.

'I should do it, so they can call her parents.' Not that her father would care. But she had five siblings and a mother. And they had to know. She deserved at least that. Eileen had given her her mother's number once, in case of an accident. Francesca had the number in her desk.

Two of the patrolmen came out and got her then, and asked her to come inside after inquiring if she was all right. They had put Eileen on a gurney, and covered her with a sheet and a blanket, and they had set the gurney down in the front hall. They asked her if she was ready, and she nodded, clutching the patrolman's hand. He had an arm behind her in case she fainted; they knew how rough this was for everyone. One of the officers pulled back the blanket and the sheet, and Francesca knew instantly that it was Eileen. Her face was beaten almost to a pulp, but she was recognizable. Francesca nodded, and they covered her up again and took the gurney out. Francesca sat down on the floor, and then they led her out of the house, sat her in one of the patrol cars and gave her a bottle of water they kept on hand for occasions like this. She knew it must look to the neighbors like she was being arrested, but she didn't care. She was crying when she called Chris again.

'It's her. He almost destroyed her face.'

'I'm so sorry. Why don't I leave Ian here with his cousins, and come into town. I don't want you there alone.'

'Thank you' was all she could muster, and hung up. She leaned out of the patrol car then and threw up.

They drove Francesca to the station and had her sign her statement. They did a composite computer sketch of Brad, according to her description, and put out an all-points bulletin for him. And then they called Eileen's mother and told her, after Francesca told them where the number was in her desk. The house was locked up after that. They said Eileen's mother wanted her cremated and her ashes sent to San Diego. There was going to be no funeral or memorial service in New York. She had no real friends except her roommates and the men she met on the Internet. In the end, her Internet obsession had killed her. Francesca knew that if it hadn't been Brad, it had been someone else she met online. She took too many risks. Francesca couldn't believe it, but the sweet little girl next door with the freckles and red hair in pigtails was dead. She had looked so innocent and cute the day Francesca had left. It had been the last time she'd seen her as she waved goodbye from the steps.

The police took Francesca to the Hotel Gansevoort. She took a room, and sat there shaking. She didn't want to go back to the house. And it seemed like hours later when Chris called her. She had lost all track of time. He was on his way in from the airport and wanted to know where she was. She told him, and he was there a few minutes later. She opened the door to him and nearly fell into his arms. He stood there and held her, and then sat down on the bed with her as Francesca cried.

'Stupid kid' was all he could bring himself to say. He was angry and sad all at the same time. And if it hadn't been Eileen, it could have been his wife a dozen times. She had just been lucky so far, but one day she wouldn't be. One day she would wind up like Eileen, only with a needle in her arm, and Ian would be heartbroken. He hated them for the risks they took, the people they hurt, the hearts they broke, all the tears that were shed for them. Francesca cried herself to sleep in his arms that night. He lay on the bed next to her, and held her as he had Ian so many times. And in the morning, Francesca got a call from the police. They had Brad. They had run fingerprints on him and from the scene. The prints matched. It was him. They would do DNA tests, but all the puzzle pieces fit. The evidence was conclusive so far. Brad had killed Eileen.

Chapter 14

Francesca woke up feeling groggy and confused, unsure if what she thought had happened had been a dream. She had fallen asleep in her clothes on the bed next to Chris in the room she had taken at the Hotel Gansevoort. As she opened her eyes, she turned to look at him. He was still lying next to her, and he was awake.

'Did I dream it?' He shook his head. It wasn't possible. That couldn't happen. It wasn't fair. Eileen was dead. Her Internet insanity had killed her. But it was more than just that, it was Eileen's appalling judgment, her addiction to bad men, and her lifetime familiarity with abuse. All of that had contributed to her sad end. They all knew lots of nice people who had met each other online, fallen in love, and gotten married. But mixed in with the good ones were terrifyingly bad ones, and Brad had been one of those. And Eileen had become too addicted to him and the abuse to save herself. She had gone back for more one last time. One time too many.

Chris had checked, and Brad was still being held on suspicion of her murder. They wanted Francesca and Chris to identify him in a lineup, and then they would arraign him the next day. They had already started the DNA tests from his skin, to match traces found under Eileen's nails. They would have partial results in three days. Her body was at the morgue, and after the autopsy she was going to be cremated, but not for several days. With her heart in her shoes, Francesca couldn't help asking herself now what did any of it matter. Whatever they did, she'd still be dead. She was such a lost girl. She kept thinking of her making papier-mâché puppets with Ian, and as Francesca thought of the scene the day before, and identifying her, she got up and went to the bathroom and vomited again. She was kneeling on the bathroom floor, as Chris rubbed her back, and held her hair, and then handed her a wet towel.

'I'm sorry,' she said, wiping her face with the towel.

He shook his head. 'I'm sorry for her. Abusive relationships are a terrible thing. Psychological abuse is almost as bad and just as addictive. I think people stay in it, or go back, so they can turn it around, and convince their abuser that they're nice people and don't deserve it. They always get blamed. And sometimes they get killed. She just wasn't strong enough, or healthy enough I guess, not to see him again.' They both knew it happened all too often. Francesca went back to the bed and lay down. The thought of getting up was too much for her. She wanted to lie there forever, as Chris sat on the bed next to her and stroked her hair.

Marya and Charles-Edouard had just come back from a walk in her garden, and were starting to make breakfast when Chris called on Marya's cell phone. It was sitting on her desk, and she didn't rush to get it. She wasn't expecting any important calls, she wanted to enjoy Charles-Edouard, and she was still in vacation mode. She didn't recognize the caller's number when she picked up her phone, but she answered anyway, and was surprised to hear Chris's voice.

'Hi, Marya,' he said in a hoarse, somber voice. He hadn't gotten much sleep, and had watched Francesca for most of the night. She had woken several times in tears. He was tired and sad.

'What a nice surprise,' Marya said happily. 'How's Ian? Where are you both? I'm still in Vermont.' She hadn't spoken to him since they'd all left New York for the summer.

'I'm in New York with Francesca,' Chris said quietly, as Francesca listened. She had asked him to make the call. 'Ian's at the Vineyard. I'm going back for him in a couple of days.'

'Is something wrong? Is Francesca okay?' It seemed odd to Marya that he would be with her, or said it that way, and he sounded upset.

'She got back yesterday, and I'm sorry to call you, but something terrible happened at the house. Eileen was killed a few days ago, probably by Brad.'

'Oh my God, how awful.' Tears instantly filled Marya's eyes, imagining it. She was such a sweet, silly, innocent young girl. Charles-Edouard was watching her and was instantly concerned, with a question in his eyes. 'Did Francesca find her?' She hoped not. She couldn't imagine a more traumatic scene than that.

'She thought something was wrong when she walked in. She called me, and I told her to wait outside and call the police. They found her. She was dead in her room. He strangled and beat her. They have him in custody now. We have to identify him today.' He didn't tell her that Francesca had identified the body the day before. Francesca was lying on the bed, listening to their conversation, with her eyes closed, deathly pale, and he was holding her hand. They were two very sad friends, and he was glad to be there with her.

'Do you want me to come down? We could be there in a few hours.' He noticed the 'we' but thought she was confused, with all the strong emotions of the terrible news about Eileen.

'There's not much you can do. We're okay.' He said it, but neither of them felt it.

'Are you staying at the house?' The idea of that was shocking, and she wasn't sure what they would do.

'We're at the Gansevoort,' he said calmly. And the police had given them the name of a service that specialized in cleaning up crime scenes. Once they had all the evidence they needed, and had taken photographs, the service would come in and strip any evidence of the crime. It would take a few days. If necessary, they would repaint the room. That happened more frequently when there were gunshots involved. It sounded like a grim job to him. 'Everything should be in order by the time you get back.' But in order or not, Eileen would never be there again. Francesca had already decided that morning that she didn't want anyone else in that room. She never wanted to see it again herself, it would make her too sad. She had genuinely liked Eileen, despite her foolishness with men, and had taken her under her wing and into her home. And now she was dead.

'I'm so sorry,' Marya said again. 'I don't want to bother Francesca, but if there's anything I can do, call me. I'll get in the car and be there in a few hours if it will help. I'll try to come back in a few days. Did someone call her parents?'

'The police. They're cremating the body after the autopsy, to send the ashes to her parents. There's no funeral in New York.'

'Maybe we can have a little service of our own,' Marya said vaguely, too shocked to think of anything right now. She reminded him to send her love to Francesca, and they hung up.

'What happened?' Charles-Edouard asked her with a look of concern when she hung up.

'Eileen, the little girl on the top floor whom you met, was killed at the house. Beaten and strangled.'

'By a burglar?'

'They think it was by a man she went out with. They have him in custody and are charging him with the murder. He beat her up very badly twice before.' Marya looked sick. She sat down on the couch with a distant expression, and Charles-Edouard sat down next to her and put an arm around her and held her. It was a sad beginning to the first day of their new life. Beginnings and endings, the birth of a relationship and the death of a young woman. The bittersweetness of life. And this was very bitter. Marya looked up at him and then sank into his arms and cried.

The lineup at the police station for the Sixth Precinct on West Tenth Street took forever to begin, and they were a motley group of men as they were led out. There were two tall ones, a short one, and three of medium height. All had tattoos. One had long hair. Three were being held on other charges, one was an undercover cop, one was on parole, and one was Brad. They both recognized him instantly as he stood in profile and full face as he was directed. The men in the lineup stood there shuffling, on the other side of a two-way mirror, and Chris and Francesca confirmed the identification without a doubt. It was him. And then the men were led out. It was over. And he would be arraigned the next day. After that, Chris and Francesca were free to leave.

They walked back to the hotel and needed the air. Ian called Chris while they were walking, and his father said everything was fine, and Francesca sent her love. He had told him he was going to New York to do some work, and to help Francesca at the house. He didn't want him to worry that something had happened to his mother in jail.

Ian was always worried about her, with good reason. But now she had been charged with manslaughter. And Chris doubted that her father would get her out of this one. And no one had been able to stop, sway, or save Eileen. Women who were bent on destroying themselves usually did, as Chris knew too well.

The police had told them that the house should be cleaned up by midweek. They were planning to stay at the hotel till then. Chris had taken his own room before they left for the lineup. And he didn't care if he used it or not, this way he had the option, and if he sat in a chair in Francesca's room every night, he didn't mind that either. That's why he had come from the Vineyard, to do anything for her that he could. They steered a wide berth of the house on their walk, and Francesca wasn't sure if she wanted to see it again. She wondered if this would haunt them forever, or if they could live there in peace now. She wasn't sure.

She hadn't eaten since the day before, and Chris finally convinced her to go to Da Silvano for some pasta. They gave them a table outside in the usual hustle-bustle of the popular restaurant, and she couldn't touch her food. All she could think of was Eileen. They walked back to the hotel after that, went to Francesca's room, and Chris turned on the TV. There was a baseball game on, and as he watched it from a chair next to the bed, she fell asleep. She stirred several times, had nightmares once or twice, and got up to go to the bathroom, and other than that, she slept until morning. He slept in the chair, fully dressed, with the TV on. But they both felt better the next day.

They ordered room service, and Marya called to see how they were. She talked to Francesca this time, and they both cried for Eileen. It made Francesca miss Marya more than ever. She hadn't said anything about the new developments with Charles-Edouard, their good news didn't seem appropriate now in the face of their collective grief.

'Do you want to come back to the Vineyard with me for a few days?' Chris suggested over breakfast, but Francesca didn't.

'I don't know what I want to do,' she said, still looking dazed. 'I don't want to see people. I have to open the gallery and get back to work.' She was grateful for the distraction. She could also stay at her father's house in Connecticut, if she needed to get away. He and Avery had just returned from Aspen.

She called Avery that afternoon and told her what had happened. She was horrified.

'Maybe roommates weren't such a great idea after all,'

Avery said quietly. She was so sorry for Francesca, and wondered if the house would be forever tainted for her now. Francesca was mulling over the same thing. She wasn't sure. She'd have to see how it felt when she went back. 'What are you going to do now? Sell the house?' It seemed an extreme decision, but living in a house where a young woman they liked had been murdered wasn't going to be easy either, for any of them. And Francesca had a lot of sad memories in that house now. Avery suggested that maybe it was no longer worth the struggle to keep it. She asked if Francesca had called her mother.

'Not yet,' she said with a sigh. 'I'm not sure I will. She doesn't need to know. She'll just hound me about it, tell me she was right all along about what a bad idea this was to keep the house and have roommates, and pressure me to sell. I need to figure that out for myself, if that's what I want. I just don't know yet.'

'You will, at the right time. It's too soon, unless you're sure you want to sell it.'

'I'm not. I still love the house. I just hate what happened there. I keep wondering if there was something else I could have done, or been stronger with her. But I was her roommate, or landlady, not her mother. I couldn't forbid her to see him. All I could do was tell her she couldn't have him to the house, but she did anyway when I was gone. And I kept begging her to get help, and stop picking up guys on the Internet. I think she was a lot more complicated than she appeared, with a bad history of abuse from her childhood. Maybe she was drawn to people like that, and she would have found a Brad anywhere. She didn't need the Internet to do it. We all have our secrets and our problems and our issues. I'm still trying to get over Todd, Marya the death of her husband, Chris is dealing with his heroin addict ex-wife and trying to keep his son safe. We all have our struggles, and I guess things aren't always what they appear. They weren't with Eileen. And look what happened to her.' Francesca was crying again when she said it, she had really liked her. And no one she knew had ever been murdered. It seemed like such a terrible way to die, strangled and beaten in her own bed. But he had given her plenty of warning that he was a dangerous man, and she'd still tried to turn it around, instead of running as fast as she could in the opposite direction, which would have been the sane and healthy thing to do. Eileen just wasn't healthy, and she had been addicted to Brad and his abuse, and had paid the ultimate price. Avery reminded her that the statistics on abusive men and abused women were horrifying. Seventy-five percent of men who threatened to kill the women they were involved with actually did. Now Eileen was just one more statistic instead of the sweet freckle-faced girl upstairs. Her dating games with total strangers and her lack of judgment about them had been her downfall.

Chris went back to the Vineyard the next day to pick up Ian and promised to return as soon as he could. Francesca insisted she was all right. She opened the gallery, and kept her room at the Gansevoort. Her suitcases were still in the front hall of the house from when she arrived, and she had them brought to the hotel. And she told Marya that she didn't need to rush back either. There was nothing for them to do. Eileen's room was being stripped and steam-cleaned and repainted, the furniture removed. Her things were being boxed and sent to San Diego after the police went through them and took what they needed as evidence. And then Francesca was planning to close the room and lock it. She didn't even want to go in there. She was eliminating the top floor of the house for the time being. She couldn't imagine anyone who would want to live there, knowing someone had been killed in that room. It meant that she would be paying half the mortgage payment, instead of a quarter, with four of them there. It was what she had paid when she lived with Todd. But she couldn't figure out any other way to do it for now. She didn't want another tenant to replace Eileen, just Chris and Marya, and of course Ian. They were adults, used good judgment, lived sane lives, and put none of the others at risk, nor themselves. She couldn't go through the trauma of someone like Eileen again, no matter how much she liked her. And you just never knew what people did in private. Neither she, Marya, nor Chris even had relationships or partners. They were three adults on their own, and one small child, whom they all loved. Eileen had been too immature and too damaged to be responsible, and Francesca blamed herself for not understanding it sooner, before something like this happened. Maybe in another living arrangement, she wouldn't have been killed. They had all been gone all summer, and she had been easy prey for Brad.

The police informed her that Brad had been arraigned and bound over for trial. He had pleaded not guilty, on the advice of the public defender who represented him. He wanted his day in court, although they said he might plea-bargain in the end. But there wasn't much they could do with cold-blooded murder. The initial DNA tests had linked Brad to the murder. They said it would take about a year to come to trial, and he would be in jail, without bail, until then. It reminded her of Chris's ex-wife, who was still in jail, pending her trial too. They were trying to make a deal for her, but the district attorney wasn't letting her off the hook. She was responsible for the addict she had shot up with, and to whom she had supplied the drugs. It was an ugly scene. And poor Ian had watched while he died, and then his own mother nearly died. And he had told Chris that he had seen them shoot up, just as he had before. Chris was planning to use it all as evidence in the custody case. He didn't want his son living with a woman who did drugs in front of him, even if she was his mother, and had unsavory people around, like drug dealers and other addicts. And he was going to ask for supervised visits when she got out of jail. He didn't want Ian alone with her ever again. And he had no hope she would clean up. She never had, despite all the fancy rehabs she had gone to for years. Her parents wanted her to clean up, and so did he, but she never did. She was too much of an addict to care. All she wanted were her drugs, at whatever price. Just as Eileen had wanted Brad. He had been her drug of choice, as lethal as heroin had been to Ian's mother's friend. Now they were both dead.

Chris called Francesca several times from the Vineyard, concerned that she was alone. She had moved back into the house. She sounded down, but reassured him that she was doing all right. She didn't admit that she would be happy when he and Marya got back to New York, and that it was upsetting being there by herself.

Marya was in no rush to come back to the house either, and thought it would feel very sad. She still hadn't shared her good news with Francesca, it just felt like the wrong time. But she and Charles-Edouard were happy in Vermont, and exploring facets of their relationship that they'd never had access to before. There were no limits for them now, since he was getting divorced. He had spoken to his lawyer twice from Vermont, and everything was on track. His wife wanted to get out quickly, so she could marry his sous-chef. She wanted half of what Charles-Edouard had, and after thirty years together, he thought it was fair. He told Marya he had enough to split it in half with Arielle and still have a comfortable life. They were content with that, and she didn't want anything from him. Just a good life, and they were off to a wonderful start. She had never expected to wind up with him, or with anyone, after John. This was all an enormous surprise, and an adjustment, but they were both good sports about it and flexible and tolerant of each other's quirks. They were both kind-hearted people who enjoyed life, and loved each other, now as much more than friends. He still wanted to get married, and was pushing her to it. And she was still firm about wanting him to prove himself faithful to her, and that he was capable of it. After a great marriage to John for thirty-six years, she wasn't going to marry a cheater now, or even stay with one. And Charles-Edouard had been one all his life, and made no claims otherwise. He said it was cultural and the fact that he didn't love his wife. Marya didn't care, she wanted no part of a man who had affairs. He swore he wouldn't.

They had a wonderful time in Vermont together, driving around, and they took a gondola up the mountain at Stowe. She drove back into New Hampshire with him. They ate lobster, and simple meals at local inns. They went to farmers' markets and cooked at home, and took turns at who did what dishes, and collaborated on some. They tried out recipes for their book, planted vegetables in her garden, picked flowers, took long walks, swam in a nearby lake, went fishing and cooked what they caught, and waded in streams, and made love at least once a day, which astounded Marya. She had never thought the sex life they had possible at their age. Charles-Edouard was a very sexy man, with the drive of a much younger man, and the ability to carry it out. Marya was thriving and flourishing with his attention and the love they shared. The only dark spot in their time together was the news of Eileen's death. Marya was deeply saddened by it, and went to church with Charles-Edouard to pray for her. She cried as she lit a candle for her soul. And she was going to miss her. She wondered if Francesca was going to replace her as a tenant.

When Charles-Edouard and Marya drove down from Vermont at the end of the Labor Day weekend, she looked healthy and brown and happy, and Charles-Edouard's bright blue eyes danced in his tan face, which made his hair look even whiter. He was wearing a blue shirt, jeans, and espadrilles, with a red sweater on his shoulders when they got out of her car in front of 44 Charles Street, and they unloaded their suitcases and shopping bags full of fresh vegetables and fruit from her garden and the farmers' market in Vermont. Marya sighed as she looked up at the house, thinking how different it would be without Eileen. She had given them all an infusion of youth.

Chris and Ian were home when they walked up the steps with their things. They were surprised to see Charles-Edouard, and it was obvious that he'd been in Vermont with Marya. Chris hadn't realized that was the plan, and they seemed to be happier than ever together. Chris was still sorry for her that he was married. They seemed like a perfect fit.

'Welcome home,' Chris said as he came down the stairs

when he heard them come in. And Ian came up just as fast from the kitchen with a milk mustache and a cookie. He smiled broadly at Marya, and threw himself into Charles-Edouard's open arms.

'I have an egg in my ear!' he shouted excitedly, and instead Charles-Edouard pulled out a coin, and handed it to him.

'You sold your eggs for money,' he said, and kissed the boy on both cheeks, and then embraced Chris. He had gotten used to Charles-Edouard's effusive French greetings by then. Ian helped him carry the bags of food down to the kitchen, while Chris whispered to Marya that he hadn't told Ian about Eileen. He had said she had moved back to California to be with her parents, which was true. He hadn't explained that she was going back in an urn, in the form of ashes. The idea of her getting murdered in the house would have frightened Ian, and he'd been through enough trauma with his mother. Marya agreed entirely, and said she'd mention to Charles-Edouard not to say anything to him about the murder or even her death. It was a sad circumstance for them all. She gave Chris a hug, and they exchanged a warm, loving look of understanding.

'So how was your summer?' he asked her. 'Ours was great at the Vineyard.' He looked like he'd been away, and so did Ian. They were healthy and tan, and so was she. With the exception of the tragedy that had befallen Eileen, they had all had good vacations.

'We had a wonderful time in Vermont,' Marya said, glowing, 'and Europe is always terrific. I've been back for a month. It feels like ages ago.' Chris and Ian had returned from the Vineyard the week before. And there was no sign of disruption in the house. Eileen's rooms upstairs were closed and locked. And Francesca had finally bought living room furniture to replace what Todd had taken eight months before. It was a very comfortable room now, and she had decided not to sell the house, in spite of Eileen. She had told Chris when he got home. It was a tragedy, but they had to go on. Chris approved of her decision and was relieved. He and Ian were happy there. It was a perfect setup for them, and he couldn't imagine his life now without Marya and Francesca as friends for him, and beloved aunts for Ian, although he knew Ian would miss Eileen too, the stories she read him, and the origami birds she made.

As they always did when Marya was home, they all congregated in the kitchen. She put some mushroom soup on the stove that she had made in Vermont before they left that morning. It smelled delicious. Charles-Edouard was playing the egg game with Ian, who was squealing with delight. Suddenly the house seemed full of good smells, and joy and noise and laughter again. It hadn't been that way when he and Ian got home, and it had felt very somber to him at first, and as though they were all in mourning. It was better now. Marya and Charles-Edouard gave them back energy and life. It had been too quiet without them.

Francesca could hear all of them laughing in the kitchen, as she unlocked the front door when she came home from work. She smiled as she walked downstairs, and saw Marya. She already had her apron on and was cooking. She had put a chicken in the oven for dinner. And Charles-Edouard put some pâté that he had made on a plate and then threw his arms around Francesca and kissed her when he saw her.

'Ahhhh!!! *La châtelaine!*' he said with delight. He called her 'the mistress of the château.' 44 Charles Street was hardly a château, but it was their home and they loved it. 'You look beautiful with a tan, Francesca.' And her hair looked like spun gold.

They were all talking at once as Marya looked around the kitchen. A few things were out of place, and she set them to rights and put things on the shelf where they belonged. And then she noticed that the kitchen computer was gone. Francesca had given it to the police as evidence. They all had their own computers in their rooms, and didn't need one in the kitchen anyway. Marya suspected that was why it had vanished, since Eileen used it so often.

The five of them couldn't stop talking, to catch up on everything, and for the first time since Francesca had returned from Maine, the house felt alive and happy again and joyful. They each brought their special magic to it, and were a family together.

They were sitting at dinner at the round table in the kitchen, trying not to feel Eileen's absence, when Francesca noticed something different about Charles-Edouard and Marya. She didn't want to say anything, but as she cleared the soup dishes with her and rinsed them, she whispered to Marya.

'Am I crazy, or is something going on with you and Charles-Edouard?' It was subtle but noticeable, and Chris had sensed it too but would never ask. He was far too polite.

Marya grinned mischievously as she answered in a whisper too. 'His wife left him this summer. She filed for divorce. She's marrying his main sous-chef.' Francesca stared at her in amazement.

'Omigod! Are you serious?'

Her voice was slightly louder in her excitement for

Marya, and she lowered it again. 'Are you getting married?'

'I don't know yet. I want to see if he can be faithful for more than five minutes. But we're happy and having a good time. This is all very recent. He showed up in Vermont a few weeks ago. It's very new.' She looked beautiful and young as she said it. And Charles-Edouard glanced at the two women whispering at the sink, and suspected what they were talking about as they giggled. He smiled at Marya.

When they sat down again, and Marya served the chicken, he looked at Francesca with a warm smile. 'Marya told you?' She nodded and beamed at both of them, while Chris looked confused.

'I'm very happy for both of you,' Francesca said with a loving look, and got up to kiss him on both cheeks, French style. 'That's wonderful news.'

'Did I miss something?' Chris looked puzzled. 'Did something happen with you two this summer?' It looked that way to him.

'We're in love. My wife is divorcing me.' He looked extremely happy about it, as he beamed at Chris.

'Good for you both!' Chris said with a broad smile. 'I'm happy for you.' He meant it, although he wouldn't have wanted to be in that situation himself. He had

253

sworn off love forever after Kimberly. He always insisted that he didn't miss it. His life was peaceful and sane, and he had Ian. 'That's exciting! When did all this happen?'

'In Vermont,' Marya filled in. Charles-Edouard got up to pour them all champagne, and they toasted the couple, and then as Francesca looked around the table, she wanted to offer another toast. She had a lump in her throat when she did.

'To Eileen. I hope she's in a better place now,' she said softly, and they each solemnly raised their glass and took a sip.

'Why did she move back to California?' Ian asked plaintively. 'I miss her. She was nice.'

'Yes, she was,' Francesca agreed. 'Sometimes people we like move away,' she said simply. Ian nodded and started cutting his chicken, and after that they talked of Marya and Charles-Edouard, their respective summers and plans for the fall. Ian had started third grade, Francesca had a heavy exhibition schedule at the gallery, including two one-man shows, and she wanted to go to Art Basel in Miami in December. Charles-Edouard and Marya had their book to write. For the first time in weeks, life felt normal again at 44 Charles Street. Eileen wasn't forgotten and never would be, but life went on.

Chapter 15

At Marya's urging, Francesca invited her mother to dinner the following week when she returned from Europe. She wanted to see her anyway, and had to, and doing it at one of Marya and Charles-Edouard's dinners was an easy way to get together.

Thalia accepted with delight. She said she had had a fabulous summer. She had sent Francesca several e-mails and called her a couple of times, which was a lot for her. She rarely stayed in touch when she was away. She usually forgot her family when she was with her friends. And never the reverse. She had stayed longer than planned in Venice, and had a terrific time. And she thoroughly enjoyed the meal prepared by Marya and Charles-Edouard when she came to dinner. She still flirted with him whenever she talked to him, but she seemed a little less outrageous about it now. She had worn a black sweater and slacks instead of a short dress and high heels. They were halfway through the meal when she noticed Eileen's absence. Francesca still hadn't told her that she died. There was a long pregnant pause after Thalia asked about her.

'She moved back to California,' Ian said simply. 'San Diego,' he informed her. No one else commented, and the conversation moved on. Francesca and Marya exchanged a long look that Thalia didn't see.

'So what's everyone planning now?' she asked over dessert. Charles-Edouard had made them a delicate pear tart. 'Any trips? I'm going to Gstaad for Christmas,' she announced. Her friends in Venice had invited her to join them at their chalet there. It was one of the fancier ski resorts in Europe, and Thalia went at least once every winter, sometimes twice.

No one else had any major plans. The holidays seemed like light-years away to them. Charles-Edouard and Marya would be finishing their cookbook. Francesca was going to be busy at the gallery, and Chris had to get through the hearing for permanent custody of Ian, but he didn't mention it to Thalia. That was hardly a pleasant plan.

Thalia had noticed the new warmth and closeness between Marya and Charles-Edouard. She asked her about it before she left, and Marya admitted it was true.

'Is he getting divorced, or did you just give in?' Thalia asked with interest. She had met several attractive married men in Venice herself. But she didn't like playing on a team.

'His wife left him this summer and filed for divorce. I got lucky,' Marya said simply. She felt a little guilty having a man when Thalia wanted one so badly.

'You certainly did get lucky,' Thalia agreed in a plaintive tone. 'I just don't get it. You didn't want a man, and I do. You get one and I don't. Talk about upside down.' Marya didn't want to tell her that maybe she tried too hard. And Marya hadn't tried at all. Quite the reverse.

'Destiny perhaps,' Marya said diplomatically, but she believed it. 'Things happen in their own time. You'll get your turn,' she reassured her.

'I hope you're right,' Thalia said with a sigh, as she put on a white jacket she had bought in Paris. As always, she was impeccably groomed and beautifully turned out, with exquisite pearl and diamond earrings and immaculately coiffed hair. She was enough to terrify any man. 'I didn't meet anyone even remotely possible this summer. St Tropez is full of Eurotrash and Russians these days. And they're all twelve years old. And everyone else in Europe is married, and cheating.'

'There's someone out there for you,' Marya reassured her, and then Francesca came up from downstairs, walked her mother out, and put her in a cab. Even when she was pleasant, it was always a relief when she left. She was a lot of work, and it was stressful being with her. But Thalia got on well with Marya and Charles-Edouard, and was perfectly polite to Chris, which made her visits easier for Francesca. It was more agreeable than having dinner alone with her, which was always like the Spanish Inquisition. Francesca was tired when she went upstairs. It had been a long evening.

She spent the weekend in Connecticut with her father and Avery after that. He was working on a new painting and in his studio most of the time, which gave her a chance to go for long walks with Avery and relax.

'How are you all doing after Eileen?' Avery asked her gently, and Francesca sighed as she answered. She was still sad about it.

'We all miss her. She put a little extra youth in the group, despite her boy-craziness. She was more like a college kid than a grown-up. I still haven't told my mom, and I won't. She doesn't need to know. She'd just give me a headache about it, and it was bad enough. She was a real example of the kind of dating risks not to take. She would go out with anything that moved. She always thought it was safe, even when you could see it wasn't. She had miserable judgment.'

'What about you? How's your dating life these days?' Avery was worried about her. Todd had moved out more than eight months before, and Francesca had made no real effort to meet someone else. She didn't seem to care.

'I don't have one. I'm not even sure if I want one. I never meet anyone I'm interested in through my work. The artists I meet are all flakes, or pompous, or narcissistic. It just seems like too much work, and the clients who hit on me are always jerks. The nice ones are married.'

'You're too young to give up,' Avery said firmly.

'I don't know. Maybe I'm not. I miss having someone in my life, but I don't want a mismatch like I had with Todd, and figure it out five years later. You invest four years, figure out he's the wrong guy, and then have a year of grief, and break up, and it breaks your heart. And five years go down the drain. I'm finding it a little hard to reenlist.'

'I hear Todd's engaged,' Avery said cautiously.

'Yes, he is. Brave guy. He was suddenly in a big hurry to get married and have kids. God knows if he's marrying

the right woman. All he wants is a brood mare and someone to take to the Christmas party at his law firm. I'm not
the type for either.'

'That's a little harsh on both of you,' Avery said gently.
She liked Todd. Just not for Francesca. She had never
thought it was right, even in the beginning when they did.
Avery had never thought he was interesting enough for her.

'Maybe it isn't,' Francesca answered. 'I don't know
what I want anymore. Arty, conservative, married, not
married, living together, not. It's all so goddamn complicated, and at this age everyone is damaged. They've all
been screwed over by someone else, and so have I.' She
was thinking of Chris when she said it. He readily
admitted to being relationship-phobic, and she was
beginning to feel that way too. 'Maybe I'm too comfortable by myself now.' She'd been desperately lonely at first
without Todd, but she wasn't anymore. She liked doing
what she wanted without having to consult anyone. 'My
roommates keep me company. I have Ian as the token
child in my life, my artists to drive me nuts, they're kind
of like having permanent adolescents in your life. Why
do I need a man?'

'When was the last time you had sex?' Avery asked her
bluntly. 'You might not want to give that up quite yet at
thirty-five. It's kind of nice.'

'Oh that.' Francesca grinned sheepishly. 'I don't even miss that anymore. I just turn it off.' It had been more than a year since she and Todd had stopped sleeping with each other, and having sex, before he left. 'And I don't have to shave my legs.'

'That's attractive,' Avery teased her. She was worried about her. She seemed turned off, or shut down. It had taken her longer than expected to get over Todd, and it had obviously been a more traumatic disappointment than Avery thought it would be at first. But five years was a long time. And her struggle to keep the gallery and the house had been frightening for her.

'I do want to do some new things though. I'm going to Art Basel in Miami this year, just for the hell of it. I'm not showing there. And next summer I want to go someplace other than Maine. I had a great time, but it reminds me too much of Todd. They're his friends, not mine. I don't know, maybe Europe next year. But not with my mother,' she said, and Avery laughed. They both agreed that Thalia was high maintenance, and traveling with her would have been a nightmare for Francesca. 'Maybe I'll take a trip with Marya next year, if she's not married by then,' Francesca said pensively. She loved talking to her stepmother. It gave her perspective about life, and she was so kind. She was a terrific friend.

'Is Marya getting married?' Avery looked surprised.

'She might. She hasn't decided yet. She and Charles-Edouard are in love. He's getting divorced.'

'That's interesting. They're terrific together. You know the old saying, there's a lid for every pot. You just have to find yours.' The trouble was that Francesca wasn't trying, and it wasn't going to fall down the chimney in a white beard and red velvet suit into her arms. Avery remembered too easily all the men she had gone out with before Henry, the bad relationships she'd had, the disappointments, the heartbreaks, and the good relationships too. Avery hadn't been desperate to get married either, but she did want to find the right man to spend time with. She never settled for less. It had taken her until she was fifty to find him, and the minute she met him, she knew Henry Thayer was it. That hadn't happened to Francesca yet, and Avery hoped it wouldn't take her as long. At least she was enjoying her life in the meantime. But Avery couldn't decide if Francesca's roommates were a good idea or not. They kind of blunted her hunger for meeting anyone, and it was too easy to just content herself with being with them, with no relationship in her life.

Her father came out of the barn that was his studio then, and smiled at both women as he put an arm around their shoulders. 'How's my favorite business partner?'

he asked as he kissed his daughter. 'Are we rich yet?'

'Maybe next year.' Francesca grinned. But the gallery was doing well. Better than it had the year before. Little by little, she was building the business, and it was making a small profit, more so than before, although not a big one yet. But it gave her hope. She was hanging in.

Before she left Connecticut after the weekend, Francesca promised to invite them for one of Charles-Edouard and Marya's world-famous dinners, and her father was thrilled. He liked them both, although he had only met Marya twice, and Charles-Edouard once, but he thought he was a great guy. And he loved the Cuban cigars he had shared with him, even if Avery disapproved of their smoking.

Francesca thought about it on the drive home, and once again Avery had given her perspective. She thought about what she'd said about dating, and finding the right lid. In her case she wasn't even sure of the size and shape of her pot, let alone what lid would fit on it. She felt as though she had changed a lot in the last year without Todd. She felt more confident and sure of herself. She had come into her own without him, more than she had with him, which told her a lot about the relationship and herself. She wasn't a half of anything now, she was a whole person. It had also done her good to have roommates and have to adjust to other people. As an only child, she'd never had to do that when she was young. She respected Marya and Chris, and they were all very different. And it was fun having Ian in her life. She'd never been that close to a child before. He was kind of a good introduction to it. Having kids didn't seem as daunting now as it had before, as long as they were as cute as Ian, although there was no guarantee of that. He was about as cute as it got.

When she got home, she could hear noise in the kitchen, and went downstairs to see what it was. It was late for dinner, and they didn't seem like happy sounds. She could hear loud noises and the clanking of pots. When she walked down the stairs, she saw her kitchen under six inches of water. Charles-Edouard was wearing a Panama hat and shorts, barefoot in the water, waving a cigar as he gave directions and asked questions. Marya was wearing Wellington boots and trying to help with a distressed expression. The kitchen table and chairs were in the garden with things stacked on them. And Chris was soaking wet in a bathing suit and sweatshirt, wading through the water and crawling under the sink, trying to locate the pipe that had exploded and flooded the kitchen.

'Oh shit,' she said, rolling up her jeans and taking off her own shoes as she waded in next to Chris. 'What can

I do to help? I'm sorry you got stuck with this.' He looked over his shoulder at her with a grin, and she felt guilty for not being there when it happened, and for all he was doing. This was exactly what Todd had hated about the house and why he wanted to sell it the year before. It was a very old house and things happened. Charles-Edouard poured her a glass of wine and handed it to her. It looked like a party in the midst of a flood. Charles-Edouard and Ian were having fun. The others weren't.

'I got the water turned off,' Chris explained. 'It happened while we were all out. It's probably been running all day. We'll have to find someone to get the water out of here tomorrow, and you need a plumber. I think this one is over my head.' As he said it, Ian took a leap off the stairs and landed in the large pool of water with a delighted splash.

'This is cool!' he squealed, and Chris told him to stop it or go back upstairs. Ian made a face and waded toward Charles-Edouard. There wasn't much they could do about it that night, although Chris made a few more passes at trying to locate the leak and finally gave up. Francesca had been holding the flashlight for him under the sink, and she was soaked now too. Her jeans were wet to the waist.

'Have you all eaten dinner?' Francesca asked

apologetically, and Charles-Edouard said they hadn't. She suggested they all go to the nearest pizza parlor, or order Chinese takeout and eat it in her living room. And then she realized that Charles-Edouard and Marya couldn't sleep in their own room that night. Their carpet was soaked through. She suggested they take her room, and she could sleep on her new living room couch. Marya resisted at first, but they had no other choice. And Francesca insisted she didn't mind sleeping on the couch.

They opted for pizza and went out to dinner. They were chattering loudly, and all of them looked a mess. Charles-Edouard was still wearing shorts, Marya had left her boots on, and Chris and Francesca had put on dry jeans. Ian said he wanted to go back and splash in the pool in the kitchen and Chris said he couldn't. They all had a good time, and went back to the house after dinner, in better spirits, although the kitchen was still a disaster. The water was slowly draining into the garden through the doors they'd left open, but there were still several inches of water covering the floor, and it had spilled into Marya's room. At times like this Francesca wondered if she should sell the house. If Chris hadn't been there to turn it off, the water would still be pouring out of the wall. She had said as much to him on the way back.

'You can always find a plumber, Francesca. It's a beautiful old house. That's not enough reason to give it up.'

'Yes, it is beautiful, and I love it. But it's a lot for me alone. Financially and every other way.' Losing the income from one of her tenants had been hard too. Owning a house, particularly an old one, was a big challenge and a lot of work. 'I'd miss it if I sold it,' she admitted. 'I hope fixing that leak doesn't cost a fortune.' Every time she got a little money put aside, some emergency came along and gobbled it up. The Pac-Man of life.

He walked her back to the living room then, and Marya and Charles-Edouard went upstairs to her room. She had changed the sheets for them before they all went to dinner. And Ian went upstairs to watch TV from his bed. When Chris had put bunk beds in their room he knew Ian would love sleeping on the top bunk. It wasn't romantic, but it worked for them and gave him more space in his bedroom than a queen- or king-size bed, which he didn't need anyway. He had no one to share it with. It was just him and Ian.

Chris sat down on the couch next to Francesca to relax. He was sorry he hadn't been able to fix the leak in the kitchen, or stop the flood before it turned into a swimming pool. They both laughed at the vision of Charles-Edouard in his Panama hat and shorts, giving directions, and Ian leaping off the stairs to make a big splash.

'This house would be miserable without all of you,' she said honestly with a grateful look.

'You don't get sick of all of us in your space? I wonder about that sometimes, and if I should get an apartment for me and Ian. But we'd miss you. It was kind of an experiment for me in the beginning. But it really works for us and it's good for him. I think he'd be lonely with just me now.'

'And I'd be even lonelier. Having everyone here puts a little happy craziness in my life.' It had been an experiment for her too, and a financial necessity, but she loved their communal life.

'Me too,' he said, grinning, and then he turned to look at her. 'You mean a lot to me, Francesca. I hope you know that. You're a wonderful friend.'

'So are you,' she said shyly. 'I couldn't have gotten through all the Eileen stuff without you.' He nodded.

'You're a godsend with Ian . . . and with me . . .' And then with no warning, he leaned over and kissed her, and she stared at him with wide eyes.

'What did you just do?' She looked as though he had hit her over the head with his shoe.

'I think I just kissed you,' he said, looking pleased with

himself. He had wanted to ever since the night they were together after Eileen died, but it never seemed like the right time. He wasn't sure it was now, but he had done it anyway. And he was smiling at her.

'I mean why,' she insisted. 'Why did you kiss me?'

'Are you mad at me for doing it?' he asked, looking worried, and she shook her head.

'Not mad. Just confused. I thought you had sworn off relationships for life.'

'I did. Maybe I just changed my mind. It was just a kiss, Francesca, not a proposal. Relax.'

'I think I'm relationship-phobic too.' She was remembering the conversation she'd had with Avery the day before.

'No, you're just bruised. That's different. I'm bruised too. It doesn't have to be permanent. It just takes time. You've probably been numb for the last year after your relationship with Todd fell apart.'

'Yes, I have been. I felt as though something in me had died, and couldn't come back to life again.'

'It's not dead. It's just asleep,' he reassured her.

'How do you know?' she asked, looking intrigued.

'I'll show you,' he said, and kissed her again. This time she laughed after the kiss. It was a nice kiss. She had liked it a lot. Maybe she wasn't so dead after all, and he was right. 'See what I mean? I think you're starting to wake up.' He kissed her again, and she kissed him back this time and melted into his arms, and then she looked worried when they came up for air. It had been a passionate kiss this time. They were both heating up, and this was totally unexpected.

'What are we doing, Chris?' she asked, looking panicked. 'I like you. I don't want either of us to get hurt.'

'Maybe we have to take that chance. No pain, no gain. Corny expression, but unfortunately true. I think I'm willing to risk it for you.'

It took some adjustment of her thinking to wrap her mind around the idea. The great relationship-phobic of all time had come out of his cave. And so had she. But it was scary as hell.

'What about Ian? Would he be upset?' Francesca asked, looking worried.

'He loves you. I think he'd be pleased.' Chris had been thinking about that for a while.

'I love him too,' she said quietly. 'I was thinking about it today on the way home. He's a wonderful boy.' And then she looked up at Chris and smiled slowly. 'And so are you.'

'You're not so bad either. Why don't we see where this goes. How about dinner this week?'

'You mean like a date?' She looked shocked.

'That's the general idea. Dinner, you know, all that stuff. Maybe a kiss goodnight. How about Tuesday?'

'I suck at dates,' she said, looking nervous again. 'I've given them up.'

'Yeah, me too. But I'm willing to try again with you.' He had known her for almost nine months, he liked everything about her. And he'd had almost a year to get comfortable and get to know her, and see her in situations that were real. He loved what he had seen and knew of her, and she was wonderful with his son. He couldn't ask for more than that. It seemed like a reasonable beginning to him. What they had was based on friendship, not passion, or blind hope. They knew each other well.

'Okay,' she said quietly, feeling as though rockets were going off in her head. She had never expected this to happen between them. Nothing really had happened, but there was a glimmer of it, a possibility, and she wanted to take a chance with him. 'What if it doesn't work? Then you'll hate me, you'll get mad and move out, and I'll never see you or Ian again. That would be terrible, Chris.'

'Yes, it would,' he agreed. 'Let's try not to let that happen. We'll work it out.' She nodded and he kissed her again, and then he pulled himself away from her and stood up. She walked him to the door of her living room, and he smiled as he walked up the stairs to his own room.

Ian was sleeping with the TV on, and Chris had a wild urge to let out a war whoop of glee. He had kissed her! She was a wonderful woman. He trusted her completely. And what better combination than two relationship-phobics who were scared to death? Better yet that they had started as friends.

Chapter 16

On Monday morning, the plumber came and fixed the pipe and they drained the kitchen. They were back in business. It had cost Francesca two thousand dollars, which was a stretch for her, but she had no choice.

Marya and Charles-Edouard baby-sat for Ian on Tuesday when Chris took Francesca out to dinner. She had to take Marya into her confidence, otherwise it didn't make sense.

'Like a date?' Marya looked shocked. She hadn't picked up even a hint of romance between them, ever, although she loved them both, and could easily see them together. But she had never thought it appealed to either of them and had been sorry it didn't.

'Yeah. Like a date,' Francesca admitted, looking

273

embarrassed. She felt awkward saying it to anyone. She didn't even feel like dating material anymore. She had been in neutral for nearly a year. 'At least that's what he said. But don't tell anyone.'

'Who am I going to tell? Page Six of the *New York Post*?' Marya was laughing at her. Francesca was a wreck.

'I don't know – Ian, my mother, Charles-Edouard. I don't want to make this a bigger deal than it is. It's just dinner.' But it was dinner with Chris, in a restaurant, and he had called it a date. And he had kissed her several times.

'Is it a big deal?' Marya asked her pointedly.

'Maybe . . . I don't know . . . maybe not . . . maybe it will be. Maybe it shouldn't be. Maybe we're both too afraid.'

'What if you're not? What if it works?'

'That's even scarier,' Francesca said, looking panicked.

'That's how I felt about Charles-Edouard. It's a little frightening getting into a relationship, at any age. And the older you are, the more defined your personality and your life, and the harder it is to put the puzzle pieces together.'

'How's it going with you and him?' Francesca asked her. Marya looked ecstatic, and so did he.

'It's fantastic. Other than my late husband, he's the most wonderful man I've ever met. I'm a very lucky woman to have two great men in one lifetime. It's probably more than I deserve, but I'm loving it,' she said humbly.

'You deserve it,' Francesca confirmed to her. 'Just don't say that to my mother. But what the hell, she's had five helpings at the buffet of life, you only had one. You have a right to seconds.' She was happy for her.

'My best advice to you is to just see what comes with Chris. Don't anticipate, don't project, don't expect him to be someone he isn't, or try to be someone you're not. Be yourself. And enjoy it.' It was good advice. 'And don't worry about Ian. I'm happy to baby-sit for him anytime. And Charles-Edouard loves him too. When Chris takes you out, sign us up for Ian. We'll make cookies or something. Have fun,' Marya said to her, as she went upstairs to dress.

For the first time in months, when Francesca sat in the bathtub, she shaved her legs. She didn't know yet if she'd wear a dress, but whether she did or not, it was a symbolic gesture. 'Welcome back to the world,' she said to herself in the tub, and then she laughed out loud.

'What did you tell them?' Chris asked her as they hurried down the steps and the front door closed behind them.

She was wearing a black leather skirt, a red sweater, and high heels. She felt a little like her mother, and worried that she'd overdone it. She didn't want to look like she was trying too hard. She couldn't even remember what you were supposed to wear on a real date and didn't have the wardrobe. Her forays into dating had been minimal so far. And for someone she actually cared about, she was aware that she was supposed to look cute and sexy. She had no idea if she did. But he had smiled at her admiringly when she came down the stairs and knocked on the door of his room to let him know she was ready. Ian was already in his pajamas with freshly washed hair and told her she looked sick.

'I do?' She looked worried.

'Sick is good.' Chris translated for her. 'Like "hot," only cooler and younger.'

'Oh, thanks, Ian . . . you look sick too,' she said over Chris's shoulder, and then they ran down the stairs and out the door. Ian knew he was supposed to report to Marya and Charles-Edouard in the kitchen for a cookie-baking fest.

'So what did you tell Marya and Charles-Edouard?' Chris repeated the question. She hadn't answered.

'I told them you hate their food and wanted to go out for a decent dinner.' With two of the most famous chefs in the world cooking daily meals for them, it was admittedly hard to justify going out. But this was different.

'Very amusing.' He knew she hadn't really said that.

'I told Marya you invited me to dinner.'

'What did she say?' He was curious at the reaction they were going to get if they started going out. Ian had already said he thought it was funny and let it go at that. He had laughed at his dad as he got dressed.

'She thought it was a good idea. So do I.' She was liking the idea better and better, although she had terrified herself for the past two days, imagining every possible disaster that could befall them if they got involved. But she had still kept their date.

'I like the idea too,' he said, looking pleased with himself as they walked to Da Silvano. He had chosen that because they both liked it. And he didn't want to do anything too fancy and make her uncomfortable. He wanted her to have a nice time. She already was. It was fun to feel like a girl again, on a date, in a skirt, with a man. Wow!

The headwaiter gave them a good table inside, and there was a chill in the air. Winter was coming, and fall had arrived. Chris was wearing jeans, a white shirt, and a brown corduroy jacket, with freshly shined loafers. He looked nice. And he had shaved before they went out. She liked that. The five-day beard stubble look had always turned her off. Trendy or not, it looked dirty to her. Chris looked immaculate and handsome, and they looked right together.

They both ordered pasta and salad, and he ordered a great bottle of Napa Valley wine. And even before the pasta arrived, they were talking and laughing, about how silly they felt all dressed up and out together, about the leak the other night, and things Charles-Edouard did and said. When she thought about it later, she didn't even know what they had talked about, but they'd had a nice time. A really nice time. It was fun to get away from the house, their work, and even Ian, and just be grown-ups out for an evening together. It was great.

They lingered over dessert and coffee and were the last to leave the restaurant. They wandered home slowly, and everyone was in bed when they got home. Ian was sound asleep, tucked in on his top bunk.

'I had a wonderful time,' Chris said, as he kissed her just outside her room, on the landing. He had walked her upstairs, like a proper date.

'So did I,' she whispered, and he kissed her again.

'I don't know why we didn't figure this out six or nine months ago,' he said, smiling down at her. 'I feel like we wasted a lot of time.'

'We didn't. We weren't ready.' And now they knew each other well. It was better this way.

Chris nodded, and kissed her again. They held each other, and he hated to turn away. She finally let herself into her room, and he ran quickly down the stairs to his own. She walked into her bedroom with a big smile on her face and then laughed. It had been an excellent first date.

Francesca and Chris tried to act like nothing was happening, but it was obvious that something was. Marya smiled every time she saw them together, and Charles-Edouard clapped him on the back with a big grin after their date on Tuesday night.

The next morning at breakfast, it was hard being together, trying to act normal. Chris kept smiling at her, and Francesca blushed shyly, which made him want to kiss her, but he couldn't. He didn't want to have to say anything to Ian yet. But his son was no dummy either. He chuckled when he saw them together.

Chris took her out again on Friday night, for Mexican food and a movie, and on Saturday morning Ian looked at both of them and burst into a fit of giggles. He was eating his favorite Mickey Mouse pancakes and bacon. Marya had made them for him, since he never tired of them and requested them again and again, and then she and Charles-Edouard had gone to Vermont for the weekend. Their romance was going well, and they both looked happy. So did Francesca and Chris. It was contagious.

'So, have you kissed her yet?' Ian asked his father when Francesca went upstairs to get something from her room. She had promised to give Chris a book she read that summer and thought he would love too.

'What are you talking about?' Chris tried to look innocent, but Ian wasn't buying it.

'If you take a girl to dinner, you have to kiss her. Everyone knows that. You took her to dinner twice. If you don't kiss her, she'll think you're gay.'

'Where did you get that from?' Chris looked shocked.

'A fifth grader told me. He said that means you're a sissy and don't like girls.'

'Well, don't go calling anyone that, or they might take a swing at you if they don't like it,' his father warned him.

'Okay. So did you?'

'It's none of your business,' Chris said defensively.

'Yes, it is. She's my friend too. I'd kiss her if I took her out to dinner.'

'That's nice to know.' Chris smiled at him as Francesca walked back into the room and handed him the book. She said she had loved it and thought he would too. It was a well-written thriller by a new writer.

'What are you two talking about?' Francesca asked innocently as she poured herself a cup of coffee and sat down at the table with them.

'I asked him if he kissed you yet, and he wouldn't tell me,' Ian said, polishing off the last of his pancake, and then he looked straight at her. 'Did he?' She nearly choked, and didn't know what to say.

'Would you be upset if he did?' Francesca asked gently, and Ian laughed.

'Of course not. I love you, Francesca. I think my dad does too. He's just too chicken to say it, or do anything about it. I told him if he doesn't, he's gay.' Francesca's eyes opened wide. She hadn't expected that.

'I don't think he's gay,' she said, and sipped her coffee, looking at Chris for cues. She had no idea what to say. Chris was nodding imperceptibly, and she looked straight at Ian. 'He kissed me.'

'Then he's not gay.' He gave his dad a high five for the kiss, and she felt like she had walked into the locker room with two high school boys. She was the object of a high five. It was a first for her.

'I figured he wasn't. So that's okay with you?' she asked Ian. She was glad that Charles-Edouard and Marya weren't there. This was definitely a family discussion.

'Yeah, it's okay with me,' Ian confirmed. 'I like it. You're our friend.'

'Yes, I am, but I don't want to do anything that makes you unhappy. You both mean a lot to me, and I don't want to mess that up.'

'You mean like my mom?' he asked. They were heading into deep waters.

'I don't know about your mom, Ian. That's between you and your dad. I just don't want to upset you or your dad, or disappoint you in any way.'

'You won't,' Ian said confidently. He had total faith in her. 'What are we doing today?' He moved on to the next subject, since they had established that they had kissed. He hopped out of his chair then, and bounced upstairs to watch TV. He wanted to go to Central Park after lunch.

'Well, that was easy,' she said with a look of relief after he left the room. 'I was afraid he'd be upset.' Chris was smiling at her.

'I didn't think he would.' He leaned over and kissed her then, and then slipped into the chair next to hers and put his arms around her and gave her a real one. At that exact moment Ian walked back into the room. They didn't even see him until they came up for air. He was laughing at them.

'Good one, Dad,' he said happily, and left the room again, and took a box of rice cakes with him, to munch while he watched TV.

'I have to get the hang of this,' Francesca said, looking a little shaken. 'I wasn't expecting a cheering section in the bleachers.' But she was glad that he approved. It was better that way.

'They talk about sex too much in school,' Chris said, looking slightly unnerved too.

They cleaned up the kitchen, and went out for lunch that afternoon, and then to Central Park. They walked around the boat pond, wandered into the zoo, bought ice cream, and threw a football between the three of them and played tag. They felt like a family, and all three of them were happy when they came home late that afternoon with some new DVDs. Chris invited her into their room, and she watched TV with them, sitting next to Chris on the couch, and Ian sprawled out on the floor. Francesca hadn't been that happy in years. And best of all, Ian approved.

Chapter 17

The morning of the permanent custody hearing, Chris was up at six. Marya had offered to take Ian to school. He knew that something was going on, but he wasn't sure what it was. He knew it was another one of those court hearings about his mom, where his dad went out in a suit. Chris didn't want to explain the details to him. And nothing was going to change. Ian was still going to be with him, whatever happened in court today. So Chris didn't want to worry him. Kim was still in jail, she was still a drug addict, and she wasn't coming out anytime soon. The only difference after today's hearing was that if Chris won, Ian would never have to live with her again. She would have visitation, but Chris wouldn't be getting calls from the police after she OD'd or slashed her wrists with Ian keeping pressure on her arteries until the paramedics arrived. He wouldn't be picking him up in juvenile detention halls after she got arrested. He didn't want Ian ever going through that again. And he wanted court-supervised visitation whenever Ian saw her in future.

Francesca had volunteered to go to the hearing with him, but he thought it would be too upsetting for her.

'Excuse me?' she said to him after Ian left for school. 'Do I look like a sissy to you? I know what a drug addict is. I know what Ian has been through. I remember when she OD'd and you flew out the door to go get him. I'm well aware that she's being charged with manslaughter and may go to prison. Why can't I be there for you?'

'What if I lose?' he said, looking worried.

'That's even more reason for me to be there for you. And if you lose,' she said firmly, 'we'll try again. You're not going to lose, Chris. She's a mess.'

'Her father is a very powerful man.'

'So is yours. You're related to two presidents, for chrissake. And I don't mean Benjamin Franklin and Thomas Jefferson. I mean recent ones. That carries some sway.'

'My family doesn't like to get involved in public messes. They love Ian but they thought I never should have married her. She wasn't on heroin then, but she was a mess. I thought I was going to put Humpty Dumpty back together and turn her into a princess. Instead, she turned into scrambled eggs, and always was. They think she's an embarrassment to us, so they ignore the whole situation, even what it does to Ian. I think they have denial about it. They don't want to know. Kimberly's father would lie, cheat, steal, and murder people so she doesn't have to suffer the consequences of anything she does. That's part of why she's never cleaned up. She's never had to. He cleans everything up for her. There's no such thing as paying the price in her life. Everyone else does it for her, even our son.'

'Can I come?' she asked again, and he nodded assent, and she kissed him. Their relationship was going well. It had only been a few weeks, but they had spent some good time together, and he had taken her to dinner several times. They hadn't slept with each other yet, but neither of them was in any rush. They were proceeding with caution, and he had this hearing on his mind. He was going to feel a lot better when it was behind him, especially if he won, but either way. And as Francesca had just said, if he lost, he would try again.

They took a cab to the courthouse on Lafayette Street. They arrived punctually at ten o'clock, and Chris's attorney was waiting outside. Because she was in jail, Kim didn't have to be there, and she wasn't, but her lawyer was, a very nasty woman whom Chris had hated for several years. Her only interest was in protecting her client, and never their son.

Chris's attorney was a serious-looking man in a suit, wearing a dark tie and steel-rim glasses. Chris introduced them, and he shook Francesca's hand. She had a good feeling about him. She didn't like the look of his ex-wife's attorney. She looked mean and threw dark looks at Chris.

They entered the courtroom at the same time, and took their places. Francesca took a seat directly behind Chris, and touched his shoulder as she sat down. And a moment later the judge walked in, and the bailiff called them to order. There was no one with Chris except his lawyer and Francesca. Ian's mother was not in the courtroom, only her attorney, and Chris had pointed out discreetly to Francesca as they walked in that Kim's father was in the room. Everyone knew he was there and who he was. He was hard to miss. He was on the cover of *Time* and *Newsweek* every year, and in the papers frequently, and the judge would recognize him too. His being there was a form of silent intimidation, but the message was not likely to be missed. His daughter had his full support, which was no small thing.

Both sides of the case were presented. Kim's immense devotion as a mother and her love for her son. How much she loved him. What a good person she was, that she was going straight into rehab as soon as she got out of jail, because she wanted to be clean for her son. The woman lawyer representing her turned to the judge, and with the most earnest look Francesca had ever seen, she said that there was nothing on earth Kim was not willing to do for her boy, and that she could swear to the judge personally that there would be no further risk to the child, and that joint custody must and should be preserved. And at all costs this eight-year-old boy should not be deprived of his mother once she got out, nor feel abandoned by her if Chris wrested custody away from her, for sole custody for himself. She said that was clearly *not* in the best interests of the boy, but joint custody was. She used everything except organ music and a choir to sway the judge. He sat stone-faced on the bench, listening raptly to everything she said, and Francesca saw him glance in Kim's father's direction more than once. She knew that Chris had seen it too. It was what he expected. Powerful people pulling strings, even just by being there and staring at the judge. It also told them that Kimberly's family didn't intend to lose. It was an important message, and Chris was afraid it could well convince the judge to maintain joint custody between them. That was Chris's worst fear, and Francesca shared it. She didn't believe for a minute that they wanted what was best for Ian. Nor did Chris.

Francesca was nervous about Chris's lawyer at first as he began to speak. He seemed professional more than impassioned. He was extremely dry and unemotional, particularly in comparison to Kim's lawyer, who had pulled out all of the emotional stops to an alarming degree. A private investigator had been working for Chris, and unearthed information that none of them had ever known before, and surely not the court. Chris's attorney explained in his opening statement that Chris was not seeking to keep Ian from his mother, that they would welcome court-supervised visitation when she was free to participate in it. They didn't want to keep the boy from his mother. All they wanted was to keep him safe, and living in a wholesome atmosphere. And given his mother's history and her poor judgment, they felt that all decisions regarding Ian should be made by Chris. That meant sole custody for him. It meant deciding about schools, taking him to doctors, making regular trips to the dentist. Everything from religious education to braces would be decided by Chris, which made sense to Francesca as she listened. Chris was doing it anyway. Sole custody for him meant that Kim would lose her voice in all decisions. It meant that she could see him, even regularly if she was in good condition, but she couldn't decide where he went to school, or put him at risk again, if the judge granted supervised visitation.

Having explained very unemotionally that Chris was not seeking to prevent visitation, as long as it was supervised by a third party appointed by the court, but only to gain full custody of his son legally, the attorney then read the essentials of the investigator's re-port. It was a list of horrifying acts, failures, episodes, misdeeds, dangerous interludes, and shocking displays of wanton and even criminal negligence. Francesca knew a little from Chris, but what she knew was a drop in the bucket compared to the rest.

Kimberly Harley had endangered her son in every possible way hundreds of times. And Chris had been fighting her and trying to protect Ian for years. The courts had always tried to respect the fact that she was his mother. But the accumulation of evidence was over-whelming now. All of what Chris's lawyer was telling them was new to the court, and some of it had been new to him. According to witnesses who had signed state-ments for them, she had left Ian with other drug addicts, abandoned him in truck stops and restaurants where he was brought home by other people, forgot she had him with her and left him by the side of highways, dropped him when he was a baby because she was on drugs, which Chris knew, forgot him on the roof of her car as an infant, where Chris had rescued him before she drove off, left him in crack houses, left him with a dead body, forgot to feed him for days, had attempted suicide several times in front of him, and pointed a loaded gun at him intending to kill him and then herself, and another addict had taken the gun away from her and saved Ian's life. The attorney said that Ian had called 911 for her countless times when she OD'd. The list went on and on and on and on. It no longer mattered that Chris's lawyer was unemotional and used none of the bells and whistles the female attorney had. It was better this way. His lack of emotion was far more effective. They were cold hard facts, pages and pages and pages of them, with police reports and signed witness statements attached. Francesca looked behind her at Kim's father, and he looked like he wanted to kill Chris's attorney for telling the truth about his daughter. It was the most damning evidence any of them had ever heard and couldn't be denied. Listening to it, and knowing Ian, Francesca thought Kim deserved a lot worse than prison. She had no idea how Ian had survived it, and it was no longer surprising that Chris was relationship-phobic. Married to a woman like that, constantly endangering the life of their son, even when he was an infant – how could he ever trust anyone again? There were tears in Francesca's eyes as she listened. The list of horrors finally ended, and Chris's attorney approached the bench and handed a copy of all of it to the judge. He was sitting silently and stared at Chris. He then asked the attorneys to come into chambers. Francesca whispered to Chris and asked if the judge knew that Kim was currently being charged with manslaughter, and he nodded. Chris was sitting there stone-faced, trying not to remember vividly each incident where she had endangered Ian. She was a public menace, and Chris had said for years that she belonged in prison.

Both lawyers went into the judge's chambers as soon as he left the bench, and Francesca leaned toward Chris again.

'Now what?'

'He can either tell us his ruling today, or he can submit it in writing after he considers the case and reads what we filed. Most judges usually do it in writing, so no one punches them out in the courtroom. People get pretty heated up about custody hearings.' It was easy to see why after what she'd just heard.

'That was some list,' she said sadly, and Chris nodded. The investigator had done a terrific job. Poor Ian. Her own mother had been an embarrassment to her all her life, but never a danger. Ian's mother had risked his life from the time he was three months old when she went back to drugs, and had been on and off them ever since. Francesca's heart ached for him, and for Chris, who was still trying to protect his son.

The attorneys came out of chambers ten minutes later. There was no expression whatsoever on Chris's attorney's face as he led them out of the courtroom. Kim's lawyer had gone straight to her father in the back of the courtroom, and they were conferring with bowed heads, as he pointed emphatically in the direction of the judge. He didn't look happy, but she had given a good performance, and that's all it was. Theater, not law, and not justice for Ian.

Chris's attorney escorted them outside, at a rapid pace. They were at the bottom of the courthouse steps before he turned to face them. He had been afraid that someone might call the press, so he got them out of the courtroom as fast as they could.

'What happened in chambers?' Chris asked him with a worried look. His attorney smiled at Chris and touched his shoulder. 'You have sole custody of Ian, Chris. The judge said he doesn't want to hear another word from them in this case. He said that as long as he's on the bench, you'll have custody of Ian, and he said that the next time she endangers him, he's putting her in jail. He said he has no idea how she kept joint custody for this long.' Tears rolled down Chris's cheeks as he listened to the words, and Francesca choked on a sob. 'Now get out of here before someone figures out who you are and calls the press. Her father won't this time.' Chris beamed at him and thanked him, and then hailed a cab, and he and Francesca jumped in. Francesca burst into tears and hugged him as the cab drove away. It had been a total victory for Chris, and Charles-Edouard and Marya were waiting for them when they got home. They knew immediately when they saw Chris's face and Francesca's tears.

'Thank God,' Marya said as she hugged him, and so did Charles-Edouard. It was an enormous relief to all of them. And Chris reminded them again not to say anything to Ian when he got home, and then he went upstairs to change into a sweater and jeans. He was shaken and thrilled. Ian was all his. At last. She could never do any of it again. The horror was over. Ian was safe. That was all Chris had ever wanted. And she had risked his life so many times. The judge had also approved court-supervised visitation by a third party. They had won it all.

Francesca tried to tell Marya about it, and she was horrified even by the few things Francesca remembered from the long list. It had been a total victory for Chris and above all for Ian. His mother would never put him in harm's way again.

It was even more meaningful and a more important victory when Chris saw an item in the paper a week later. Francesca could see his teeth clench and his jaw work as he read the piece, and she was worried. She asked him what it was when he finished reading, and he silently handed her the paper. This time Kim's father's attorneys had won, for his daughter, if not her son.

They had somehow claimed, and probably paid people vast sums to corroborate the story, that the addict who had OD'd next to her was a dealer, that he had endangered her life and not the reverse. Because the deceased was allegedly a criminal, it shed new light on her guilt. They had claimed psychiatric issues for Kim, delicate health, and everything else they could think of to plead her felony manslaughter charges down to a misdemeanor. The district attorney had been willing to plea-bargain with her. The judge had meted out a six-month sentence, with credit for time served since she'd been there, and time off for good behavior. Kim was not going to prison. She would be out of jail in a few weeks and home for Thanksgiving. The article stated that she would spend time at a famous country club rehab to restore her health after her time in jail. She could leave any time she wanted, and knowing her, Chris was sure she'd be calling soon and wanting visitation with Ian. But at least now it would be with court-appointed supervision. Chris was furious that she'd been allowed to plead to lesser charges and was getting out of jail. She'd be back in his face in no time, wanting to see Ian and screw up his life again.

'I didn't think he'd pull it off this time,' Chris said, looking livid, referring to her father. 'She belongs in prison. She's a danger to herself and everyone around her.'

'Yes, but at least now Ian is protected,' Francesca said sensibly. 'You have sole custody, and she'll have supervised visits.'

'I was hoping she'd be gone for a few years,' he said, looking grim. It made Francesca more grateful than ever that he had won at the custody hearing. No one could have denied or refuted that list.

Chris put the paper in the garbage, where Ian wouldn't see it, and then he went back upstairs to work without saying another word. It was no secret how much he hated his ex-wife. And Francesca felt sorry for both of them that in a few weeks she'd be back on the streets, and in Ian's world.

Chapter 18

In the weeks after the custody hearing, their romance burst into full bloom. Chris started to relax, and make his peace with the fact that Kim wasn't going to prison, and would be back, wanting to see Ian. Francesca reminded him that there was nothing he could do about Ian's mother. He had won a major victory. He had full control and sole custody, and all their visits would happen with supervision. Ian would be safe from now on. It allowed Chris to finally think about something else. He was spending more and more time with Francesca. They were in her living room and bedroom at night, after Ian went to sleep, but they didn't dare do more than kiss, in case he woke up and came upstairs.

They went on wonderful outings together on

weekends, the Bronx Zoo, the Staten Island ferry, the boat museum at the tip of Manhattan. She took them to see her father and Avery in Connecticut, and Chris and Henry got on well. The three of them wore costumes and went trick-or-treating on Halloween, and watched the parade in the Village. Francesca hadn't had as much fun in years. The next morning, as Ian lay in bed with a plastic pumpkin full of candy, Chris came upstairs to find her in her room.

'I'll trade you two Milky Ways for a Snickers,' he said, as he walked into the room.

'No deal. The lady on Jane Street gave me the dark Snickers bars. That's worth at least six Milky Ways, and a bag of peanut M&M's. I saw you slip two of them into your pocket at our last stop.'

'You're a crook,' Chris accused her as he kissed her. He was starving for her. Years of monastic solitude had finally caught up with him. 'I have a proposition for you,' he whispered as he ran a hand under her sweater, and she caught her breath. 'I want to go away for the weekend with you.' They didn't dare get too passionate, with Ian so near, but they had come close. Very close.

'When?'

'Now!' he said, and she laughed. They had Ian on their own for the weekend, because Marya and

Charles-Edouard had gone back to Vermont for a few days to work on the book. 'How about next weekend? Maybe Marya will baby-sit.' He sounded desperate.

'I'll ask her when they get back.'

'If she won't do it, I warn you, I may go crazy and rip your clothes off in a public place of my choosing.'

'Take it easy. We'll work something out,' she said, and teased him as they kissed. They were both anxious for an adult weekend somewhere where they didn't have to behave, be circumspect, or think about Ian. They needed time for themselves now. They had been very respectable for almost two months. It was long enough.

Francesca asked Marya on Sunday night when they got home from Vermont. As always, she was delighted help out. She loved Ian, and heartily approved of their romance.

'Where are you two going?' She was happy for them. There were two happy couples in the house now. Charles-Edouard was wonderful to her, and promised her he was a reformed man. He wanted no other woman but her. Francesca had long since told her about her father, who had been exemplary ever since he had married Avery. She told Marya it just took the right woman.

'We haven't figured out where we're going. I wanted to see if you'd mind baby-sitting first.' And then Marya had an idea.

'Why don't you go to my place in Vermont? It's quiet and peaceful. It is beautiful this time of year, even if it's chilly. And it's nicer than being in a hotel.' Francesca loved the idea, and so did Chris. They made their plan. They were going to leave on Friday afternoon and come back on Sunday night. It was a long drive, but it was worth it. They thought of nothing else all week, and Marya was busy making plans with Ian. They were going to a movie, a play, and a museum. Ian was delighted, and Chris and Francesca could hardly wait. Francesca got one of her artists to work at the gallery for her. They were covered.

It felt like a getaway scene in a movie as they drove away from the house on Charles Street late Friday afternoon. There was rush-hour traffic, but neither of them cared. They had actually pulled it off. Even Ian paid no attention as they left. He kissed both of them, and didn't even ask where they were going for the weekend. He was too busy with Marya. And Chris promised to call him.

They both started laughing as they left the city, and congratulated each other on having done it.

'I kept worrying all week that something would happen and we couldn't leave. Like Ian getting chicken pox,' Francesca said with relief as he drove.

'So did I,' Chris admitted. 'I was sure one of us would

301

get sick, or Marya couldn't do it, or Kim would break out of jail or go nuts. We have two whole days together!' he said victoriously. 'I can't believe it!'

'Neither can I!' She was beaming.

Even the drive was relaxing and enjoyable. They stopped at a little inn on the way up and had dinner. And then got back on the road and continued driving to Vermont. They got to Marya's place just before midnight. It was a pretty little house with an orchard, tall trees, and beautiful grounds. Francesca and Chris were thrilled to be there. Marya and Charles-Edouard had been enjoying spending time there lately and he loved the area. It was a perfect counterpoint to their city life in New York. In France, he had a farm in Normandy, which he had just given to his wife. He wanted to buy another one with Marya, when they were in France next summer. He liked the country better than the beach. He loved her home in Vermont.

It looked and felt like a honeymoon cottage as Chris unlocked the door and turned off the alarm. And Francesca looked around at all of Marya's pretty things. It was a beautiful room with wood paneling and a fireplace. And upstairs, the guest room had a big canopied bed. They set their suitcases down, and before Francesca could even take her coat off, Chris had her on the bed and was kissing her. They were both out of breath and frantic with passion within minutes. They had waited so long for this, and they had wanted each other so much in the past weeks. They had been circumspect for Ian's sake, but there were no constraints on them now. They were both naked within minutes and under the covers, learning each other's bodies and fondling each other. They were both aroused, and neither of them could wait any longer. Francesca welcomed him, and Chris plunged into her, burning with desire. It was the hottest, fastest, most unbridled sex either of them had ever had. They were like two starving people who had finally found food after years on a desert island. They came at the same time, and lay breathless and panting half off the bed afterward, and they both started to laugh.

'I think I'm too old for this,' Chris said, trying to catch his breath, and she was lying on top of him, dripping with perspiration, her eyes closed, with a huge smile on her face.

'I think I died and went to heaven,' she said, as out of breath as he was. It had been worth waiting for, and they rolled over in bed and looked at each other. 'Do you suppose it's like this for Charles-Edouard and Marya?' she asked him, propped up on one elbow, admiring him, as she traced a lazy finger down his chest, and he laughed.

'I hope not. It would kill them.' He kissed her then, and she fondled him. He was totally sated, but easily aroused again. He had years to catch up on, and it had been a long time for her too. They made up for it that night. And again the next morning. Neither of them wanted to get out of bed. They just wanted to lie in each other's arms.

Francesca went downstairs to make them coffee, and there were some rolls in the freezer that she heated up for them in the microwave. And then they went back to bed. There wasn't a house around them for miles, and the view was beautiful. They finally got up and walked around the property, just so they could tell Marya they had, and then they went back to bed for the afternoon.

And they called Marya to thank her for the house and tell her how much they loved it.

'I'm so glad you do,' she said happily. 'It's very romantic, isn't it?' She giggled like a girl, and Francesca smiled.

'Yes, it is,' she agreed.

'I never realized that until recently. I just thought it was a pretty house.'

Francesca knew that they would never forget the days they spent there. They made themselves go to a local tavern for dinner, where Marya said the food was very good, and she was right. And they took a walk in her orchards afterward by moonlight, and then they came back and sat on the porch, and huddled together and kissed. Neither of them wanted to go back to New York. They wanted to stay there forever. She envied Marya the house, and would have loved to spend weeks there with Chris instead of just a few days.

She smiled as she looked up at him, as they sat on the porch swing, swaying slowly. 'You know, for two relationship-phobics, I think we're doing pretty well. What do you think?'

'I think you're turning me into a sex maniac. It's all I can think of,' he confessed with a grin. 'Are you putting something in my food?'

'Yeah, saltpeter. I can hardly sit down.' They both laughed. It was the perfect honeymoon weekend and just what they needed. It was the final bond to each other, and the only one they'd been missing. They had the friendship they'd built over many months, the romance that had sprung up between them since the summer, and now this, the union of their bodies to complete what they felt for each other. The circle of their love was complete.

'Would you ever want to get married, Francesca?' he asked as he held her.

'I never have before. I was afraid I'd end up like my mother, married fourteen times.'

'Be nice. Only five,' he teased her.

'I figured once was too many. My father cheated on everybody. My mother married everybody. I never wanted to do either, and I was afraid to have kids,' she said honestly. 'That seemed like too much to me. What if you screw it up? You ruin a whole human being.' Chris was struck by the irony of it, as he listened to her. She would have made a wonderful mother but hadn't had children because she was afraid to hurt someone or do something wrong. And Kim, who was a walking mine-field and human disaster area, hadn't hesitated to have Ian, and wanted more. Once he realized what a mess she was, Chris wouldn't let her, although he would have loved to have more children. 'I think Ian is the first child who has ever made me wish I'd had some of my own. But I'm still not convinced you have to get married to have them. That's a double jeopardy I was never ready to face.'

'I think it's nicer if you are. It's a statement about commitment and believing in the other person.' He thought about it for a minute and then shrugged. 'What do I know? Look what a catastrophe my marriage was.' But look at who he had married.

'It probably helps if you marry the right person.'

'I couldn't have married a worse one. I must have been blind, but she talked a good game, and we were both young. I'd know better now.'

'Would you ever marry again?' She didn't think he would and was stunned by his answer.

'I would with you,' he said softly, and she didn't respond. It was a long time before she did.

'That terrifies me. I don't want to screw up what we have.'

'If it's right, it makes it better. If it's wrong, it makes you wish you'd never been born. I can't imagine feeling that way with you.' She kissed him and put a finger to his lips then. She didn't want him to say anything she wasn't ready to hear. But he told her he loved her that night, in the big four-poster bed. And she told him she loved him too. They fell asleep in each other's arms.

They woke up when the sun rose the next morning, and had breakfast on the porch. It was cold, but the air was crisp, and they drank coffee in their bathrobes and sat on the porch swing again under a blanket. She was thinking about their conversation of the night before, about marriage, but she didn't mention it, and neither did he. It was also on Chris's mind, but he didn't want to unnerve her, so he didn't bring it up again.

They made love again that afternoon, and changed the

sheets on the four-poster for Marya. They had done their dishes, and Francesca left her a note on the kitchen table. 'Thank you for the most beautiful weekend of my life.' Chris looked at it and crossed out the last two words and wrote 'our lives.' She smiled and kissed him.

'Thank you too,' she said to him, and he carried their bags out to his car.

They turned on the alarm and locked the door. They drove away just as the sun was setting, and Francesca leaned over and kissed him, and he smiled. 'I love you, Chris.'

'I love you too, Francesca.' He reached over and touched her cheek, and they drove in silence for a while. There was so much to think about, and remember. Everything felt exactly the way things were meant to be. Neither of them had ever felt that way before.

Chapter 19

For the next few weeks, all Francesca and Chris could think about was the wonderful weekend they had had in Vermont. Marya was thrilled that they had used the house and said they could go there anytime they liked.

They had been planning to behave until they could go away again, but by the next day they realized how impossible that was for both of them. They waited for Ian to fall asleep, and then Chris sneaked upstairs to be with her. They locked her door and made love as passionately as they had in Vermont. And afterward he went back downstairs to Ian.

Chris complained about it one night when he had to leave her. He hated to get out of bed, and go back downstairs and spend the night without her. But they had no other choice.

'You can't just move up here and leave him down there,' she said sensibly. 'Then he'd resent us.'

'I know. I just miss you when I'm downstairs. You're too far away.' She loved that he felt that way, and she did too.

They overslept one morning, and Ian nearly caught them. She called Marya on her cell phone and asked her to lure him down to the kitchen. A few minutes later Chris walked in with the newspaper under his arm, and claimed he'd been picking it up outside. Ian never suspected that he'd been upstairs in bed with Francesca, and without Marya's help, they would have been trapped.

Sometimes after they made love, they took a bath together in her huge tub and just talked. Most of the time, afterward, they wound up back in bed. They were golden days. It was a November they both knew they would never forget. And everyone in the house was excited about Thanksgiving.

Thalia had announced to Francesca that she was going to spend it with friends in San Francisco. There was a man they wanted her to meet there who had a big yacht. And her father and Avery were going to Sun Valley to spend the holiday with old friends. Chris's family was gathering in Martha's Vineyard for the holiday, as they always did, but he wanted to stay in New York with her this year. Charles-Edouard and Marya offered to cook a traditional turkey dinner, and Chris and Francesca accepted with glee. Francesca had nowhere to go, and Chris didn't want to go home. He wanted to have Thanksgiving with Francesca and Ian, at home. The house on Charles Street was their home now.

The meal Charles-Edouard and Marya prepared for them was a feast. There was every possible kind of vegetable and trimming, a turkey that looked like a photograph in a magazine, and some touches that were purely French. Others were traditional, cranberries, and chestnut purée, mashed potatoes, biscuits, peas, carrots, spinach, asparagus with Marya's fabulous hollandaise. It was easily the best Thanksgiving the Americans in the group had ever had. They could hardly move when they left the table, and Charles-Edouard and Chris stood in the garden, smoking their cigars and drinking Château d'Yquem, their favorite sauterne. Charles-Edouard had definitely introduced them to some of the finer things in life. Chris loved his Cuban cigars but never smoked them in the house, and only one after a great meal, like now.

Marya and Francesca cleaned up in the kitchen, and Ian fell asleep on the bed in Marya's room, watching TV.

Chris introduced Charles-Edouard to American football, and they were a cozy group. They weren't four strangers as they had been in the beginning. They were two couples now and a child. They were a solid unit of people who loved each other. For Francesca, it was a Thanksgiving where blessings were easy to count. In spite of the tragedy with Eileen at the end of the summer, it had been a good year.

And Francesca wasn't prepared for the announcement Marya and Charles-Edouard made after the game was over. Marya looked at him with a hesitant expression, and he nodded.

'We're going back to France,' she said with tears in her eyes.

'For Christmas?' Francesca asked her. It sounded like fun to her, but Marya shook her head.

'For six months, maybe longer. A year. Charles-Edouard has some business to do. He wants to close his restaurant, and find something else. He needs to tie up the details on the property settlement with his wife. And we need to spend some more time in Provence to finish the book. We just rented a house there. I hope you come and visit us,' she said, looking from Francesca to Chris, with tears brimming in her eyes. She didn't want to leave. But she was half of a couple now, and she didn't want to be here without him either. There were worse fates than spending a year in France, or even moving there, which they were discussing too.

Francesca looked shocked and very sad. 'Are you selling the house in Vermont too?' Marya shook her head. 'I couldn't. You can use it anytime you want. Charles-Edouard promised that we can spend a month there next summer. I don't think we'll be back before then.' His life was really in France, he had spent the past four months in the States for Marya, but he needed to get back. He had a lot to do there, and a business to run or sell. It was running off the rails in his absence. He had to go back and make some decisions.

Francesca couldn't imagine the house without her now, nor could Chris. And he knew Ian would be sad too. She was like a grandmother to him, and much nicer and more present on a daily basis than the ones he had. He was the grandchild she would never have, especially since Charles-Edouard had no children either.

'I want you two to promise that you'll come over to see us, whenever you want. We're family now,' she said, hugging both of them. They felt that way too.

They went up to Francesca's living room then to talk about their plans. Chris put Ian to sleep in his own bed, and the child had never stirred as he carried him upstairs. And then he came down and lit a fire.

Francesca asked them if they were getting married, and Marya smiled. 'Not yet. But Charles-Edouard has been very well behaved! I'm impressed.' And so were they. He was still totally French in all the best ways, but his roving eye seemed to have been checked. He only had eyes for Marya. She trusted him completely, and he assured her she was right to do so. He had never said that to his wife. He was an honest man, even if he hadn't been a faithful one until now. He had always admitted to his affairs when asked. He didn't lie to Arielle, nor would he to Marya.

Marya said they had only decided to go back to France in the past few weeks. And it had been a hard decision for her. But it made sense and felt right to both of them, and was a whole new life for her, and for them.

'When are you leaving?' Francesca asked with bated breath.

'In a month. Charles-Edouard wants to be back in Paris for Christmas. We'll probably leave on the twenty-third of December.' Francesca knew it would mean their giving up their room on Charles Street. They didn't need a room in New York if they were living in Paris. They could stay with her whenever they came back, but there was no reason for them to pay rent in New York. It was going to be a financial challenge for Francesca, but this time she didn't think about selling the house. She and Chris and Ian were happy there. She'd have to find a way to make it work. But she didn't want to take in roommates again. There would never be another Marya. And she didn't want to risk another Eileen. It had been too traumatic.

'I hope you stay here when you come to New York,' Francesca said sadly, and Marya hugged her.

'We will. And you'll have a home with us in Paris. You can send Ian over to visit anytime,' she said to Chris. 'It would be wonderful for us and exciting for him.'

'Do you think you'll ever live in the States again if you two get married?' Francesca asked her.

'We don't know. It depends what Charles-Edouard does when he reshuffles his business.' He had to make some adjustments after giving half of what he had to his ex-wife, which seemed fair to him. Divorce was expensive. He never complained about it, even to Marya.

Their announcement was a big change, and bittersweet for all of them. They were losing beloved friends, or at least on a daily basis. And Charles-Edouard was part of their family unit now too.

Ian cried when they told him about it the next morning, and Francesca felt that way too. She'd been depressed since Marya announced it. And Ian didn't want them to

315

leave. Marya told him he could come to visit in Paris and see the Eiffel Tower and the Arc de Triomphe and ride on the Bateaux Mouches on the Seine.

'But I don't speak French,' he said mournfully.

'Lots of people in Paris speak English,' she reassured him, 'and Charles-Edouard and I will help you. We'll take care of you, and I want your dad and Francesca to come too.' He nodded, but he wasn't convinced. It was too far away. Ian loved them both, and they loved him.

And on Sunday Chris found Francesca poring over the bills in her office. It reminded her of the days when she was trying to save her house and her business, and afraid she could do neither. Marya leaving was going to make things very tight. She was struggling with the numbers again, and they didn't look good. She had never rented Eileen's room again and she didn't intend to. The top floor had been closed since August, and Francesca wanted to leave it that way. The memories in that room were too awful, and she didn't want anyone up there, out of respect for Eileen. The rooms were clean and empty and kept locked. She hadn't been up there herself since the murder. And Brad still hadn't gone to trial and probably wouldn't for many months. The police had stayed in touch with her. She had often thought of calling Eileen's mother, but she never had. She had the feeling they wouldn't welcome her call. She was planning on sending them a note over Christmas, and had written a heartfelt condolence letter when Eileen died, saying what a wonderful girl she was. They had never responded. Maybe they just didn't know what to say or how to do it.

Chris saw her worried expression as Francesca went over the bills.

'Bad news?'

'Sort of. I don't know why, but we had a bad month at the gallery in November. We hardly sold anything. October was great, and September was pretty good. Every time I think we're getting solid, something slips. I don't have a lot of cushion from it, and I'm still paying that damn plumber bill from the big leak.' Two thousand dollars was a lot at one gulp for her. The plumber had allowed her to do it in two payments, which helped, but she still had to pay it. 'It's kind of a blow that Marya's leaving, in more ways than one,' she said sadly. 'I'm going to miss her so much.' She was both surrogate mother and friend to her now, and good at both. Francesca loved chatting with her every day. They all did. 'And I don't want to rent Eileen's room again. I just can't. And no one would want it anyway. What happened there is too heavy for anyone to want to live in that room. And I don't want to take strangers in again. It's too risky.' In the end, she

317

had decided that her mother was right for once, although she'd been lucky. But it seemed too high-risk now, and too intrusive.

'You did okay with me,' he teased her, and she smiled. She was so happy with him.

'Yes, I did.' But now she was losing two-thirds of her income from the house, with no Marya and no Eileen. That was a big chunk to her, and made things very difficult for her again. Marya's lease had been about to end anyway. And so was his.

'How did you manage when Todd was here?' he asked, curious about it. He had never asked her that before.

'We each paid half of the mortgage payment. It was tight, but I managed, and it worked. I can't carry it alone.'

'What if I split it with you, and we don't rent to anyone, and just live here like a family, the three of us.'

'That would work,' she said thoughtfully, 'but I don't think that's fair to you. You only live in two rooms.' He laughed when she said it.

'I was thinking I could move upstairs with you, if you like that idea. And Ian can stay in my room. I can even pay two-thirds if you like, since there are two of us, and only one of you.' He was being generous and fair, and he wanted to make things easier for her. He could afford to. He lived simply and there was nothing showy about him.

His graphic design business did well, and she suspected he had family money, given who his family was. He was a modest person, but he didn't have to struggle as she did. For her, everything was tight, and she didn't want to sell the last of her father's paintings if she didn't have to. She was still sad she had sold the others.

'I think we should split it fifty-fifty, if you want to,' Francesca said cautiously, grateful for his help. 'We could turn your whole suite into Ian's room, with a playroom, use the living room downstairs, sleep in my room, and we could turn Marya's room into a den or an office for you. It would make a nice office.' It was sunny and bright with a view of the garden. 'You can smoke Cuban cigars there,' she teased him. But it all made sense and would work.

'I like that idea. I don't want you taking tenants in again either,' Chris said simply. 'I think it's too risky too.' And at least the house was hers now. If Chris ever left, and they broke up, she could think about roommates again, but if he paid half, for now she wouldn't have to.

'That would work,' Francesca said again, gratefully. 'I was getting worried.' He could see that she was, and he was sorry it was so difficult for her. He had suspected that Marya leaving would put an additional burden on her, and didn't realize how heavy. Francesca lived with very little to spare. And Chris wanted to help her. He would be by splitting the mortgage payment with her, although it doubled his rent, but he'd have use of the whole house now. And they were going to be living there like a couple with a child, not just four roommates. 'I've got some other ideas about how to make things easier for you,' he said simply. 'Maybe we can talk about that another time.' She nodded, wondering what they were. But for now he had solved her problem, and she was deeply grateful.

Marya asked her if she was going to be okay, when they cooked dinner together that night. 'I feel terrible leaving you in the lurch on such short notice, but Charles-Edouard kind of sprang it on me a few weeks ago, and I didn't agree to it till last week. Will you be all right here?'

'I will now,' Francesca said, looking relieved. 'Chris is going to help me.'

'I was hoping he would. What are your plans now, the two of you?'

'No plans for the moment.' Francesca smiled at her. 'We're just going to live here and hope for the best and see how it works out.' Marya hoped they would get married eventually, and Francesca was hoping the same for her. Charles-Edouard wanted to marry her as soon as his divorce came through. The dissolution papers were going to court in a few weeks, to be stamped by the judge, and then he'd be free. But Marya was in no hurry.

Nor was Francesca. She'd been avoiding marriage all her life, and didn't want to change her mind about it now, no matter how much she loved Chris, and she did. 'I don't want to be like my mother.' She had said that to Marya before, and to Chris.

'You couldn't be in a million years,' Marya reassured her. 'She's a completely different woman than you are. I like her, but you're just not playing in the same league she is.' Marya saw Thalia for what she was, a frivolous, spoiled, selfish, superficial woman, even if she was amusing, and a bit of a caricature of herself. But Marya respected Francesca profoundly, and loved her, like a daughter or a niece. 'Even if you got married ten times, you wouldn't be anything like her.'

'I'd rather not risk it. I wonder if she'll ever find another victim. She's been shopping for number six for years. You'd think she'd get tired of it and forget it, but she never will. She'll want to get married again when she's ninety.' They both laughed and suspected it was true.

She and Chris talked about their plans for the house that night. She was wondering when they should tell Ian.

'Do you think he'll be upset if you move upstairs with me?' She looked worried, and Chris kissed her.

'Stop worrying. He'll be thrilled to have his own

playroom. I'm going to get him a big TV so he can watch movies. And we'll just be up one flight of stairs.' They were both excited about finally sharing a bedroom. It was becoming a real life, not just a romance.

They had a lot to think about and to talk about, and Francesca reminded him that the following weekend they were going to Miami for Art Basel. It was one of the finest art fairs in the world, second only to the one held in Basel, Switzerland, in June. And there were a dozen other smaller art fairs being held in Miami that weekend too. Francesca could hardly wait, and Chris was coming with her. She was still shaken by Marya moving to Paris, and especially so soon, but they had a lot to look forward to, and their life together was just beginning.

He wanted her to come to Boston to be with his family for Christmas. Francesca had said she would, and Ian wanted her to, but the thought of it scared her to death. What if they hated her or thought she wasn't good enough for him? She was just a little art dealer in the West Village, and the daughter of a famous artist. His family was chock full of important people.

'They're going to love you. I promise,' Chris reassured her. She decided to postpone worrying about it till after Miami. Between Marya leaving, switching the house around when she left, Christmas with his family, and the art fair in Miami in less than a week, December was going to be busy.

Chapter 20

Marya and Charles-Edouard had agreed to baby-sit for Ian, when Chris and Francesca left for Miami for the weekend. She could hardly wait to see the different art fairs. There was Scope and Red Dot, and fourteen others, along with Art Basel, which was the finest in the world. The work that was exhibited there would sell for a fortune. Her father's dealer had a booth, her father and Avery went every year, and she had promised to call them. Francesca and Chris were staying at the Delano, and when Chris saw it, he loved it. Each of the elevators was lit up in a different color, and the rooms had been designed by Philippe Starck. The weather was balmy and warm when they arrived, and Chris was dying to spend some time at the pool. Francesca wanted to go straight to the fair and get started. They'd be seeing more art in the next few days than most people saw in years.

Art Basel was at the Convention Center in Miami Beach in an enormous hall, and the others were at the Ice Palace and scattered around the city in different locations. Some of the smaller fairs had taken over hotels, and each room was rented by a different dealer. And there were parties in a dozen locations, in discos and hotels and restaurants. Francesca had received a stack of invitations. It was Chris's introduction into the serious art world, by total immersion. He was excited about sharing it with her, and willingly put himself in her hands. But he stopped her before they left the room, and they wound up in bed for half an hour. It was a nice way to start the trip. They showered, changed, and went out.

They caught a cab at the hotel, and went to the Convention Center. There was a separate building for younger artists and more avant-garde work. Francesca's dream was to show at one of the smaller fairs in Miami one day. She was planning to apply to Red Dot the following year, but didn't feel she was ready for it yet. And she expected to spend several years on the waiting list. Getting into art fairs was extremely political, and often depended on who you knew. She had a great in through her father, but she hadn't traded on it yet. She would if she absolutely had to.

'I'm never afraid to grovel for my artists,' she said to Chris, and he laughed as they got out of the cab at the huge hall. She had a pass from her father's dealer to get in, and a few minutes later they were walking down the aisles, stopping at each booth to check out the art. Chris was amazed at what they saw. There were an infinite number of traditional dealers, selling important paintings. He saw three Picassos in less than five minutes, at astronomical prices. He saw a Matisse, a Chagall, two de Koonings, a Pollock, and two of her father's paintings were exhibited by his dealer. One had a red dot next to it, which meant it was already sold. The other had a white dot, which meant it was on hold for a client. You had to have a big budget to buy there.

'Where does all this stuff come from?' Chris said in amazement. He had never seen so much art in his life, and the high caliber of the artists shown there was impressive.

'Europe, the States, Hong Kong.' Dealers from all over the world were showing there, and had flown in from everywhere. There were also a vast number of avant-garde galleries that were showing art that was intended to shock. There were video installations, conceptual art, and in one booth a huge mound of sand on the floor. It was selling for a hundred thousand dollars, and installed by the artist, who was well known.

Chris made comments as they walked along, and Francesca told him who some of the artists were. She loved being there with him, and they stayed until nearly eight o'clock, and after that they took a cab to a party she'd been invited to at a restaurant called Bed, where people sat and lay on mattresses and ate dinner. Every conversation they heard around them was about art and artists, the quality of the show, the expensive pieces that had already sold. Francesca ran into a lot of people she knew and introduced them to Chris. She was having a ball and loved every minute of it, and he was enjoying himself too. This was her world, and it fascinated him. Everyone seemed to know her.

They didn't get back to the hotel until two A.M., after stopping at another party hosted by a dealer at a disco. They danced for a little while and then went home, and fell into bed in their stark white room at the Delano. They were dead to the world when Ian woke them up the next morning. He had just bought a Christmas tree with Marya, and they were making decorations. They were going to bake some of them to hang on the tree, and he sounded excited. Chris smiled at Francesca proudly after they hung up. Ian promised to call them back later.

'He's such a great kid, isn't he?' Chris said, cuddling up to her in bed.

'Yes, he is,' she agreed, 'and so are you.' She kissed him, and they got up a few minutes later. And an hour after that they were back at the fair. They stayed there all day until Chris begged for mercy, and said he couldn't look at another piece of art. They had almost finished with Art Basel by then, and she still wanted to see Red Dot and Scope, but she agreed to take a break, and spend an hour with him at the pool. He lay gratefully next to her, and looked ecstatic, as he held a beer.

'Jesus, they're not kidding when they say this is the biggest art fair in the world.' She laughed at his look of exhaustion. There was still a lot she wanted to see, although she didn't think they'd get to all the fairs. She had five on her list for the next day. They weren't going back to New York till the afternoon, on Monday, and that still didn't give them time to see it all.

By Sunday, Chris said he was on art overload, and she laughed and said he looked just like Ian. He wanted to go back to the hotel and watch football. So she agreed to meet up with him later that afternoon.

They had dinner at a trendy restaurant in South Beach

that night, with her father and Avery and his dealer, who was a fascinating man. Chris had an interesting conversation with him about Italian art in the Middle Ages, which he had studied in school, and enjoyed a lengthy conversation with Francesca's father about his work. The two men seemed to get along famously, and Avery winked at Francesca from across the table, while she listened to their conversation with one ear. So far so good. She could tell from her father's expansiveness with Chris that he liked him, and she was pleased. 'I really like your guy,' Avery commented to her in a whisper as they left the restaurant. 'And I can tell your dad does too.' It would have been hard not to. Chris was intelligent, interesting, solid, nice to be with, and loved what he was learning about her world.

It was a nonstop art bath all weekend, and by Sunday night even Francesca was tired and happy to go back to the hotel. There were only three more shows she wanted to see the next day, and Chris flatly refused and said he was going to lie by the pool. She didn't mind his doing that. There was so much to see, and so many people she knew, that she was fine being on her own. And she and Avery went to two of the smaller art fairs together, set up in small hotels, on Monday morning.

'I really like Chris,' Avery said casually as they strolled through the booths. 'And so does your father. He's intelligent and fun to talk to, and crazy about you. I like that a lot for you,' Avery said, smiling at her.

'I'm crazy about him too. I'm not renting to any more roommates when Marya leaves, by the way. Chris and I are going to split it.' Avery was relieved, and started chatting with a friend from a gallery in Cleveland, when Francesca heard her cell phone ring in her purse. It was Chris, and he sounded panicked.

'Where are you? How fast can you get back here?'

'I'm at one of the smaller fairs at some hotel near the beach. Why? What happened?' There was a lot of noise from people talking around her, and poor cell service in the hotel. She stepped into a hallway to try and hear him better. She had no idea what he was talking about, but she had never heard him sound so frightened.

'Kim grabbed Ian. From school. She's got him.' He was in tears.

'Oh my God. How did that happen?' Francesca was panicked for Chris and Ian. Especially Ian. They knew that she had gotten out of jail two weeks before, and was at a fancy rehab in New Jersey. She was due to stay there till Christmas, but she could walk out of it anytime she wanted to, and Chris had been sure she would. He had told Marya to be careful. They had hardly gone out all weekend, except to buy the tree. She had kept Ian busy making decorations and baking cookies.

'She showed up at his school this morning and said she had visitation with him and was taking him to a doctor's appointment for a booster shot. And they believed her. I guess Ian was happy to see her, and went with her. The school just called me to verify it. But she had already run out the back door. I don't know where he is,' Chris said. 'I have no idea what she'll do with him, or where she'll go.'

'She can't be that crazy,' Francesca said, trying to calm him down, and he shouted at her for the first time ever.

'Yes, she is!' he roared over the phone. 'I'm going to kill his fucking school. They know he's not supposed to be with her without supervision. I gave them a copy of the court order. How fast can you get back here? Where are you? There's a one o'clock flight to New York. I want to be on it.'

'I'm not sure exactly where I am. We went to another fair before this.'

'I'll pack your stuff. Meet me at the airport. United Airlines.' Francesca went back to find Avery and told her what had happened. And Avery looked as worried as she was.

'Do you think he'll be all right? She wouldn't hurt him, would she?'

'I don't think so. Not intentionally. She's more likely to hurt herself, doing something crazy. Maybe she just wants to scare Chris, or show him she can do whatever she wants. She's pretty nuts.' All she could think of was the list of horrors she had heard at the hearing. But Ian was eight years old now. He was resourceful and could take care of himself better than most kids his age. He had had to whenever he was with his mother.

Francesca kissed Avery goodbye in haste, ran outside and caught a passing cab, and told him to take her to the airport. She was wearing running shoes, jeans, and a T-shirt, but she would have boarded the plane in a bathing suit to be with Chris. He looked frantic when she found him at the airport. He had just checked her bags in, and was carrying her coat.

'Maybe she took him to her apartment,' she suggested. 'Can you call the police?'

'I already did,' he said, looking tense. He looked as though his nerves were raw. 'I don't know why Ian went with her. He knows better, and he knows he's not supposed to.'

'She's his mother,' Francesca said gently, as they ran

toward the gate. They had barely made it, and were the last passengers on the flight.

'She's not answering her cell phone. The police are looking for her now. I told them I think Ian is in danger. And I believe he is. The woman is insane.'

They boarded the plane, and took their seats. And Chris hardly spoke on the flight. It was the longest three hours of her life, watching him, and knowing he was dying inside. He was terrified for his son. Francesca didn't even try to talk to him after a while. She just held his hand. Chris drank two straight scotches on the plane. And he dozed for a few minutes after that. There was nothing they could do until they landed.

They took a cab at the airport, and Marya was waiting for them at the house. It wasn't her fault, but she felt terrible anyway. Chris had checked with the police the minute they landed, but they had nothing yet. They had gone to her apartment, and she wasn't there. The elevator man and doorman hadn't seen her since she got out of jail and left for rehab. Chris sat in the kitchen on Charles Street, with his head in his hands, trying to figure out where she was. Where would she take him? And then suddenly he had an idea. He looked like a madman as he stared at them both, and right then he was.

'If she's not out buying drugs, or dead in an alley

somewhere, there's a bar on the West Side where she used to take him. They have pinball machines and arcade games. He loves it, and it's close to her dealer.' He had given the police her dealer's address too, or the last one he knew of, from Ian.

Chris ran out of the house before they could stop him, and Francesca followed him down the stairs at full speed. She didn't even bother to take her coat although it was cold.

'Go back inside. I'll call you if I find him.' He looked distracted and still frightened as he hailed a cab.

'I want to come with you,' she said, as he hesitated and yanked open the door. He didn't want her to see what this was like, but she loved Ian too, and she was part of his life now, even this. He slid over, and she jumped in. He told the driver where they were going and said they were in a hurry. The driver made good time up the West Side Highway, and they were there in ten minutes. It looked like a sleazy place that would have frightened Francesca otherwise. They were open. And Chris pulled open the door and walked in. It was dark inside, and all he could see were the lit-up machines that blinded him for a minute. There was a bartender wiping down the bar, and two waitresses with heavy cleavage, short nylon uniforms, and fishnet stockings. Two men were playing with the machines. And then he saw him, in a back corner, play-ing an arcade game, a tiny figure standing in front of the machine. There was a woman with him, sprawled across the table next to him. She looked like she was asleep. Chris had the boy in his arms in a minute, lifted him off the ground, and took a long hard look at him. There were tears streaming down Chris's cheeks, and he didn't even know it. Francesca was crying with relief. Ian's eyes were huge in his face.

'Are you okay?' Chris asked him, and Ian nodded.

'I'm fine.' Ian's voice was small as his father held him. 'She's sick.' Which meant she had just shot up. She looked it. This was not a new scene to Chris, or Ian.

'I'll take care of it,' Chris said through a clenched jaw and handed him to Francesca. Kimberly hadn't stirred. 'Take him back to the house.' Francesca nodded, and Ian took her hand as they walked out, as Chris jabbed his finger into his ex-wife's shoulder. She didn't move, and he suddenly wondered if she had OD'd while Ian played the machines. He felt for a pulse in her neck, and while he was looking for it, she groaned, and then threw up all over the table where she lay. Her face was lying in it. One of the waitresses saw what happened and came over with a towel. Chris pulled her head back with a hunk of hair clenched in his fist. She opened her eyes as the vomit dripped off her face. And hating her, he cleaned it. Heroin always did that to her, especially if she hadn't had any for a while. And she'd been in rehab for two weeks. It was an easy way to OD after being clean.

'Oh . . . hi . . .' she said vaguely. 'Where's Ian?'

'He went home.' And then without even knowing he'd done it, he put a hand around her neck and squeezed. Her eyes opened wide as she stared at him, but she was too high to even be frightened, just confused. 'If you ever do that again . . . if you ever touch him, grab him, take him anywhere . . . see him without supervision . . . I swear, Kim, I'll kill you.' And as he stood there nearly choking her, he wanted to. For one crazed uncontrollable moment he wanted to snap her neck, and then with his whole body shaking, he let go. 'Don't you *ever* come near him again and take him with you when you shoot up and to a place like this.' Without another word, he pulled her to her feet then, and she staggered toward him. He dragged her outside into the sunlight, and she threw up again and then looked better. 'I hate you,' he said when she glanced at him. 'I hate everything about you, and what you did to our life . . . I hate what you do to him. He doesn't deserve this.' And worst of all, Chris hated who he was when he was anywhere near her. She was a poison that filled him with rage. For an instant in the bar, he had wanted to kill her. No one could do that to him except her, and she wasn't worth it. She never had been. A sob caught in his throat as he held her up with one hand and hailed a cab with the other. An empty cab came to a stop next to him. He opened the door and pushed her in. She reeked of vomit and so did he. She was thirty-two years old, and a once beautiful woman, but there was nothing left of what she had been.

Chris gave the driver forty dollars and her father's address, and he looked down at Kim with disgust and the dying embers of his fury. 'Go see your father. He'll take care of you. And stay away from Ian until you're clean.'

'Thank you,' she said, trying to focus on him, and then she laid her head back against the seat and closed her eyes. Chris looked at her and slammed the door of the cab. He was shaking all over as they drove away. He had almost killed her. He had wanted to, which terrified him. He walked for a few blocks and hailed another cab and got in. He gave him the address on Charles Street, and stared silently out the window all the way there, realizing that his life and Ian's would have been destroyed if he had lost control and killed her. He never wanted to see her again. She was the worst thing that had ever happened to him. And Ian was the best thing. He tried to focus on that on the ride home.

Chapter 21

Chris could hear Marya and Francesca in the kitchen with Ian when he got home. Charles-Edouard was cooking something for them. And Chris went upstairs, took a shower, and changed his clothes. He was still shaken by what he had almost done to her. He had been terrified all the way back from Miami. He never knew what kind of life-threatening situation she would put their son in.

He looked shaken and subdued as he walked down the stairs to the kitchen. Ian looked up at him with the thousand-year-old eyes that ripped Chris's heart to shreds.

'Where's Mom?' He was worried, and afraid that his father was angry at him. He wasn't. He was scared. By what had happened, what could have happened, and what he had almost done. It was a wake-up call to him. He couldn't let her get to him again. Ever. He had almost lost control.

'I sent her to your grandfather's. He'll know what to do with her.' He would take her back to rehab, for the ten millionth time, and she would walk away again. Until one day she was dead. Chris didn't need to kill her. She was already dead, and had died years before when she started shooting up. She had done it even before they met. He just didn't know. 'She'll be okay, Ian.' For now. For a while. But not for long. She'd never be okay again. 'I'm sorry. I didn't mean to frighten you. I was very worried. I don't want you going off with her again. You can see her, but there has to be someone there.' Ian nodded, and Chris walked toward him and gave him a long hug. 'I'm sorry you had to see that.' He had seen it a thousand times before. He wondered how you apologize to your son for giving him a mother like that. Or worse, if he had killed her. The thought made him shudder and Ian felt it. He felt sorry for his dad.

'It's okay. She wasn't too bad. Just a little sick.' It was pathetic that that was his definition of 'not too bad.' They had both seen her much worse. Chris wanted to take another bath, to scrub his insides and his mind, and all the memories from Ian's memory too. But he knew he couldn't do that. And one day Ian would have to sort it all out for himself. It was the legacy she had left him. They had been to hell and back with her. Chris turned and saw Francesca then for the first time. He hadn't even noticed her when he walked into the room. He smiled at her and saw how upset she was too. It had been a horrifying scene, and it only got worse after she left.

'Thank you for bringing Ian home.' He sat down at the kitchen table, and Francesca sat down next to him and looked into his eyes.

'It's okay, Chris. You're both going to be fine.' She smiled at Ian then, and he cuddled up next to her, and she took him in her arms. 'Well, that was a little bit of excitement.' She smiled at Ian, and he laughed, and they all slowly began to unwind.

Marya made them something to eat, and then she and Ian showed Chris and Francesca all the Christmas decorations they'd made over the weekend. The little tree looked beautiful, and Ian looked proud. And little by little the nightmare they'd just been through began to slip from their minds. It could have been much worse.

'Why don't we all go up to Vermont next weekend?' Marya suggested. 'It's probably going to be our last chance, and it would be fun to be there together.' Francesca loved the idea. It was where their life as a couple began. Ian loved the idea too, and even Chris smiled.

It wasn't until late that afternoon that Chris had a moment alone with Francesca in her room.

'I'm sorry you had to see that. It's not a pretty part of my life.' He was as ashamed as though he had done it. He was more ashamed at what he had almost done to his ex-wife.

'It's not your fault,' she said quietly, and put her arms around him. 'I'm glad I was there.'

'So am I.' He might have been even crazier if she weren't.

He kissed her, and felt as though he were being lifted out of the past. With her, it was a whole new life. Kim was the nightmare, and Francesca was the dream.

As Marya had suggested, they all went to Vermont that weekend, and they all had a good time. They played in the snow, went for long walks, and took photographs of each other. They went to local restaurants and taverns. Chris took Ian to a nearby ski resort early Sunday morning, rented skis, and took a few runs with him. They all wanted to cling to every minute. They didn't know when they'd be together again. Charles-Edouard decided it for them.

'You're all coming to the South of France next summer. Marya and I are going to rent a villa. In July. We want the three of you to come over.' Ian clapped his hands and looked thrilled, and Chris and Francesca agreed. Marya and Charles-Edouard were coming to Vermont in August, so they would see them again then. This wasn't the last chapter in their friendship. It was just the beginning. They were all starting new lives now. Chris had told Ian that morning that he was moving upstairs with Francesca, and Ian was going to have his own room from then on.

'That's good,' Ian said solemnly, ''cause you snore.' Francesca laughed when he said it.

'Now you tell me,' she said, but she was relieved that Ian wasn't upset.

They sang Christmas carols in French and English on the ride back to New York, and Marya had given them the keys to the house in Vermont and told them to use it whenever they wanted. It was going to be wonderful for them.

Ian fell asleep on the drive home. And Chris carried him in when they got back. He stirred for a minute and looked at his father as though he had something important to tell him.

'Can we get a dog?'

Chris laughed. 'Sure. What kind of dog?'

'A Great Dane,' Ian said with a sleepy smile.

'Forget it. Maybe a dachshund, or a Lab.' Ian nodded and went back to sleep in his father's arms. And a minute later he put Ian on the top bunk and covered him with a blanket, and then he walked upstairs to see Francesca. She was unpacking from the weekend in Vermont, and she turned and smiled when he walked in. He couldn't believe his good luck in having found her. And she felt the same way about him.

'Can I sleep here tonight? My bunk mate is dead to the world.'

'Sure.' She liked the idea too. It had been nice sharing a room with him all weekend, and hard to be apart once they got home.

He lay in bed, watching her undress and put on her nightgown. He could hardly wait to watch her do that every night.

'I'm really going to miss Marya,' she said sadly, as she got into bed next to him. He slept in his T-shirt and boxers. His socks were on the floor with his jeans and shirt. He was already at home in her bed.

'We'll see them in Europe next summer. That'll be fun.' She nodded. And they were both excited to use the house in Vermont. It was an incredibly generous gift to them. They were very special friends.

'Do you think they'll get married?' Francesca asked him as they lay in the dark in her bed. She loved having him there next to her, and waking up with him in the morning.

'Probably. They act like they already are.' Francesca was looking forward to getting to that point with Chris. They weren't there quite yet. In some ways it was going to be good for them to have the house to themselves, although they would all miss Marya and Charles-Edouard.

'Goodnight,' Francesca whispered to Chris, as she cuddled up next to him and drifted off to sleep. Chris smiled at her, and lay looking at her for a long time. And then he drifted off too and held her in his arms all night.

Chapter 22

Marya and Charles-Edouard's last week in New York was totally chaotic. Francesca helped Marya pack. They were sorting everything and shipping things everywhere, to Paris, and to Vermont. She gave most of her cooking utensils to Francesca, and threw a lot of things out.

'It's amazing what you can collect in a studio apartment in one year,' Marya said, looking around. There were boxes everywhere, and even a stack of things for Goodwill. They'd been packing for days. And Francesca's mother came to say goodbye to her too. She was flying to Zurich in two days on her way to Gstaad.

'I'll call you in Paris the next time I'm there,' she promised. 'And don't invite me to the wedding if you marry Charles-Edouard,' she teased her. 'I'd be much too jealous.' The man with the yacht that she'd met in San Francisco over Thanksgiving hadn't panned out. She was still looking for number six, but Charles-Edouard wouldn't have fit the bill either. Marya was more his type than she was.

'We're not in any rush,' Marya reassured her.

'What's happening with Francesca and Chris?' Thalia asked her as Marya handed her a gift. It was one of her cookbooks that Thalia had said she wanted and couldn't find because it was no longer in print. Thalia thanked her and smiled.

'They seem very happy. They're just getting started. I think it'll take a while for them to figure it out. He went through an awful lot with his ex-wife. And Francesca is very cautious, as you know.' Marya poured them both a cup of tea. Thalia was going to miss her. She was her only conduit into her daughter's life. Francesca never told her anything.

They chatted about Paris for a while, and then Thalia stood up and hugged her. 'Take good care of yourself,' Thalia said softly. 'I'm going to miss you too, and not just to fill me in about Francesca.' She had become a good friend to them all, and Thalia was happy for her. Marya deserved all the happiness she had found with Charles-Edouard. She brought joy to a lot of people, and it was nice to see her getting her fair share of it back. The two women promised to stay in touch.

Thalia left Christmas gifts for Francesca, Chris, and Ian, and she told Francesca she'd call her from Gstaad. She was leaving for Europe the day before Marya, but she was going to be busy now until she left.

Avery dropped by to say goodbye to Marya too, and leave Christmas gifts for Francesca, Chris, and Ian. The one for Francesca was enormous, and it was easy to guess what it was. It was one of her father's paintings, to replace the five she had sold.

Francesca was thrilled when she saw it that night, and she had Chris help her hang it in the living room, and took down one she had never liked, by an artist she no longer represented. Chris loved the new one too. They had told Marya and Charles-Edouard all about the show in Miami, and Chris had admitted to being totally overwhelmed. 'I've never seen so much art in one place in my life.'

Marya said she would have loved to see it. She had always wanted to go to the June show in Basel. Maybe now, living in Paris, she would. There were so many things she wanted to do. She was sad to be leaving, but getting excited as the day approached. They were planning to spend Christmas in Courchevel with friends of

Charles-Edouard. It was a very fancy ski resort, with some excellent restaurants Marya was anxious to try out. It was going to be a much more exciting life than the one she'd had on Charles Street for the past year, or in Vermont before that. And Charles-Edouard moved around Europe a lot. He said he wanted to take her to Prague and Budapest.

And then the day finally arrived when they had to leave. It was wrenching, and Francesca and Marya both cried. Marya could hardly let go of Ian, and Charles-Edouard shepherded her gently toward the door, where a car was waiting to take them to the airport. She promised to e-mail, and she and Francesca stood for a last moment holding each other tight.

'Take good care,' Marya whispered, and Francesca was crying too hard to talk.

'I'm going to miss you so much,' she said finally through her tears. This felt like a huge loss to her. And Ian looked mournful too.

'I'll see you next summer, and talk to you long before that,' Marya promised as she bent to kiss Ian for a last time. Chris kept an arm around Francesca and held Ian's hand as the car finally drove away, and they all went back inside. The house was going to be deadly quiet without them. Francesca was glad they were going to

Boston in a few days, for Christmas with Chris's family. She was still nervous about meeting them, but it was going to be better than staying home in a house that seemed too big now without Marya and Charles-Edouard.

'I think our kitchen just lost five stars,' Chris said, smiling wistfully at her.

'What do you want for dinner? Pizza or Chinese takeout?' Francesca asked him, and he laughed, as Ian voted for Chinese.

'I think we're in trouble. One of us better learn to cook.' But Marya had actually taught her a number of her little tricks, if Francesca had time to do them. And Ian had become an expert at making all kinds of cookies. Charles-Edouard had left Chris a box of his favorite Cuban cigars. But the treasures they had left for them were no substitute for the people they had lost. It was going to be a big adjustment without them, and the house felt empty and sad for the rest of the week. It was going to be a relief to fly to Boston, and Ian was excited about seeing his cousins. Francesca was scared stiff. Chris had been giving her little hints about his family, that sounded like warnings. 'Conservative, stuffy, not as uptight as they look, religious, Old Guard.' They sounded like danger signs to her.

'What if your parents hate me?' she asked Chris in bed, the night before they left.

'Then I won't see them anymore,' he said matter-of-factly. 'You forget who I was married to before. She's not exactly a tough act to follow. My mother's a little serious, but my father's a good guy. They'll love you,' he reassured her.

'How is Kim, by the way?' Francesca asked carefully. 'Did you ever hear from her father?'

'My lawyer says she's back in rehab. It won't last. It never does.' He had given up hope. They had filed a report about her grabbing Ian from school, and she had been strongly reprimanded by the court through her attorney. They considered it a serious violation. Even Chris didn't think she'd do it again. She hadn't sent anything to Ian for Christmas. She always forgot, just like she did his birthday. There was no room in her life for holidays. She was too busy either trying to buy drugs, or get off them. It was a full-time job for her. Her addiction was her life.

Francesca's mother had given Ian a cute little leather bomber jacket, and he loved it. Francesca was touched that she had made the effort. She bought a silver pen set for Chris, and an evening bag for her, which she wasn't likely to wear often, but it was pretty. The bomber jacket for Ian more than made up for it. And Avery and her father had given him a beautiful drawing set with paints and pastels and pencils and colored pens, and he loved that too. His new substitute grandparents had done well by him. And Francesca loved the painting from her father, and went into the living room to see it every day.

She was going to get busy turning Marya's room into an office for Chris as soon as they got back from Boston. And he was excited about that. They were spreading out all over the house. It was starting to feel like her house again, not having to make space for roommates. Ian seemed to feel it too – he had left a pile of toys in the kitchen, and loved watching TV with his father in Francesca's bed at night, and climbing into bed with them on Sunday mornings. Chris and Ian had come home.

Chapter 23

It took Francesca hours to pack the night before they went to Boston. She wasn't sure what to bring. Dressy, not so dressy, polite suit for church on Christmas Eve? Cocktail dress for dinner? Too sexy? Too short? Too low cut? Too dreary? She didn't want to make a faux pas, and was terrified she would. Chris told her to forget it and wear jeans, but she knew that would be wrong too. She expected them to be conservative and stuffy, from everything Chris had said. She was hoping he had exaggerated a little. But she was worried. In the end, she took all the options with her, and had two heavy suitcases for the plane. Chris groaned when he saw them.

'What did you bring?' he asked with a look of dismay.

'Everything,' she said, smiling happily. She had taken

no chances and brought it all. And then she appeared with a third smaller suitcase full of presents for Chris, Ian, and Chris's parents. He managed to get it all in the car. And when they got to the airport, it was a zoo and the flight was late. It was snowing in Boston. They didn't get out till ten o'clock, and they landed in Boston before midnight. Chris's father was waiting for them, despite the late hour. He was a tall man like Chris, but had broader shoulders, a deep voice, and a firm grip as he shook Francesca's hand. He looked like the linebacker he had been at Harvard fifty years before. He gave Ian a warm look and shook his hand, which seemed unusually formal to Francesca, but he seemed like a nice man. They closed the airport in the snowstorm right after they landed, and the roads were covered as they drove slowly into Boston. The two men talked football and politics in the car. Chris had already warned her that he was considered the family black sheep for not going to Harvard and moving to New York. He didn't mention their objections to her house. He said they couldn't understand why he'd want to be a graphic designer instead of a politician or a banker. And Kim had been the icing on the cake. So they didn't approve of him, whatever they thought of her now. It made entering their world somewhat dicey for Francesca.

Chris's parents lived in Cambridge, on Brattle Street,

where the president of Harvard lived as well. All the men in his family had gone to school there, before becoming senators, governors, and presidents. They were an impressive bunch. Chris seemed so humble and unassuming, given the family he came from.

When they got to the house, his mother was waiting up for them. She was a small grandmotherly-looking woman with white hair and gray eyes like Chris. She was wearing a dark gray wool dress, and a string of pearls. There was nothing fashionable about her. She was totally unlike Francesca's mother. And she showed Francesca to her room herself. Sharing a room with Chris would have been out of the question, even if Ian weren't there. Chris's mother had put Francesca in a guest room as far down the hall as possible from Chris. Her room assignment made it clear that there was to be no hanky-panky in their house. Francesca was nervous as Chris winked and left her in her room, after his mother said goodnight. Francesca wondered if he'd be back later. And Ian was sleeping in the room with his father. It was Chris's boyhood room, and they had a full house, with Chris's brother and sister and their families and numerous other relatives and their children staying with them. The house was huge. Chris had explained who would be there and she couldn't keep track of any of them, the second cousins, an aunt, his siblings and their children. It was very confusing, with relatives and in-laws and their children, many of whom had the same first names. Francesca was sitting in her room, feeling a little dazed, when Chris walked back in, and quickly closed the door. Francesca had realized by then that his mother hadn't spoken directly to her, other than to greet her, and say goodnight.

'My mother is still wandering around. I'll be back later,' he said quickly, and Francesca rapidly understood that when he was at home, he followed their rules. Breaking them was not an option, even for him. It was one of the reasons he lived in New York, and had gone to Stanford on the West Coast. His parents had considered it treason.

'I take it you can't sleep here,' she whispered, and he laughed.

'My mother would call the vice squad and have us both thrown out. She's a very proper woman.'

'Got it.' He was thirty-eight years old and not allowed to have a girl in his room. But Chris knew his way around the system. They made her family look like wild libertines. And this was Boston. Old Boston. Old Guard.

Half an hour later, the house had gone quiet, and Chris tiptoed back in, barefoot in jeans. 'All set.' He had his toothbrush with him. All he had to do was escape back to his own room in the morning by seven, when his mother came down to breakfast, religiously, every morning. She ran a tight ship. And kept a close eye on what went on in her house, just as she did at the Vineyard. Nothing escaped her eagle eye.

'She's very old-fashioned,' he explained. He hadn't mentioned it before, and hadn't wanted to frighten Francesca. And as she thought about it, Francesca couldn't even imagine the chaos Kimberly must have caused there when they were married, doing drugs and getting drunk. His parents must have loved that. And they would like even less what she'd been doing lately, recently out of jail, and absconding with their grandson. Chris said they hated her, and it was easy to see why. She just hoped they didn't hate her too. Francesca was determined to respect them while she was there, even if their rules seemed silly to her.

They spent the night together in her room, and Chris set the alarm on his cell phone for quarter to seven. He bounded out of bed the moment it went off, kissed her, put on his jeans and shirt, and ran down the hall to his own room, where Ian was still sleeping. It was going to be an interesting weekend playing hide and seek in the hall, and musical bedrooms, to avoid his mother discovering them in the same room. He didn't mind standing up to them on important issues, and always had, but he didn't want to make waves now, and prejudice them against Francesca. If at all possible, he hoped they'd like her, and also relax their negative outlook on his living in her house. He wanted them to see what a good person she was, and how sweet to Ian.

Francesca almost expected Chris's mother to do room inspections, and was afraid she would. She had brought them a bottle of wine and wondered if it was enough of a gift for a whole weekend. Maybe she should have sent them flowers instead. They were so proper, she was afraid to do the wrong thing. Nothing about them put her at ease. And his mother had been polite but not warm the night before.

Chris had breakfast with his mother, and then came back to find Francesca while she was getting dressed. She had breakfast in the dining room with assorted house-guests at eight-thirty and found herself sitting next to Chris's sister Hilary, who was too busy taking care of her four-year-old twin boys to say more than hello. They were all going to church at ten, and Chris said it would be a good idea if she went. She had no objection, but clearly these people were used to doing everything together. It was a little like military school, or camp. And

Chris was much more uptight here than he was in New York. All the men were supposed to play golf together that afternoon, but Chris said they wouldn't if it snowed. And in summer they played football at the Vineyard. There were trophies for various athletic events all over the house. One of his cousins had won a gold medal in the Olympics. And his brother had been captain of the rowing team at Harvard. Francesca met him after breakfast, and he looked her over and said a cursory hello. He was four years older than Chris and planning to run for a congressional seat in the coming year. He introduced Francesca to his wife, and then they went upstairs to dress for church. They all seemed so different from Chris. They seemed like very competitive people to her. Tennis was a big deal to them, and football. All she knew anything about was art, not sports. She could barely contribute to the conversation at breakfast and hardly spoke. Chris could see how nervous she was when he found her afterward. She had worn black leather jeans and a black sweater. All the other women were wearing twin sets and plaid skirts, and none of them short. Francesca didn't own a plaid skirt, of any length.

She sat next to Chris's mother in church, with Chris next to her and Ian between them. His siblings and their families were on either side. She had the feeling that his mother could tell if she was praying or not, or faking it, and she had X-ray vision. Francesca had changed into a black suit to wear to church, and she felt overdressed. His mother was wearing a navy blue twin set and gray skirt. Francesca couldn't think of a single outfit she'd brought that seemed right. They had a kind of sporty but formal style. But his mother was extremely polite and very pleasant. His cousins seemed nice, and his father very jolly. And his siblings were distant but friendly. His grandfather had been governor of Massachusetts. They were a daunting lot. She couldn't imagine telling any of them that her mother had been married five times. His mother would have fainted. His parents had been married for forty-four years, to each other and not a whole collective. Francesca recognized that these people were the real deal, old-fashioned American aristocrats. It was a closed world, and Chris was the only one who seemed different. They were the definition of Old Guard.

It was stressful being there, but by late afternoon Francesca had started to relax. Several people had gone to play tennis at their club, or squash. The children had been whisked away somewhere. It snowed, so no one played golf, and they were expected to be downstairs for cocktails at six-thirty sharp. Dinner was at seven-thirty, and since it was Christmas Eve, it was a fairly formal event. The children would be eating at a separate table in the hall, adults in the formal dining room. And they were going back to church at eleven-thirty for midnight mass. His mother said it was optional, which Chris said meant you had to be there under penalty of death. Nothing Chris had said to her before had prepared her for these people. They were the rock-solid foundation of the establishment. Chris had none of their stuffiness, but these were his roots. He was worried they would scare her off. And he kept watching her for signs of panic but so far there were none. What she had noticed more than anything was that they weren't warm. They were perfectly behaved and polite to everyone. They were nice to the children whenever they were around, but there was no sign of affection or warmth. No one was laughing, no one was hugging, there were no family arguments. They were all intelligent and very polite, and watching them made Francesca feel sad, especially for Chris. What was missing from what she saw around her was love.

Francesca was in the living room at exactly six-thirty in a black cocktail dress that looked demure enough, with heels that were too high, and an evening bag that was too jazzy, with rhinestones on it, a gift from her mother from Paris. She wore her hair in a bun, which seemed right. His mother wore a plain black dress with a high neck and long sleeves, and her regulation pearls that she wore with everything, and that Francesca suspected she probably slept in. The fantasy of their two mothers together nearly made her choke.

'How did you and Chris meet?' his mother asked her over cocktails. Francesca had no idea what to say to her. *He was living in my house* didn't sound like the right answer. *I'm his landlady . . . I run a boarding house . . . In church?* There was no right answer. Chris had warned her not to say she lived at 44 Charles with him.

'We met through friends.' Chris had been listening, and wandered by to fill in. Francesca smiled silent thanks. She was constantly afraid to do or say the wrong thing.

Chris's father asked what kind of work her father did, and she said he was an artist. She mentioned his name, and they were impressed by that, which was a relief. And she mentioned that her mother was in Gstaad for Christmas. They looked a little shocked by that. Her father being in Sun Valley was okay. They knew it and liked it. But a ski resort in Europe sounded like Sodom and Gomorrah to his mother.

'The only way to get through these dinners is to get blind drunk and keep smiling,' one of his cousins told her in a whisper as they headed to dinner, and she laughed. The suggestion had a lot of appeal, but she wouldn't have dared do it. You had to be alert to field their questions. They wanted to know where she'd grown up, where she'd gone to school, whether she went to boarding school, whether she'd ever been married, and of course she didn't have children, and where did she spend her summers? Maine was good. Running an art gallery was question- able, but since her father was an artist, it was forgivable. His sister and brother spoke to her from time to time. She felt like she'd been playing tennis all night by the time they finished dinner, and she collapsed in her room for a minute, before they went to church again. They were so much more impressive than she had expected, and being face to face with them was even dicier than she had imagined. Particularly his mother. The thought of his mother in the same room with hers made her feel faint. It was a frightening prospect that meant that if she ever married him, they'd have to elope. There would have been no way to have her family and his under one roof, let alone at a wedding. Only Avery would have passed muster. Her father was much too racy and un- conventional too. He hadn't gone to Harvard, he hated sports, and knew nothing about football. And intro- ducing her mother to this very proper conservative group was out of the question. They were as white-bread, pure, holy, church-going, and athletic as it got. And they were successful, social, and important on top of it. There didn't seem to be one rebel in the group, except Chris, who was a renegade by their standards and no one else's.

Chris burst out laughing when he saw her sprawled out on her bed before church, looking like she'd run a marathon, and exhausted. She had ten potential outfits spread out on her bed for upcoming events.

'Having fun yet?' he teased her. 'Don't mind my mother. She's a little like Scylla and Charybdis, or whoever they have posted at the gates of Hell these days, but when you get past her and she gives you her seal of approval, you can pretty much do what you want. All you have to do is show up for meals on time and not do anything to seriously annoy her.'

'She's your mother. I don't want to offend her.' Francesca couldn't remotely imagine ever getting his mother's approval.

'It's rude to ask people that many questions. She should be worried about offending you. Start asking her stuff, like where she went to school. She loves that. She went to Vassar when it was an all-girl school. She's very proud of it.' It was an easy entree to a benign conversation with her.

'I've never been to church twice in one day in my life,' Francesca said with a look of desperation. 'If God sees me there, He'll throw me out, and the whole congregation will be hit by lightning.' He laughed, grateful for her patience.

'It's good for you. Brownie points in Heaven,' he said, as he pulled her off the bed. 'Speaking of which, I'm sorry to do this to you, but it's time to leave for church.' There were twenty of them going to midnight mass. Francesca couldn't remember their names or who they were, except his siblings, with whom she had nothing in common. They were just Harleys to her, en masse. The only one who stood out to her was Chris. She was almost angry at him for bringing her here, but staying home alone in New York would have been depressing too, and she loved him. So here she was, on her way to church again, for the second time that day. Her father would have laughed, and even her mother would have been amused. Thalia hadn't even gone to church for her last three weddings.

Francesca dozed off in church during the homily. And afterward they all went back to the house, and then mercifully everyone went to bed. The vice patrol in the form of his mother said goodnight and went to her room after wishing everyone a merry Christmas, with the emphasis on the 'Christmas,' not the 'merry.' Francesca noticed that no one kissed, and fathers and sons shook hands. There were no bear hugs in this group.

Chris was in Francesca's room half an hour later. She was thirty-five years old, and she felt fourteen and like a juvenile delinquent. She was afraid to wind up in juvenile hall, or detention, or jail.

'Merry Christmas, baby,' he said as he kissed her then, and he handed her a box he had carried in his jacket. It was a long slim box from Tiffany's, and when she opened it, she saw that it was a gold bracelet with hearts on it. He put it on her arm and kissed her. She had bought a gray cashmere scarf for him, and he loved it too.

She was relieved that she only had two more days to get through. But the next day was better because it was Christmas. They had present opening, a big meal, with the table set for thirty, with the children at the table in the hall again, the girls in velvet dresses. There was touch football outside afterward on the frozen ground, from which she was exempt because she was a girl. And then they all drank hot toddies and sat around the fire. Chris's mother played bridge with her husband, her daughter, and one of her nieces. And Chris sat next to the fire with her. Ian was playing upstairs somewhere with the other kids. And by midnight she was back in her room with Chris. Only one more day to go, and then they could leave. She could hardly wait.

'Are you having fun?'

'Yes,' she lied, 'but I'm scared all the time that I'm going to do the wrong thing. I feel like a kid.' That part was the truth.

'You just have to ignore them. They think they created the world, but they didn't. That's why I only come home twice a year. And it's better at the Vineyard. It's more relaxed.' He was well aware that his family could drive most people insane. They were major overachievers in everything they did, and expected everyone else to be too, and conform to all of their rules. He hadn't in years, but no longer confronted them about it. He just led his own life, he always had. But he liked coming home for Christmas, for all the traditions, and was grateful she had come with him. He knew this wasn't easy for her, to be constantly scrutinized. He readily admitted to her that his family lived in a cookie-cutter world, where everyone was the same and all the pieces fit. She came from a world where nothing fit, neither her mother nor her father. One was outrageous and the other was artistic and eccentric. But both she and Chris were their own people, independent of their parents' ideas and lives.

'Your mother would have a stroke if she ever met my parents,' Francesca said ruefully.

'Yes, she would,' he agreed. 'But, so what? I don't approve of my parents either. They live an incredibly limited life and they bore me to tears.' At least he agreed with her about it, but she didn't want to be rude about his family. They were decent, respectable people. She just felt ill at ease and off-kilter in their midst. She didn't fit. But neither did Chris. She was comforted by that.

He slept in her bed again that night, and was gone before seven, and he had breakfast with his mother again. It was the day after Christmas, so everyone was more relaxed, even his mother. And for once, they didn't have to go to church. Everyone played tennis and squash again, which seemed to be a daily ritual when they all got together. Francesca still couldn't remember anyone's name, and she felt like she had dementia. She was the only 'Francesca' in the group. The men all seemed to be named Chris, Bob, or William, and there were at least five of them with each name. The women were Elizabeth, Helen, and Brooke. His mother was Elizabeth with countless offspring of all ages named after her.

The only one who seemed to be having any fun was Ian, who loved his cousins and was unhappy to leave. Chris had a last breakfast with his mother on the day they left. His father drove them to the airport and said he had loved meeting Francesca, and she felt like she had been in the twilight zone for three days. It had been the weirdest Christmas of her life, and in spite of that, she still loved him, but she couldn't wait to get back to New York and relax. She wanted to scream with joy the minute they got back to the house. They had been there for ten minutes when her mother called her from Gstaad.

'I hope you had a nice Christmas,' she said blithely. 'I met the most divine man at dinner on Christmas Eve. He lives in New York, he's Swiss, he's a banker, and he's taking me to dinner as soon as I get back.' Francesca could tell her mother was beaming, and she almost groaned. It sounded like number six was on the way at last. Wait till the Harleys heard about that.

'Don't rush into anything,' Francesca said wanly. There was no stopping her mother when she had a potential husband in her sights. And she hadn't had one in too long, according to her. And it wasn't for lack of trying.

'Of course not. It's just dinner, for heaven's sake, not marriage.'

'That's refreshing,' Francesca said, and her mother laughed.

'You don't trust me, do you?'

'No, I don't. I figure you're going to find number six one of these days.'

'What's so wrong with that, if it makes me happy?' her mother asked her, and for a long moment Francesca didn't answer as she thought about it.

'You know, you're right. At this point, it doesn't make much difference. Five, six, and if you're happy, to hell with what everyone else thinks.' She had just spent three days with the most conservative, boring people on the planet, and they were a lot more obnoxious than her mother. At least her mother had some style and spirit. 'Go for it, Mom,' she said, laughing. 'Do what makes you happy. But if you throw me the bouquet at your next wedding, I'll kill you.'

'All right, dear. See you when I get back. I may stop in Paris first.' When Francesca hung up, Chris was looking at her. He was grateful she had gone to Boston with him and been a good sport. His parents even said they liked her.

'My mother is crazy,' she told him matter-of-factly. 'But I think I just figured out that I like her that way.' It was a whole new way of looking at things, and she realized that it probably meant she had grown up and accepted her mother for who she was. It was a first for Francesca.

They went upstairs to bed that night, and Francesca had never been happier to be in her own bed, with Chris lying next to her. She didn't have to answer anyone's questions. He didn't have to leap out of bed and run down the hall to his own room before seven, and she didn't have to satisfy anyone's assessment of what she should look like, wear, or say. She was her own person even if she didn't fit in. She fit in here in her own house and world. And she was totally happy in her own little universe with Chris next to her in his boxers and T-shirt, and Ian sound asleep downstairs. And it was a very nice little life they shared.

Chapter 24

At the last minute, with nothing else to do, Chris and Francesca decided to go back to Vermont with Ian for the New Year's weekend and use Marya's house there. They had no baby-sitter for Ian now with Marya gone, and they were happy to have him with them for a family weekend.

They liked being together, and the revelry in the city didn't appeal to either of them. He had been invited to a few parties, and so had she. But being in Vermont seemed like a nicer way to spend it, so they drove to Vermont the day before New Year's Eve.

Francesca went to the grocery store when they got there and got food for them. Chris lit a fire in the living room, and Ian had brought DVDs and toys with him to keep busy. It felt like the perfect way to spend the holiday to all three of them. And it looked like a Christmas card when they woke up on the morning of New Year's Eve. It was snowing. Francesca only wished that Marya could be there with them. But she was in Courchevel in the Alps with Charles-Edouard and his friends. Francesca had had several e-mails from her and she sounded happy.

Francesca and Chris played Monopoly and Clue with Ian that night. The two of them played Scrabble, and Gin and Go Fish with Ian. And they slept in in the morning, and then played in the snow. They made a snowman and had a snowball fight, and went skating at a nearby lake that was frozen, although Francesca was nervous for Ian. She didn't want him to fall through the ice, but he didn't. They toasted marshmallows and made s'mores. They did all the things that all three of them liked, especially together. It was a totally perfect weekend.

Francesca heard her cell phone ring on the day after New Year, and she was almost too lazy to answer. She finally got up and answered it, annoyed that it wouldn't stop ringing. It went to voicemail twice, and they called again. Francesca finally picked it up and was glad she did. It was Marya, calling from Paris.

'Guess where we are?' Francesca said happily. 'In

Vermont. It's been snowing for two days and it's gorgeous.' They were sleeping in Marya's room, and Ian was in the four-poster in the guest room, as Marya had suggested the last time they came here with her. 'Happy New Year.' She assumed that that was why Marya was calling. 'How's Paris?'

'Beautiful. It snowed yesterday here too. I think we found a flat on the rue de Varenne.' It was exactly where they had wanted to be, in the seventh arrondissement. 'Charles-Edouard has been negotiating for it all week.' She hesitated for a minute and then went on. 'I have something to tell you.' Francesca waited, and missed her fiercely. 'We got married yesterday. Just the two of us and a few friends. His divorce came through before Christmas. The papers were here when we got back. I feel a little crazy, but I'm glad we did it. And if he ever cheats on me, I'll kill him.' They both laughed, and Charles-Edouard got on the phone a minute later, and Francesca congratulated both of them. It was amazing how destiny intervened and life worked out. Marya had thought she was going to be alone forever, and then his wife left him and everything changed. Now five months later they were married. A year ago she would never have dreamt that this could happen.

'I'm so happy for both of you,' Francesca said. She

meant it, and Chris was beaming too. They sounded so happy, and they deserved it.

'I wish you'd been here,' Marya said wistfully, and Francesca wished she had been too. It was one wedding she would have liked to be at, with two people who meant so much to her. She and Chris were still smiling when they hung up, after talking to them for a few more minutes.

They lay in bed afterward, talking about it, and how happy they were for them.

'So when are we going to do that?' Chris asked her. For a long moment, Francesca didn't answer.

'I don't know. What's the hurry? Things seem to be working like this.' They had only been dating for four months.

'I'd like it better if we were married. You're not going to turn into your mother if we do,' he said, and she laughed out loud.

'That's probably true,' she admitted. 'I wouldn't have the energy for five husbands. And I sure as hell wouldn't be looking for a sixth.'

'How about just one?' That had always seemed like one too many to her before. 'What do you think?' He rolled over on his side, and looked at her, propped up on one elbow in bed, and he was smiling. So was she. For the first time, she wasn't scared when she thought about it. She didn't need to get married, but maybe it wouldn't be such a bad thing, and it might even be nice for Ian.

'Maybe,' she said, and grinned. It was as far as she was willing to go at the moment. She wasn't her mother, or Marya. She had to find her own way with him.

'That'll do for now,' he said happily. 'I'll settle for that.' He kissed her as they lay in bed, just as Ian bounded into the room. They were going back to New York that afternoon. It had been a heavenly three days.

'Let's make another snowman,' he said, looking excited, and Francesca got out of bed. They made two more snowmen to go with the one they'd done before. There was a family of them now, right outside Marya's windows.

Ian waved goodbye to the snowmen when they drove back to New York. On the drive home, Francesca was relaxed and peaceful. She had heard recently that Todd was getting married in the spring, and she wasn't upset about that anymore either. She had her own life without him. And Chris was perfect for her. The pot had found its lid, and it was a perfect fit. All she had had to do all along was find the right one.

They got to New York late that night after a long drive, and Francesca helped Chris carry their bags into the house after he carried Ian up to bed, sound asleep. She looked around as she set down their things in the hall. The house seemed quiet and empty, and she looked surprised as she turned to Chris.

'I want to sell the house,' she said softly. He looked stunned.

'Are you serious? Why? You love it.' They both knew how hard she had struggled to keep it, even recently. And a year before, she had been willing to live with three strangers so as not to lose it.

'I do love it, or I did. I want a fresh beginning for us, a new start . . . a clean slate . . .' She was thinking of Todd and Eileen when she said it. 'Too much happened here. There's too much baggage.' She was instantly sure, as sure as she had been when she wanted to keep it a year before. And Chris didn't disagree with her. He just didn't want her to sell it if she loved it and wanted to stay.

'Why don't you sleep on it and see how you feel about it in the morning?' he said, and she nodded, and then they went upstairs to their bedroom. Ian was sound asleep in his own.

She said the same thing to Chris the next day. She looked at him over breakfast with a determined look. 'I want to sell it. I'm sure.'

'Okay.' He nodded. 'Let's put it on the market.'

'It could take a while to sell. It's an old house,' she said cautiously. That afternoon, she called the realtor she had used before. They agreed on a price, and then she raised it a little bit. They were putting it on the market that weekend. She called Avery and told her what she was doing.

'I think it's a good idea. The market is high right now, and you should get a decent price for it. I haven't felt right about that house for you since Eileen was killed there, but I didn't want to say it.'

'It's not about her. It's about me. I think I outgrew it. I kept it when I wanted to. But I think I want a life with Chris. I don't want a house that was part of another life. Todd has a new life. I want one too. I feel like I'm dragging four hundred tin cans tied to my tail. I want to be free. And we need something new.' It all made sense to her. She told her the price that the realtor had quoted her, and it sounded fair to Avery too.

'You're not giving up the gallery, are you?' Avery wondered if she was making a clean sweep, but Francesca was quick to answer.

'Of course not. I just feel like I outgrew this house. It's an albatross around my neck. It's too heavy, in too many ways. Eileen, the cost of running it, the size of the mortgage payment, the repairs. It's too big for us without other people living in it, and I don't want to do that again. Maybe an apartment or a smaller house. We can rent something for a while.'

'See how fast it sells and how much you get for it,' Avery suggested. Francesca was fully prepared to do that, and Chris was pleased. He liked the idea of finding something with her.

There was an open house that weekend, and two weeks later she had an offer. It was for almost the full asking price. And they had disclosed what had happened to Eileen there. It made no difference, the people who wanted it loved it. They had four children, and they could afford it. Francesca was thrilled, and so was Chris. He would never have asked her to sell it, and he would have helped her keep it if she wanted to, but he was happy she wanted to move on. And he loved the idea of a fresh start for them. She wanted a whole new life that was only theirs, not a hand-me-down from someone else, even if it was now hers.

The house was due to close on the fifteenth of March. On Valentine's Day, they found an apartment to rent that they liked and was just the right size, and moved two weeks later. Things were moving fast, which told her that everything was right. And the family that was buying the house was thrilled with their new home. It was a blessing for all concerned, and especially for Ian, Francesca, and Chris. They had a new home, they were a new family, and they had a new life together.

The day after they moved, Francesca went to the house alone to close it. Chris and Ian were waiting at the new apartment, but she wanted to turn on the alarm and lock up at Charles Street on her own. A service was coming to clean the place up and make it sparkle for the new owners. The realtor had arranged it, and Francesca didn't need to be there. But she wanted to say goodbye to the house.

She wandered from room to room and remembered the good times they'd had there, and the bad ones. She didn't go upstairs to Eileen's room, which was open and empty now. But she went everywhere else. And she smiled standing in the kitchen, remembering all the wonderful times and meals with Charles-Edouard and Marya.

The house had served its purpose in its time, and Chris was right, she had loved it, and part of her still did and always would. But like people, sometimes you had to let them go, and houses were no different. It was a question of timing, of who belonged in your life when. And she was letting this one go. She stood in the front hall for the last time, and looked back at it as she set the alarm. She punched in the numbers and locked the door. She whispered goodbye and ran down the steps, and she took a cab to the apartment where Chris and Ian were waiting for her. It was a whole new life with people she loved and who loved her.

The apartment smelled delicious as she walked in. Ian had baked her cookies.

'Look what we made for you!' Ian said, looking excited. They were four-leaf clovers for St Patrick's Day, and he had sprinkled them green.

'Those look like lucky cookies to me,' she said, and bent down to kiss him, and then she kissed Chris. 'And I am a very lucky woman,' she said to them both. The pot had found its lid, just as Avery had said. And she didn't even have to go out looking for it. It had found her. She knew she had been right to fight to keep the house. If she hadn't, she would never have found Chris. Everything had worked out just right, except for poor Eileen. But there was nothing they could have done to save her. Sometimes you just couldn't.

Francesca helped herself to one of the cookies, and looked around. There were boxes everywhere. They had tons to unpack, and a lot to do. It was exciting to be here. And more exciting still to be here with them. Francesca had found her people and her place. And it was no longer 44 Charles Street. Charles Street was part of another time, another life, and now it was gone, to a family who would love it just as she had. 44 Charles Street was a chapter in her life, more than just a house. The chapter was closed. And a new one had begun.

Betrayal

Danielle Steel

At thirty-nine, Tallie Jones is a Hollywood legend. Her work as a film director is her passion and the center of her life; one after another, her award-winning productions achieve the rare combination of critical and commercial success. With no interest in the perks of her profession or the glitz and glamour of Los Angeles, Tallie maintains close and loving relationships with her college-age daughter and her aging father, and has a happy collaboration with Hunter Lloyd, her respected producing partner, confidant, and live-in lover. Rounding out the circle and making it all work is Brigitte Parker, Tallie's devoted personal assistant. Friends since film school, they are a study in contrasts, with Brigitte's polished glamour balancing Tallie's artless natural beauty, and her hard-driving, highly organized style a protective shield for Tallie's casual, down-to-earth approach.

As Tallie is in the midst of directing the most ambitious film she has yet undertaken, small disturbances begin to ripple through her well-ordered world. An outside audit reveals troubling discrepancies in the financial records maintained by Victor Carson, Tallie's longtime, trusted accountant. Mysterious receipts hint at activities of which she has no knowledge. Soon it becomes clear that someone close to Tallie has been steadily funneling away enormous amounts of her money. In the wake of an escalating series of shattering revelations, Tallie will find herself playing the most dangerous game of all—to trap a predator stalking her in plain sight.

In this riveting novel, Danielle Steel reveals the dark side of fame and fortune. At the same time, she brilliantly captures a woman's will to navigate a minefield of hurt and loss—toward a new beginning.

COMING SOON

Big Girl

Danielle Steel

'Watch out, world. Here I come!'

For Victoria Dawson, growing up isn't a happy experience. Born to picture-perfect parents, she never feels pretty enough to meet their expectations. But when her parents have a second child, Victoria is thrilled – she can't help but adore her new baby sister Gracie. And since Gracie is the image of them, her parents finally have the perfect daughter they always wanted. Meanwhile Victoria still never seems to get it quite right – she battles with her weight, she's told she'll never find a man if she's too clever, and the one career she feels passionate about her parents don't approve of.

And so Victoria decides to move to New York to fulfil her dreams and escape her family. Though her new life is exciting, the old temptations remain, and she continues to wage war with the scales.

Victoria struggles to find a life far from the hurt and neglect of her childhood, the damage created by her parents, the courage to find freedom, and become who she really is at last.

9780552159005

Happy Birthday

Danielle Steel

Time to blow out the candles, say goodbye to the past, and make a wish for the future . . .

For April Wyatt, turning thirty is not what she had expected. She's single, with no interest in changing that in the foreseeable future. Her popular, successful restaurant in downtown New York – where she is chef and owner – consumes every ounce of her passion, attention and energy. Ready or not, though, April's life is about to change, in a tumultuous discovery on the morning of her milestone birthday.

April's mother Valerie is a popular TV personality and the queen of gracious living. Since her divorce long-ago, she has worked tirelessly to reach the pinnacle of her career and to create a camera-ready life in her Fifth Avenue penthouse. But she's having trouble equating her age with how she feels, and all the hours with her personal trainer, the careful work of top hairdressers and her natural good looks can't hide the fact that she is turning sixty, and the whole world discovers it on her birthday.

It is also Jack Adams' birthday – the most charismatic sports personality on TV, a man who has his pick of desirable younger women. But he fears his age may finally be catching up with him when he wakes up on his fiftieth birthday needing an emergency visit to the chiropractor . . .

A terrifying act of violence, an out-of-the-blue blessing, and two very unlikely love affairs soon turn lives inside out and upside down. As these three very different people celebrate their birthdays, they discover that life itself is a celebration – and that its greatest gifts are always a surprise . . .

9780593056851